Praise for *Toxic Spirits*

"A complex and enthralling international intrigue with a treasure of remarkable detail neatly packed into a short novel that dances on the edge of John le Carré territory. A rich read from start to finish."

Frederick Barthelme, author of New Yorker stories, five story collections, and eleven novels including *There Must Be Some Mistake*

"Mani writes Thailand beautifully with heart and a lot of souls."

Colin Cotterill, author of *The Coroner's Lunch*, from the Dr. Siri Paiboun mystery series, and sixteen other novels set in Laos and Thailand

"*Toxic Spirits* is a striking debut. Its prose, fluid, will tug you along; its dialogue, rendered gracefully, sparkles with authority; its plot is loaded with much to love, plenty to leave you in the kind of wonderment your soul has sought in books."

Mark Wisniewski, Pushcart-prize winning short story writer and author of three novels, including *Watch Me Go*

"A fabulous writer whose sensuous and affecting prose both beguiles and transforms."

Tom Vowler, author of story collection *The Method* and novel *What Lies Within*

Toxic Spirits

Mani

CALUMET EDITIONS

Minneapolis

Excerpts from Toxic Spirits were previously published in the following journals:

"Last Rites." STORGY (April 15, 2018).
https://storgy.com/2018/04/15/fiction-last-rites-by-inderjeet-mani/ .

"Genes." Eclectica, 21, no. 1 (January/February 2017).
http://www.eclectica.org/v21n1/mani.html .

"Mother's Day." Unsung Stories (September 16, 2016).
http://www.unsungstories.co.uk/short/2016/16/9/mothers-day.

"Mimi." Short Fiction: The Visual Literary Journal, no. 10, (2016): 68-79.
https://www.shortfictionjournal.co.uk/.

10 9 8 7 6 5 4 3 2

ISBN: 978-1-959770-42-8

Cover and book design by Gary Lindberg

Toxic Spirits

Mani

**CALUMET
EDITIONS**
Minneapolis

Also by Mani

Nonfiction, as Inderjeet Mani

Computational Modeling of Narrative, Artificial Intelligence, 2012, Morgan & Claypool Publishers

Interpreting Motion, Computational Linguistics, 2012, Oxford University Press, (Co-Author)

The Imagined Moment, Narrative/Literary Theory, 2010, University of Nebraska Press

The Language of Time, Computational Linguistics, 2005, Oxford University Press, (Co-Editor)

Automatic Summarization, Artificial Intelligence, 2001, John Benjamins Publishing Company

Advances in Automatic Text Summarization, Artificial Intelligence, 1999, MIT Press, (Co-Editor)

Acknowledgements

I would like to express my thanks to the dozens of hill-tribe children I taught from 2010-13 as a volunteer with the Children's Organization of Southeast Asia in Chiang Mai. I also visited many of their families in the mountains of Thailand's Golden Triangle. These experiences informed my characterization of the Palin tribe in *Toxic Spirits*. The organization and its children were featured in the documentary film *The Wrong Light* (2016) from Run Riot Films.

I am also deeply grateful to Daniel Burgess, who provided the first detailed comments on the ur-text; Mary Beth Rathgeb, who offered encouraging reader feedback; Ian Graham Leask, who, as publisher, supplied extensive feedback on multiple drafts; and last but not least, the patient and ever-tolerant Mani family of readers.

1. Siri

The Irish Pub in the small seaside resort of Prajawan was a cottage of wood and bamboo that had since 1998 provided nourishment and entertainment to expats in Thailand. Benton headed down the orchid-lined pathway to the entrance, passing the miniature spirit house guarded by a statue with four faces, one of which, long and mustachioed, stared quietly at him.

The proprietor, Apple, smiled broadly at him and called out to the bar staff, "Makareeta for Bento!"

The Pub had a well-stocked bar, a huge television for sports fans, and hefty teakwood tables that Apple kept shiny and spill-free. Benton took a table beside the long mirror at one end that made the place look twice its size. The wall in front of him was festooned with photos of Apple and her boyfriend Klaus, posing with patrons and local celebrities, the collage of inebriated smiles hanging a respectful distance from the gold-framed pictures of the ruling monarch in different guises, as monk, sailor, and saxophonist. To the far right was a small stage that featured live music performed by aging Western expats as well as younger Thai bands. Benton liked coming there in the evenings around eight to eat Western food and listen to music without being hassled by bar tarts.

The margarita arrived in a tall glass, its rim studded with salt crystals. Benton took a long sip and then looked aside to the mirror, which reflected his spectacles and—as he inspected them—the series of spectacles within. His grandfatherly African-American face revealed a truly American mix of ethnicities, including high cheekbones with more than a hint of Native American and East Asian ancestry and velvety brown eyes that might have come from anywhere. As for his straggly white beard, he had been growing it out, as if to remind himself that Sylvia wasn't there any more to object.

People drifted in—a Scandinavian family, a backpacker couple with matching tattoos, and a group of Chinese tourists. Then came Little John, who pulled up a chair beside Benton.

"Wot's wi' the beard, Benton?" he said. "The secret agent's now a fuckin' padre?"

Benton shook the small hand of the retired Glasgow greengrocer, whose head looked pointy and whose flappy ears betrayed his advanced age. Benton, already large and overweight, always felt especially huge and heavy beside the tiny Scotsman.

Little John pointed to the television, where the British news had just come on from the ThaiVisa Expat channel. Knowing that her patrons would be interested, Apple turned the volume up. The bodies of six infants had been found at one of Bangkok's most popular temples, wrapped in gold leaf. A suspect, an immigrant from Hong Kong by the name of Chow Hok Fuen, was wanted by the police.

"Jesus suffrin' fuck!" Little John said. "The shite tha' washes up in the Land O' Smiles."

"That's *Krungthep*, the City of Angels," Benton said. "That shit wouldn't happen here."

"*Sanae dum*," Apple said. "Black magic. *Farang* kill baby and give Lord Buddha."

She shuddered as the camera provided close-ups, with the babies' heads fuzzed out, and before anyone could object, changed the channel to the English Premier League. It was a rerun from the night before, with Arsenal playing Manchester United, but Benton had no interest in it. He stared into his half-empty glass.

Little John smiled. "Kat Klub reopened last week. Lovely birds, wi' strobe lights an' all. Yer gem fer it sometime, big man?"

"Not my thing," Benton said.

"'Scuse me, Padre," Little John said, extracting a cigarette from a crinkled package. "Lest we forget, you agents got higher standards. Perks o' yer job an' all."

"I told you the other night," Benton said, "I'm retired."

He looked over his freshly arrived pork chop. Forcing a change of subject, he asked, "How are things with Nellie?"

Nelly was Little John's Thai girlfriend, a tribal woman from a village in the Golden Triangle. She was a good thirty years younger and had no doubt rejuvenated him.

"Wee one's due in two weeks," Little John said, lighting up.

"Congrats again, man," Benton said.

He remembered reading somewhere that having offspring late in life increased one's life expectancy, expenses notwithstanding. It gave one something to look forward to. Renewed life's promise. But not for him. Sylvia had been eager to adopt, but growing up an orphan, he had doubted his parenting skills. And now it was too late. Once he had started to put himself back together after Sylvia had gone, all he had wanted was an affordable overseas destination suitable for retired agency hacks—Panama, Costa Rica, Thailand, where didn't much matter.

He raised his glass and downed the rest of his margarita.

Sylvia had foreseen what would happen. In that last year she had urged him to not be so dependent on her. She asked him then to accept the verdict and return to the world of light and life. He had reached out to lift her hand from the piano, but she had gently drawn it away. "Leave me be, Ben. It's you who's gotta sort yourself out."

She had always tried to act wisely, but he had ignored her advice and stayed by her side, making his own future dependent on her existence. He was bargaining then, begging the universe for at least a partial remission, while knowing that nothing could change the final outcome.

He sighed at the memory and slowly cut into his chop.

"Likin' it?" Little John asked, sipping his Thai whisky and soda.

"As good as it gets, this being Thailand."

"Get outta yer shell an' enjoy," Little John said. "Last calls an' all."

He knew what the man meant. A retiree was expected to step out of his skin and relish the fruits of long labor. It was a time for tattoos and riding into the wind, for dancing away from geriatric doom and gloom, for checking off the last items on a bucketlist. Whereas he would always stick out among the other expats, a highly educated and overweight black *farang* who did not ride a bike and had neither a girlfriend nor a desire for one.

"Here I'm just another chickenshit foreigner. You say I got to ham it up and enjoy?"

"It's the same shit fer all o' us. They doan't hear a fuckin' word I say."

"But Nellie gets you, right?"

Little John heaved a sigh. "Ay, she does. Got tha' gift fer it."

"It's different for me."

"Yer mean bein' widowed an' all? Or bein' black?"

"Black and white are color terms, John. Not suitable for people."

Little John nodded and said, "So what d'yer call yerself?"

Benton chewed on a tough bit of rind from the chop and then took it out with his finger and stuck it on the lip of his plate.

"John, I guess you see before you a well-fed, dark-complexioned African-American male?"

Little John made a fake frown. "That's not wot these eyes're seein'."

"Laugh on, my friend. But what you see is not entirely what you get. You know I'm proud of who I am and would never allow myself to be cowed by racism. Which I've seen a lot of. And I'm not one to forget civil rights... and slavery—even wrote a thesis on it at university. But that aside, I'm my own man. I've got more in common with people my own age than my race."

"Right. But doan't yer care about yer ancestry then?"

"Sure I do. Before leaving the homeland, I swabbed some spit from my cheek and sent it to one of those genetic testing outfits."

"An' found wot?"

"My mother's stock is mainly Malagasy—from Madagascar, an island off the east coast of Africa. The rest is Gambian, from way across on the west coast."

"Like mixin' Scots an' fuckin' Greeks. An' yer pop?"

"He's 60 percent Southeast Asian."

"I might have guessed tha' from yer chinky cheeks," he said, smiling. He signaled to Apple for a refill of his whisky.

"My father's folks included seamen from Bali, in Indonesia. They wound up sailing across the Indian Ocean to Madagascar, where my mother's folks were from. Some of the family were captured and shipped from there."

"Yer folks did some hard travelin'. An' the 40 percent?"

"Similar to so-called whites like you, John."

"Yer fuckin' wi' me, Benton."

"I kid you not," Benton said, sliding his plate away. "My DNA indicates migrants from the Steppes of Eastern Europe and refugees from Central and West Asia. Under our skin, John, we're nothing but a bunch of crazy mutts. I've even got a sprinkling—thankfully invisible—of Neanderthal."

"I did not fuckin' get tha'!" Little John laughed, banging his hand on the table.

The band started playing. The electric guitar was wielded by a large woman with long hair and makeup plastered on her face, and the drummer had tattoos on his arms and wore a leather waistcoat, his neck dripping with amulets. But it was the thin, pale singer, Siri, who was the star. Her hair was part blond, part brunette, and falling across one eye in the style favored by Korean pop stars. There was a basket for tips near the drums and a box of T-shirts on sale with the band's name, Exploding Heads.

"How you doin' tonite?" Siri asked.

She made a quick Thai bow or *wai*, with her head lowered and palms pressed together, her sequined top flashing.

"A braw bird," Little John said. "Me Nellie knows her, same tribe an' all."

"She's got the looks," Benton said. "But that doesn't mean she can sing."

The guitarist strummed a few chords, made sure she had the right tone, and nodded to Siri, who cleared her throat, smiled at the audience, and then looked into the microphone and launched into her song.

> Come on naow try n understan
> The way I fee when I'm i yer han
> Take my han come undercover.

Siri bent low, almost swallowing the mike, her fingers raised in a defiant V.

> They cain hur yer naow,
> Cain hur yer naaaaaoooooooow
> Lemme hear yer!

The Scandinavian child was standing on the table and clapping, at her father's behest. The backpackers banged their palms on the table. Little John clapped briefly, and Benton joined in. He liked Siri's touch, the mysterious way she had channeled both Patti Smith and Springsteen.

At the end of the song, Siri did a high-five with her team, and then they started again. She was gyrating now, with sharp pelvic thrusts, her rings glittering in the light. Benton could see a cross dangling on her neck.

"Say yer wan me to stay?"

The audience couldn't understand the question, but it didn't matter. Other songs followed. She did a decent cover of Dire Straits' "Money for Nothing," and then she turned to Benton and Little John.

"Money for nothin' an chix fer fee—is that the truth?"

People laughed. The Scandinavian child went on clapping deliriously, as if an insect had entered its brain. The Chinese paid for their drinks and left, and then Little John departed, as Nellie was feeling unwell and needed him home.

Siri took a few requests, including "Smells Like Teen Spirit," from one of the backpackers. Then the Exploding Heads took a break, and when they returned she was wearing a cowboy hat with sequins, and her lipstick was orange-red. She looked pale and childlike as she climbed on the stage, bending low before the microphone. Benton noticed a scar under her jaw, and then she was swiveling up, gyrating, babbling obscenities and meaningless words, her eyes smoldering with dull rebellion.

He hadn't enjoyed himself like this in a long while. He lingered until eleven, following which he was ready to call it a night. Bedtime for him, although Siri was still belting out old standards.

He stepped out into a thickening drizzle. Realizing that he had left his umbrella at home, he pulled the back of his shirt over his head and hurried on down the *soi*. He heard a thunderclap, and then the gods were raining down on Thailand, providing much-needed relief for the rice crop and promising fertility and abundance. He could feel his sandals squelching on the pavement, muddy with sewer water. He turned, passing a group of ladyboys huddled in a shop front, waiting for the downpour to pass. As he stared at them, he almost collided with a food vendor who was draping his stall full of sour-smelling and no doubt ultra-spicy dishes with sheets of thin plastic.

The only other person on the pavement was a legless man sitting silently beside his begging bowl. Benton reached into his pocket and flung the beggar some change and then stepped across the street. A slew of motorcycles wove around him, the riders shooting past in their plastic capes like specters. When he reached the other side, someone called out to him.

"Hello handsome! Hello, sir. Welcome!"

He passed a series of bars with red and yellow lanterns swaying from the rafters. He could hear soft music and quiet chatter as he dodged a tangle of electric wires that loomed low at his head. The rain slanted down, drenching his spectacles, so he ducked into the next bar. As he passed the little spirit house at the entrance, a swarm of girls greeted him.

"*Sawadee-ka*," they sang out. "Come and sit here, mister."

One of the sirens gently led him by the hand to a small table in the back. The girls were tastefully made-up, without the ghoulish rouge and powder he had expected. He couldn't help lingering over their fluttering eyelashes, their dark lipstick and fingernail polish, their small, tight bodies with smooth-looking thighs and pedicured feet. How soft women were, and what a blessing to have them in the world! For one woman had given him everything, yielding every inch of herself as she led him into the dark regions of her soul. His thoughts were getting a little ahead of him, and as one of the girls leaned close enough for him to inhale the scent of patchouli, he felt a wave of exhaustion.

He finished two more Jack Daniel's. Then he found himself sitting next to a dusky lady, almost as dark as him, wearing shiny earrings. She thought Bento was a nice name, though he did not look American, more like an African. Where was he really from? Oi was her name, which meant sugar cane. With the lanterns swinging in the rain gusts, he could see only a dim outline of a stunning moon-shaped face looming up from the background of tables and chatter, smiling at him with a chipped front tooth. But that blemish only served to enhance her beauty.

Behind the glistening wine glasses a woman in high heels cradled a small dog. People seemed relaxed, drunk and happy. He ordered more drinks, and the smell of the rain came through to him, a wet loam scent that brought with it the goodness of nourished earth and fat crops. He leaned back, and there was talk of the bar fine for taking a girl out, and he handed Oi a wad of notes from his wallet and told her to take care of it. He felt different, realizing that a new curiosity and energy had been stirred up and that it went far beyond desire.

He was soon in a dark alley and then barefoot in a tiny room. He had a moment of panic when he heard a man's voice nearby. He waited, his heart beating faster, until Oi came in with her toothy smile and led him to the shower. She pointed to where the body shampoo was. He had showered earlier that evening, but decided it was best not to argue and washed quickly and emerged, worried that he had left his wallet unattended. It was only when he climbed in that he spotted his clothes, phone and wallet arranged neatly in a plastic basket on the floor, with his spectacles folded on top. Oi entered in her towel and then cast it off. He noticed the earrings, her small breasts, and then the rounded belly with its closely shaved pubis. Then she knelt over him and tore open the condom wrapper with her teeth.

The light flickered, a flurry of little moths chasing each other around the swaying bulb. Her breath was sweet peppermint with a faint odor of fish paste, and her other red mouth was soft and toothless inside. He was sticky beside her, made of mud, but hardened, beautifully molded like the dark one beside him, curving together, her flute in harmony to his trumpet. They were now gliding, black on black. What could be sweeter than that even if he was still partly flaccid and kept slipping out. Then he was in a small craft lifted up by waves, back in the arms of the woman who had raised him, and he could hear the rain thundering down on the roof of the house in Baltimore where his aunt had brought him up, and then he was thanking her and all the women and eventually Sylvia… who would not mind, he knew. She wanted him to be independent, to have his pleasure. He was not doing wrong by her… he was past all judgment.

Now Oi too was crying out "You are *big* man, Bento," which was true right then and "Please, more. Oh, I come now," which was probably not. And then there were three strong shudders, and he was aware of the fact that he had slipped out again. He lay back in her arms, the coils of sleep swirling around him. Oi was stroking his head, and he saw a pink orchid behind her ear, and then the last thing he heard was "I take good care. I take care old man."

2. Prayers

The next morning he woke up with a slight headache. The light bulb was still on and swaying in the breeze. He dressed and then stepped out. It was still early, and the birds were twittering. For the first time in a while, even with the headache, he felt light, prepared for a new day.

"*Sawadee ka*, Bento! You sleep good?"

Oi was dressed in a blouse and neatly ironed jeans. She had brought him a cup of coffee and Thai *conjee*.

"Just the coffee, thanks."

He gulped it down, noticing that her face seemed older than he had thought, with pock marks and a strange rash under the eyes, and then she was leading him by one hand and carrying a small bamboo basket in the other.

"Today is *wan pra*. Monk day. You come I show, okay?"

He followed her to the boardwalk. A line of ochre-clad monks approached. They were barefoot, their heads cleanly tonsured, their alms bowls extended. Oi reached into her basket and took out a ball of rice, handing it to Benton. The first monk, a young man with gaunt cheeks, said nothing as Benton plopped it into his bowl. But his eyes lingered on Benton's face, seemingly oblivious to the presence of Oi.

On the way back they stopped at Wat Santisuk. He had passed by the temple often but never bothered to enter. Now he removed his sandals and followed her in. The monks were chanting, blathering their singsong to the morning world.

"What are they saying?"

"Pray to Lord Buddha," she said. "*Jayamangala sutta.* Lord Buddha fight with Mara."

He could make out the rhythm, short and long syllables following each other. He realized it was a kind of poetry, the rhythm and meter conspiring to help people remember the message of the final triumph over all worldly passions.

Oi lit a small incense stick, which she stuck in a clay jar. She kneeled down thrice. He thought of following suit, but instead bowed to a bespectacled monk seated deep in a meditative trance. The man's skin had an olive sheen, and his stillness seemed unruffled, without even a twitch or breath.

Benton had heard rumors of the Thai custom of preserving their most revered monks, but now he felt a little shiver in the company of an actual embalmed person. Someone who had died maybe twenty or thirty years ago was sitting next to him, and nobody seemed bothered. Thailand was going to take some getting used to if the dead were going to be regular companions.

Oi was meanwhile genuflecting before a splendid gold-plated Buddha whose hand was pointing to the ground, which he knew meant that the earth was a witness to the reality of liberation. Staring at the idol, he felt something had changed in him as well, as if he were being prepped for a radically different mode of living.

As they left, the monks in the courtyard were sweeping away the leaves that were congealed after the night's rains. She asked him if he had children, and he said none... that his wife had died. Then she smiled sadly and wanted to know when they would see each other again.

"Going on trip," he said.

"You have *fan*," she said sadly.

"No girlfriend. Don't want one either."

They parted, but only after he had handed her an extra tip.

He could not see her again. He knew she was just trying to meet her *bun khun* or parental obligation, while hoping to win the heart of a kind and generous customer. But Benton had not come to Thailand on a rescue mission.

The next evening, he returned to the Pub. Siri wasn't there.
He waited for her, but she did not come back, and neither did her band. When he asked Apple about her, she gave one of those sad Thai smiles. Then she summoned Klaus out of the back room, where he sat all day watching videos.

"Band is kaput." He shrugged, the rolls of fat on his body shaking along. "No show."

"You know where Siri's playing? In Bangkok maybe?"

Klaus remained silent.

"Got her number?"

"Bento," Apple interrupted.

"Yes?"

"You have good heart, Bento, *jai dee*. You lonely man. Apple find lady for you."

He wondered if word had gotten around about Oi. But he had been with her only once.

"I know girl from village," she said.

He hurried away.

"Lovely lady, pray aller time," she called out after him.

3. Toy

Nora arrived, a cheerful baby with not a trace of her father's features. She sat in the Pub one evening in Little John's arms, chortling and gurgling. He and Nellie took turns holding her, as everyone came over to inspect and admire the infant. She was wrapped in a lovely petticoat with an embroidered waistcoat, matching the one worn by her mother.

"Nice outfit," Benton said, as he tickled her under her chin.

"Tribal kit," Little John explained. "Yer true-blue Scotch-Palin."

Palin. Why was the name familiar? Benton thought about it, scanning his memory banks and then trying harder, but he couldn't remember for now.

Apple leaned down to nuzzle Nora's cheek.

"Doan yer love bein' winched," Little John said, gathering Nora up again.

Soon it was time for the young mother and her child to retire. Little John stayed on to keep Benton company. A new band had started playing, but even after several more drinks Benton found their techno-tainted sound stultifying. The audience didn't seem that engaged; their eyes strayed to the soccer games unfolding silently on television. It made for an early night.

On the way out, Benton asked Little John if Nellie could find out about what had become of Siri and her band. John agreed to make inquiries.

Mani

It was a week before Benton heard back. Siri wasn't replying, so Nellie had to get hold of the guitarist Toy's number. Benton texted Toy, and she texted him back the next day. She would pick him up at five p.m. on July the sixth, right outside his guest house.

Toy arrived on time, wearing her characteristic heavy makeup and a T-shirt that declared, over pendulous breasts, "D. O. A."

He hopped on behind, the scooter creaking under his weight.

"Nellie vouched for you," she said, turning her head. "You can never be too careful over here."

"What happened to the band? And Siri?"

She reached back to tap his knee. "Let's go to a quiet beach where we can talk."

He held on tight to the sides of his seat as she picked up the pace. She cruised past the boardwalk with its seaside guest houses and beach shops, passed Wat Santisuk, and then left the town, crossing the Vietnam-era air force runway. They were now in open country, flanked by a green sea and rectangular rice paddies crisscrossed by coconut trees and telegraph poles. People were trudging through the fields bearing tools on their shoulders. A truck came skittering past, loaded with migrants in straw hats. In the evening light, the creamy *thanaka* sunscreen on the women's faces gave them a ghostly allure.

"You been with the band from the start?"

"Yeah." She turned her face to him, shrugging. "But we've had to change our tune. Nobody wants punk." She rolled her eyes. "Singing 'Fuck the Police' goes against Thai values. *Sabay sabay.* Everyone calm and happy, going with the flow."

"Don't know much about punk," Benton said. "Though I get the need to protest." Against the idea of life itself, he thought. Of being thrust into the universe as an orphan with the odds stacked against you.

"Bento, isn't it weird that you care so much? When you hardly know Siri."

He didn't understand it himself. But he was going with the flow.

"While we played you were staring like she was your kid or something," Toy said. "After the show, she wanted to talk to you. But you left without a word."

14

She honked and braked hard, barely missing a sidecar motorcycle turning from the opposite lane. The sidecar had been fitted with a small table and two chairs, on which a wife and child were seated, their hair blown back by the breeze.

The scooter turned down a rutted road, leaving the rice fields and entering the wilderness. The jungle was thick here, lapping at the road. As they bumped along, he saw enormous red flowers sprouting from a tree whose base was littered with rotting pomegranates. A long, scaly lizard was feeding on the fruit, its forked tongue darting in and out. Branches waved at him, their arms rippling like anemones. Benton dodged, holding on tight, as a limb studded with white thorny blossoms lunged for his head. The scooter turned, passing a settlement of termite mounds from which puffs of vapor emerged.

They came through a field, and then he saw rhododendron look-alikes bursting with black sugarplum fruits, banana bracts with their white flowers dangling like chandelier crystals. Flowers with the face of a monkey inside. And splashes everywhere of bougainvillea, blood-red in the evening light. Trees grew in all directions, their leaves sprouting like the generations of men. They had their lives, those unnamable ones, each tree distinct and idiosyncratic. They dwarfed him, their ancient branches drooping over the landscape like spidery hands. The wind picked up and began to tug at the scooter, forcing Toy to hold steady, and then the branches moved as one, waving in the same direction. As the scooter maneuvered onto a track between the trees, the gusts suddenly stopped, and Benton felt his hair standing at attention.

Toy's back was drenched in sweat. She drove through a swarm of gnats which then dispersed into smaller formations, a cloud following her head. The scooter slowed down as they came to a small settlement, marked by little stalls selling dried squid. Their translucent brown corpses hung in rows, suspended upside-down like desiccated brown bats. Women stood by their carts preparing coffee and bubble tea, their offerings of papaya salad with fruits and condiments neatly laid out. A man on a motorcycle offered rotisserie chickens in a glass casket. People crowded around, filling up their plastic bags to take home.

Mani

The village was at the mouth of a small inlet where a dozen fishing boats were moored. On the pier, people with scorched faces squatted, staring at them as they drove by, and then a group of half-naked children chased after the scooter, shouting *Farang*!

A half-mile beyond the village, Toy stopped at a sign for Brassiere Beach. Benton dismounted, glad to be back on solid ground. He followed her as she strolled towards a shack, a paltry affair with poles driven into the sand and a tarp top. The tables and chairs were makeshift arrangements of bamboo and termite-eaten wood.

The shack was deserted, except for a huge Thai man wearing sunglasses and sitting near the bar with a tall, gray-haired fellow in boots, possibly an East Asian. Toy guided Benton to a seat at a log table a little farther out on the beach.

Benton wrinkled his nose, smelling the fetid and fruity odor of durian, as the shack owner arrived from the kitchen in the rear. She was a tiny woman with sunglasses pushed up over her hair and a pack of cigarettes in the front pocket of her faded denim jacket.

They ordered beers, with a Thai steak salad for Toy.

Toy turned to him. "Would you like to be daring and try it too?"

"For you, *mai pet*," the owner suggested kindly, offering the low-spice option. "Very delicious."

He agreed to give it a shot, surprising himself. "But none of that MSG, thanks."

As he sipped his beer his lips felt salty. The durian odor now came mixed with sea wrack. It was a pervasive smell of decay, of marine creatures that had died and decomposed into briny offal. He gazed at the beach. A dog was wriggling on its back, kicking its legs as it tried to rid itself of fleas. Behind it, the sun was leaving bloody streaks on the sky, its yolk-like eye sinking steadily into the ocean.

"What's the deal with your band?" he asked Toy.

"Exploding Heads is a recent thing. Siri and I played before with a hardcore band. On Din Dang Road in Bangkok. I was back from a crazy year abroad, and we became close. Siri used to sing in a much higher pitch then. People would hear us from the street and come in and become friends."

He could understand that, friendships born from a song. It took him straight back to the time in college at Fisk, when he was walking by the stately Victorian chapel with its Tudor-style belfry and heard a chorus of women's voices singing spirituals. He entered the chapel, and it was then that he first saw Sylvia. She had short hair and wore fake pearls, and her voice was an octave higher than the other girls in the choir. He waited until the choir was done, and then as Sylvia passed by, complimented her on her singing, which brought out her radiant smile. Within two weeks, they had fallen in love, and after that his life took off like a spinning top that twirled even faster when he got the prized offer from the agency.

"You must be thirsty," Toy said, noticing he had drained his bottle. She called out for another Singha.

He nodded, still absorbed in an old man's memories. The job had not only handed him a career but propelled them instantly into a middle-class existence, starting with the one-bedroom rental in Foggy Bottom where there was no room for a piano, and then their first real home, a Victorian row-house in Adams-Morgan when it was crack-free and his childhood friend Daniel Thigpen played his brand of fingerpicking blues in the funky bars of their neighborhood.

Until everything fell apart. Ending in self-imposed exile in a country where the food was too spicy for him.

The steak salad arrived. He sniffed it carefully. The fish sauce was offset by the more subtle scents of fresh mint, papaya and lime. The meat came thickly sliced, with layers of yellow fat underneath. There was one token chili pepper, the kind called *prik kee nu*, or mouse shit pepper, sliced crosswise. Toy took it off his plate with her chopsticks and popped it straight into her mouth.

"It's real beef," Toy said. "Not buffalo meat."

"Needs tenderizing," he said, chewing slowly.

"Bento, the papaya is a natural tenderizer."

A mosquito was now feasting on his ankles. He kicked his feet. "Why only me? Is Thai blood not sweet enough?"

Toy laughed. "So, you've hung up your boxing gloves and retired here for good? Even though you hate spicy food?"

"Yep. This is the home stretch." He was looking forward to a time of steady decay, with lots of old wounds to pick at. But at least life was by now predictable, and there would be no more surprises.

"And then?"

"Then my life will be over, and that will be that."

She took a piece of gristle out with her chopsticks. "Don't count on it." She rotated her finger. "The universe may spin you back."

"I expect to be reincarnated as a worm."

"I know I'll end up a *Krasue*, because Toy has battles to fight."

"*Krasue?*"

"A yucky ghost who keeps hanging on. Hard to translate." She patted his shoulder. "You need to learn our language, Bento. Or else you'll be like the frog under a coconut shell."

"What frog?"

She smiled patiently. "The one who thought his world was just the coconut."

He shook his head. "I'm past the stage of trying to learn languages. And memory loss doesn't help."

"That's just an excuse. Not real living."

"And who are you to teach me about living? What do you even fucking know about me?"

She did a quick and mortified *wai*. "*Khotord ka*. Sorry Bento. Did not mean to disrespect you."

"You win," he said grumpily. "*Jai yen yen.*" His heart would remain cool and unruffled.

He finished the steak salad, which left a fishy aftertaste. He wondered if they had mistakenly added fish sauce.

The sun had now completed its descent into the sea, abandoning the sky to an eerie grey glow. The world felt indistinct, hovering in twilight. A last bird fled, flapping its wings hurriedly.

Toy was taking her time beating around the bush.

"Bento." She touched his hand, as if she had just read his mind.

"Yes?" Her fingers felt sticky and cool.

"Siri knows that you've been asking for her."

"You've been in touch?" He could feel his sluggish heart quickening.

"She's had to go underground. Because in Thailand the nail that sticks out gets hammered down."

"But why?"

Toy looked around before speaking quickly. "Because of the shit happening in her community."

He remembered to be patient. "What shit?"

"Siri's a Palin. Did you know that?"

"Yes. I also know her Palin friend Nellie, who just had a baby."

"I've met Nellie. But Siri's different, and in real trouble. Do you know much about the tribe?"

He scanned his memory banks again, and this time he remembered.

"I first heard about them at the National Geographic Society in Washington. The speaker was a French-Japanese woman, I think. She showed us slides of these hot-looking Palin women in smart outfits, from the mountains of Yunnan. It was a great talk."

"What did she say?"

"She told us how the Palin had lived in seclusion for many generations and violently resisted all contact. Then they got into cultivating rice and then opium. Their men and women fought on the Allied side in World War Two and for the Americans in Vietnam. And they had this weird ritual. Blood paddy, I think she called it."

He took a sip of his fourth Singha, remembering the black-and-white slides of tattooed warriors carrying severed heads on top of a bamboo contraption filled with rice, and the shocked murmurs from the audience. The blood-soaked rice was to be scattered across their fields in some sort of fertility rite while the skulls were for mounting on village fence posts. The Palin were of course soon forgotten by the Americans.

Toy tapped his hand. "Bento, the Palin up north are having a really tough time right now."

"Is that right?"

What Toy told him wasn't surprising. The Palin who stayed on in their mountain redoubts were eking out a precarious existence, preyed upon by the Thais from lower elevations. They had lived in Thailand for decades but remained stateless, deprived of the right to work. Opium had once been a cash crop, but now they barely made a living growing coffee and vegetables. Some of the younger women who came down to the lowlands for work had wound up in the sex industry. It was the same old story of survival at the margins.

And now it was far worse, because the drug companies had been running trials on them.

"There's a doctor from India who's in charge of the experiments. His name is Pierre."

"Pierre doesn't sound like an Indian name."

"And yours doesn't sound black, Bento."

"Haha, nor Japanese, for that matter. What are the drugs doing?"

"They're causing terrible side effects. Chronic illness. Deformity. Siri has been speaking out, trying to stop it."

He took a long draught of his beer. "But why the Palin?"

She lowered her voice. "They have preserved something unique from their history."

"Let me guess. They have a map to an ancient treasure?"

"It's in their genetic makeup," Toy said, a little cross. "Their pseudogenes."

"Their what?"

She began to explain. Pseudogenes, or *sous* for short, were leftovers of genes that were once in use. Sous were mysterious creatures, the dark matter in genes. They lurked about like ghosts while making up almost half the human genome. They were no longer essential for survival, so evolution had disabled some of their functionality.

"Like the sous for scent. Dogs, elephants and sharks have highly developed genes for smell. But they turned into sous in apes and monkeys."

"Why?"

"Because their color vision improved," Toy said. She held her nose. "So our ancestors no longer needed to stick their noses everywhere."

"How do you know all this biology?"

"I was a grad student. Even did a year's fellowship at the MRC Lab, at Cambridge, before dropping out to join our hardcore band."

"A smart career move. And why are drug companies interested?"

"You see, Bento, some sous still have the power to do good. Like friendly elves, producing proteins that zap tumors."

"What's an example of a friendly elf?"

"Google PTEN. It's a tumor-suppressing gene. And its sou PTENP1 is like an elf, gobbling up cancer-inducing molecules that would otherwise attack the PTEN gene."

Benton, scratching his beard, felt he was back at work at the Fort, teasing out analytical possibilities. "What's so special about Palin sous?"

"The Palin are an ancient tribe, right? Who lived for a long time in deep jungles. So, Bento, put two and two together."

He thought hard for a minute, while feeling an unpleasant rumbling in his stomach.

It was then that he heard a whining. It was soft, like a fan belt beginning to give way.

"Did you hear that, Toy?"

"Bento, your nerves are shot. All I can hear is the sea."

The dog, or whatever it was, was approaching, pleading for something, as the darkness closed over them. He was trying to talk, and Toy was trying to answer. But his mind was going around in spirals, and nothing he had learned was holding together. He felt delirious.

"I took your advice and ate that crap," Benton said. "Now I feel like puking."

"Me too," Toy said. "I'm taking a dump."

She got up and hurried to the bathroom.

Benton remained seated. He put his head down and tried to vomit, but nothing was forthcoming. His malaise mounted. A tangle of telephone wires grew out of his fingers. Into the dark the wires went, with prayer flags waving on them. The wires sizzled, giving off sparks and an acrid odor that he couldn't quite place. His eyes watered.

When he raised his head again, hoping his thoughts would steady, he felt someone's eyes on him. He turned around quickly. Nothing was visible in the dark. There was still some beer in his glass, and he drained it. Where the heck was the waitress?

There was a gulping sound, and he again felt someone watching him. All his thoughts seemed to be amplified, including his own breath, slow and deliberate like that of a pervert breathing on a phone.

He waited for Toy, his heart beating faster. After a few minutes, he staggered to his feet. He had to find her. He lurched towards the toilet in the back. It was open, and he switched on the light. Only a few cockroaches were scurrying about. He went to the kitchen.

The shack owner had a knife in her hand and was hacking away under a dim bulb. It could be chicken, from the yellow grains scattered over the cutting board. Or even a bat, judging by the flaps of black skin and the smooth red flesh.

"Did you see Toy?" He could hear himself shouting.

She turned around, wiping her hands carefully on her dishcloth.

"Your friend?"

"Yes."

"She leave with *farang*," the woman said.

"Which *farang*?"

She shrugged, then returned to her work. He asked again but she didn't answer.

"Your food sucks," he said.

His head was spinning as he steadied himself against a bamboo pole. He remembered then what Little John had told him. One should never make a Thai lose face. Especially a woman. She was now muttering under her breath as her fingers clenched the knife.

The acrid odor wafted up again. This time his brain recognized it, for he had smelled it once before, back home in the Washington suburb of Vienna, Virginia.

4. Soot

Benton and Sylvia Sims lived on a Vienna cul-de-sac in a three-bedroom colonial that they had bought as a foreclosure, shifting there after many years in DC's Adams-Morgan neighborhood.

They had initially loved living in DC. In those days he worked out of a top-secret office in Foggy Bottom, and after work he would hurry along to the university to attend evening classes for his graduate degree. He needed the classes like a drug, for they exposed him to far-reaching ideas that helped clear his brain of the Cold War fog that blanketed every moment of his working life with its oppressive ideology, based on dividing humanity into *us* versus *them*. After class, he would return home exhausted to Sylvia, who would be waiting up, if she had had a good day, with his *ragu* Bolognese followed by a dessert of panna cotta. Even on a bad day, her presence made him remember that for love to thrive in the world, there could only be *us*.

On weekend evenings he took a break from his studies, and his time was then Sylvia's. She came alive during those outings in the Adams-Morgan bars, amid the reassuring chorus of humanity, her eyes lit up and face aglow as they listened to the lilt of local black speech and the strange cadences of people from El Salvador and Ethiopia. The music made everyone sing and clap and chant and jig, and after they did that it spilled into the streets where he and Sylvia stepped out lightly together, high and happy. Benton's childhood friend Daniel Thigpen showed up on occasion to play his brand of funky blues, and afterwards there were beers and memories that Daniel shared with them as they sat together on the stoops along with newfound friends.

Returning home, the couple usually wound up in each other's arms on the living-room couch or carpet, or standing in the kitchen. Wrapping her short legs around his waist, Sylvia would fling her heels against the wall with its poster of Harry Belafonte smiling down at them. Benton had a thing for her nipples, bobbing like buoys in the heaving seas of her breasts, and she would allow him to play with them as he wished.

She drew the line when he wanted her to put on a pair of boots.

She laughed, yanking his neck closer. "You crazy! When's the last time you seen me in kickers?"

"In the basement of Jubilee Hall," he said, squeezing her coffee-colored tush. "Remember the SNCC meetings?"

Mentioning the Student Nonviolent Coordinating Committee made him remember that he wasn't her first love in college, and that he had to battle to displace his rival Paul Tetrault. But that thought made him love her even more.

"Say it loud, Ben," she said, their relationship being advanced enough for her to sense his thoughts. "Say you gonna love me well till the end."

He promised, feeling the sweetness of her breath upon his lips, and then she repeated her promise, and they promised to do so every day until they died, as he sank deeper and her inner muscles began to vibrate with an ecstatic energy that outdid the drumming they could hear from the park in nearby Meridian Hill.

In the gaps between these exertions, Sylvia would get an ache in her sweet tooth, and no matter what the hour of the night, he had to dress and venture out into the street, shaky and zapped, to fetch ice cream or whatever other treat was available. When he returned, Sylvia would fling her arms around his neck, kissing him until he couldn't breathe. He understood then that it was mainly the little—and sometimes seemingly minor—threads of kindness that would weave together the clinging fabric called love.

Those happier times came to an end in the mid-1980s, when DC became blighted by urban decay. The local economy tanked, and the restaurants run by Central American refugees were shuttered. Graffiti grew like a wild fungus on the walls and bus stops as the old convenience stores yielded to liquor shops. Dealers took over the street corners, and there were gunshots outside the bars at night. Among those who fell prey to crack was Daniel Thigpen, who had stopped playing. By then, it became clear that Adams-Morgan was no longer the right place to think about raising a family.

Vienna, in contrast, was a quiet, mostly white suburb, with a few old Greek and Mexican diners and plenty of junk food joints. Instead of jazz on the streets, they had to get used to the sounds of lawn mowers and leaf blowers in the afternoons and weekends, and to an ice-cream truck that drove down Maple Avenue blaring the "Entertainer" rag precisely at four p.m., which drove Sylvia wild. There were fewer night outings, and their lovemaking grew more predictable.

Meanwhile, they became friendly with a few other families in their suburb, including the Passelskys three houses down. Bert Passelsky was a big Afrikaner with a gap-toothed grin and a Nelson Mandela T-shirt who worked as a doctor at Fairfax Hospital. His wife Nadine, red-haired and mousy, was a bank teller. Sylvia used to babysit their daughter Bev after school while taking a break from her piano. Sometimes the five-year-old also stayed over Saturday afternoons when her parents played golf.

The child knew how to charm her way. She would use pretty-pleases and pretend pouts of her freckled face to wheedle a trip to Baskin's for ice cream or to demand more time in front of the television. She told Benton all about her cat and chanted the nursery rhymes she had picked up on Sesame Street, as well as one in Afrikaans, Bert's native tongue.

Sylvia, who adored children with that special fervor of the infertile, liked to do Bev's hair, dolling her up with fancy makeup and clip-on earrings while Benton snapped pictures. At the last minute, Bev would stick her pert little tongue out of the corner of her mouth. When the parents came to collect their darling, Bev would ask "Please please

25

can I stay at the Bentons?" And Nadine Passelsky would pretend that Bev didn't need to come back home.

When the Passelskys invited the Sims over for a brae one Sunday, things were tense that first time over. Benton, who usually enjoyed barbecues, helped grill the steaks, which were served with arugula salad and home fries. Apart from Bev, the two couples did not have much to talk about. They went through a six-pack of Sam Adams, and then the men started on Tecate. The afternoon culminated in the women hanging out on the patio and the men going into the den to catch the latter part of a Springboks game on cable. Benton steeled himself; the only ball game he liked watching was basketball.

The television came on, showing a flurry of sprints and clashes among warriors bereft of helmets or armor. After a few minutes, Benton's attention turned to the wall unit, where there were pictures of Bert and Nadine hugging in swimsuits on a beach with palm trees and a lovely family shot with Bev on Bert's shoulders, sticking her tongue out.

Bert offered him a jerky-like snack called biltong. It was tough and gave his jaw a workout, but there wasn't a convenient way to spit it out.

Bert laughed. The biltong, he said, brought back memories of Africa, of how he used to hunt eland with the lads along the cliffs and gorges of the Drakensburg Mountains. As he spoke, his eyes lit up. He was nostalgic for the open country of his childhood, but he was glad, he said, to have left a land under apartheid.

Benton eyed him and decided he was telling the truth, and from that moment their friendship started.

"I better not ask what it is you do for the government," Bert said, displaying his charming grin. "But I can keep a secret."

"It's not like in the movies," Benton said, as he chewed valiantly on the jerky. "Pretty dull stuff, actually."

He had started off well at work, with his Meritorious Civilian Service award carefully framed and hung by Sylvia in the living room.

"I learned about intel during military service," Bert said quietly. "A lifetime ago. More biltong?"

Benton declined, but he accepted another ice-cold Tecate, with which he downed the rest of his biltong. He now felt more relaxed.

"For me, the shitstorm started two lifetimes ago," he said. "During Vietnam."

Vietnam for him meant sitting in his Foggy Bottom site analyzing SIGINT reports from Phu Bai. The work was challenging, and for a while he even derived a cold pleasure from trying to figure out the enemy's plans, even though the overall mission stank. But in the final analysis it mattered little. That war was lost along with its warriors and ideals, and other pointless wars followed.

Bert became quiet. He watched a scoop pass being intercepted by an All Blacks player who managed to sprint all the way to the five-meter line before he was brought down.

Benton drank his Tecate staring at a corner of the screen, as if a second picture had popped up there. He thought about the long arc of his career, now in freefall. He had managed to stay on top of his game for three decades, until he was hit by an early warning system called MENTIS. The system generated fancy visualizations that wowed the junior analysts, but its threat landscape was spun out of vague information about an ever-swelling horde of potential terrorists. He rejected most of its suggestions, preferring to rely on his own intuition. The 9/11 postmortems did him in. MENTIS had not predicted 9/11, but it had indicated a month earlier that an attack was imminent somewhere on the mainland. His boss David Sardanian kept his job, but Benton was reprimanded and, in the ultimate humiliation, transferred to Digital Access Operations, where he now worked.

"Boks are back in the red zone," Bert said, sensing Benton's puzzlement at all the noise.

Benton tried to share his friend's enthusiasm, but it was like watching a foreign movie without subtitles. The sight of the large men clashing only served as a further depressing reminder of how he had allowed himself to be sidelined. The DAO youngsters, hired from the black-hat hacker community, ignored his fine-grained analyses about the intentions and capabilities of adversaries. They were supposed to be cyber-warriors, but they behaved more like fire ants, getting into a feeding frenzy whenever the sensors that monitored undersea cables detected a target. They would hoot and high-five each other and hurl strings of abuse at the victim as he landed on their spoof website, slurping up his contacts and life history before obliterating him.

The week before, they had turned their antennae on Benton. His laptop screen had filled up with arrays of color bars like a television test pattern, which melted into chocolate-colored glops before frying the hardware.

And Benton was still hanging on, waiting to be humiliated further. He wondered sometimes if he was being singled out because of his race, with his managers getting their jollies by bringing down yet another highly educated black man. History told him that it was likely, but complaining about his performance reviews to Human Resources was impossible. The HR people were powerless flunkeys, and his work and its outcomes could never be discussed with them since it was top secret. What was clear, however, was that his age was against him, his craft of painstaking analysis being considered passé. The end result was that he had been toppled from his once-lofty perch, leaving him scrambling in the dark.

"Oh bugger all," Bert said.

"What happened?"

"It's over. Boks lost 18-21." He switched off the television.

Benton got up slowly, his knees creaking. "It's my age," he said, apologetically.

"It's called a lack of exercise," Bert said, a fleck of biltong stuck between his teeth. "You should get out more. Shed some of those pounds."

Then it was time for Bert to do the lawn, as he was off to a seminar the next morning. Sylvia was in the kitchen, helping Nadine with the last of the dishes. Benton wandered out onto the patio to say goodbye to Bev as he had promised. He gave the girl a few firm pushes on the swing set and watched her swinging happily back and forth, her legs bent low like a skier's.

"Higher and higher, Mister Benton!"

As he pushed he remembered how, nearly half a century earlier, he would curl his knees, riding the swing up at Heckering Downs in Baltimore. He would go there with his pal Joey and later with Daniel Thigpen. They would swing until they got bored and then head off to the creek. It had chubsuckers and pickerel, and when he came back late one night gloriously muddy from a fishing foray there, Aunt Zora, already hunched by then, gave him a lashing on his butt. It left him squirming for a week. But Daniel's father had spared him.

A bluesman, Daniel played several instruments and loved ogling the legs of beautiful girls. He taught Benton to free himself of his hang-up about wearing glasses and most of all to be proud of his skin. Daniel was much darker than him, "like a fuckin' god," he liked to say, with his brilliant smile. He wore flowery daishikis that showed off his blackness. Benton spent many an afternoon in the Thigpen home, which came with a proper set of parents and an older brother. The family kept the radio on, hearing about the civil rights marches and the war but most of all listening to music. It was also where he learned how to dance. The twist, the fly, the pony, the wiggling hucklebuck, and later the Calypso-themed limbo rock, with its "How looow can you goow." They did them all, before trying them out with the girls at the Downs. There they danced until dusk fell upon the creek, the couples awkwardly exploring each other, then heading home.

After that visit, Sylvia started to stop over at the Passelskys' place more often. Once, when he got home and Sylvia wasn't there, Benton went over to their house and found her with Nadine, sharing a bottle of wine in the kitchen. Nadine was in her casual dress, barefoot with her red hair flowing over a man's shirt, and no slacks. Sylvia later reported that Nadine was bitching about Bert and his long work hours and the lack of help around the house.

The families were soon getting together regularly at each other's place, becoming close. Until the year Bev was finishing elementary school.

One Friday afternoon, Benton arrived home early after feeling uneasy at work. He kissed Sylvia on the cheek, then went to his room and lay down. She decided to make some butter popcorn to cheer him up. Soon he could smell something burning, and he rushed into the kitchen. But it wasn't the popcorn. Sylvia pointed outside, and they saw smoke rising from the Passelsky home. Within a minute, a sheet of flame shot up accompanied by several explosions.

After calling 911, they gathered outside along with several neighbors. Within five minutes, three fire trucks arrived, and the firemen asked everyone to move away.

He and Sylvia stood watching from their front window, holding each other, hoping no one was inside. She asked him mechanically if he wanted the popcorn, and he stared at her as if she were mad. The fire raged on, spreading from the roof to the surrounding trees. It crackled and popped, shooting out long yellow tongues into the evening sky as a brown cloud formed above. The firemen bashed in an upstairs window, but they had to beat a retreat due to thick smoke. Then Nadine arrived and was taken away in an ambulance.

After the fire was put out, one of the neighbors rang the bell at the Benton's. The old lady, one Mrs. Eiden, wanted to share the devastating news that their decent and kindly neighbor Bert and his angelic child Bev were no more.

Benton and Sylvia stood there in shock, forgetting to invite Mrs. Eiden in. They soon closed the door, and then Benton hugged Sylvia tight as his throat tightened and they both grew overwhelmed with silent tears.

Bev was like the child they always wanted, and now she was gone. The tragedy left them worn down as if by an unbearable weight. Sylvia was even more devastated than Benton, and it sent her spiraling down into a deep depression. They kept the front window curtains drawn, and it was also the end of their evening walks down Maple Avenue.

The local newspapers and television furnished more details, drawing Benton in, though it was too much for Sylvia. The forensic analysis made the Channel One news. The floors of the Passelsky home were caked with dark remains, which looked like a dense sediment curling with fibers. Two bone fragments had been found in the basement, a left elbow and a small right hip, but they were too far apart to have been blasted by the fire. They had been identified through DNA analysis as Bev's, suggesting that the body had been mutilated. No such desecration had taken place in the case of Bert, whose respiratory and digestive tracts had also been discovered in the basement, burnt and shrunken to a doll's size.

Benton couldn't discuss it with Sylvia, but Nadine later stated to the police that the couple had been having marital problems and that she had told Bert a few days earlier that she was considering leaving him. She was taken to Shreveport to her mother's place where she continued with psychiatric care. Bert's relatives were untraceable.

Benton knew there was no evidence to incriminate Nadine. The fire had started when she was at work. She had been there since morning. It was Bert who had picked up Bev from school. He also heard from the newspapers that they had no life insurance and only basic homeowner's insurance. The possibility of a third person breaking in and slaughtering the pair was discounted by the police for various reasons. Their neighborhood had always been safe, with the typical incidents being no more serious than bicycle thefts, DUIs, and the odd pit-bull encounter.

The staff at Bert's hospital were willing to speak off the record to the *Fairfax Times*. He was a caring physician who had served the community for nearly fifteen years working with thousands of patients and delivering along the way hundreds of healthy and beautiful babies. He had studied medicine at UCLA, where he met Nadine. He was known as a family man but didn't socialize much, not even on the golf course.

The case was deemed a probable murder-suicide, and closed.

Benton had doubts about that conclusion. Bert looked every inch the doting father when he was around Bev, and the child's eyes always lit up when she saw him.

"He was a fantastic dad," Benton said.

"Let it go, Ben," Sylvia said, for the umpteenth time, stroking the back of his neck. "They're now in a better place."

Mani

She was a woman of faith, and in times of trouble was able to count on an external source of strength. Whereas he couldn't.

The last time Benton had seen Bev was when he had let her play on their back patio with a piñata that they had brought with them from the Adams-Morgan house. As he held her up blindfolded so she could smash the cardboard candy container with her stick, he had an uncanny feeling that the child, so light and mobile in his hands, was doomed. And he had done nothing about it.

5. Taenia

The Passelsky case was closed, as far as the authorities were concerned. And Benton resigned himself to learning nothing more from them. The burned-down home was eventually replaced with a tall colonial occupied by a quiet Indian lawyer. Benton and Sylvia tried to get on with their lives, but life came with surprises.

Benton's transfer from DAO to Investigative Services, or IS, was his final demotion. The work called for eyes and ears but not brains. All he had to do was run background checks for US contractors needing top-secret clearances. The ones who passed muster would be summoned to the appropriate department for polygraphs and interviews. His job was essentially grunt work, designed for dinosaurs hoping to retire with full pensions. He hated it, knowing he was made and educated for far better things, but as Sylvia reminded him, it beat waiting tables or licking envelopes.

In IS, he became a power user of TAENIA, the agency's legacy who's who system. It had been seeded with the standard Form 86s used for background checks, but over the years the system had swollen to enormous proportions, bursting with everyone's juicy details. Benton had to sift through the candidates' bios, assessing the steadfastness of their hearts and minds based on information TAENIA had siphoned off from government and corporate records as well as chat and email communications. The system used high-precision porn and hate speech filters, but he still had to wade through a deluge of drivel and pap.

TAENIA's persona was as intrusive as its content. It switched between male and female voices, put on a posh British accent knowing it would irritate him, recorded his bathroom breaks and tracked his calorie intake. It made him feel guilty for visiting the cafeteria for his daily dose of raspberry-filled donuts. And its mood detector guessed, incorrectly, that he was a steady depressive.

It was all bad. But Benton was a super-user. Addicted to typing in a name of a person or a street address and seeing the shit that came churning out. One morning at the office, his fingers keyed in *Passelsky, Bertrand*. What he saw occupied him for the rest of the day.

The old police and autopsy reports were there for him to peruse. So were the Passelskys' credit histories. The doctor had ordered a fancy barbecue grill that he and Sylvia had once dreamed about, and he had a regular subscription to the Rugby Channel. The couple had purchased crab cakes and merlot from Dean & DeLuca in Georgetown. Nadine, it turned out, had a couple of DUIs when younger. She had been prescribed Ramelteon for insomnia, but seemed normal in other respects, chatting with her friends from college about relationships, diets and home remodeling. The couple had traveled to France, Italy and Thailand, where Nadine had studied Thai massage. There were tagged pictures and video mashups synthesized by TAENIA, not all of them in good taste. And on October 20, 2005, Nadine had given birth to a child weighing six and three-quarter pounds.

He called Sylvia from the office cafeteria and told her about his findings.

"Ben, what d'you have for lunch?" She was trying as usual to soothe.

"Same old crap," he said. Though the donuts weren't crap, not in the least.

"All your digging," she said. "It's no use now." Her voice sounded husky.

"I owe it to Bev," he said.

"Let her go, Ben. You ain't a real cop."

"At least you got your piano to bang on," he reminded her.

He immediately regretted saying that.

Back in the office, he explored further, clicking on Bert's picture and dropping it into TAENIA's search box. The eleventh match from the reverse image search was a Robert Bardeski, from a database recently shared by the NIA of South Africa. The black-and-white picture, blurred around the chin, showed a younger, more muscular Bert-like figure with a crew cut and sideburns. As a young man, Bardeski had been conscripted as a science graduate into their Defense Force. He had topped his batch in marksmanship and wilderness survival and was also a champion boxer. He was voted the best all-rounder and was posted to Soweto. Then an infraction appeared on his record: *disciplining of hotnot by means of excessive force*. It was followed soon after by another: *damage to property at a kroeg*. Which, TAENIA verified, was a type of bar. Within a year, he was arrested for inappropriate use of a weapon, a Vektor SP1, while off-duty. A court-martial was initiated. There was also a note, scribbled in hand on the form before it was scanned—"…absconded before trial, believed to be in Thailand."

6. The Law

Noi, the owner of the shack where he had eaten with Toy before keeling over, drove Benton right away to the San Paulo hospital.

"I not cook bad," she whispered along the way, as she gunned the pickup into the fast lane. "I very sorry, *ka*."

Benton was too nauseous to reply. His mouth tasted of rotten eggs, and his churning stomach had become swollen and rigid, requiring Noi to unbutton his pants. At San Paulo, the nurse at the reception asked if he had come from West Africa.

"Because of Ebola," she said, smiling as he started retching.

Doctor Roussel, the aging Frenchman from Papeete, gave him ipecac, and then he barfed a spectacular mash of blood, bile and glistening chunks of half-digested beef. A sample of it was sent to Bangkok. He had to stay in the ward until the results arrived.

Meanwhile, the nurses flirted with him. How many children did he have? They shook their heads sadly when he told them. The head nurse asked him to report after each toilet visit on the consistency of his shit on their rock-water scale, one meaning rock to ten for water. They cracked up after each report. They seemed to find everything hilarious, smiling and joking as they worked, except when the doctor was present.

Later that week, Roussel came back to the ward to explain that they had found traces of zinc phosphide, a rodenticide. Along with an unidentified plant base. He was lucky it was only a small dose, Roussel said. Rats roamed freely in Thai kitchens, but restaurants had to be more careful.

"You're free to go," Roussel said. "But go easy on the Thai food!"

Benton stared at Roussel. Thai food culture was supposedly one of the world's most sophisticated, and it was hard to believe the local chefs would be using rat poison instead of relying on cats. It was clear someone had tried to take him and Toy out, or at least send them a message.

Back at his guest house, he found Win, his landlady, sitting in her usual place near the coffee machine, her eyes glued to the television. She was a large woman draped in a shower of necklaces and amulets from the night bazaar.

"Honey, you in some kinda trouble?" Win asked. Her fingers were nagging at her beads. "You away one week."

"I was in the hospital," he said. "Food poisoning."

"Eat here, *ka*," she said. "Win cook delicious *farang* for you."

She handed him a plastic bag on which the price had been scrawled with a blue marker.

"Thanks… I sort of forgot." Win had a knack for neatly ironing his clothes with just the right amount of starch and folding them into small parcels. "Okay to put it on my room bill?"

"Sure thing, honey. How about a morning coffee?"

The latte had a rosette shape in the milk on top. He gulped it down, destroying Win's pattern. Then he thanked her again and went upstairs to his room.

Sylvia's picture sat in its frame on his bedside table, next to the fan. He wished he could tell her what had just happened. She was looking gorgeous, wearing the Fair Isle sweater he had bought her, her eyes sharp, her face youthful, her hair neatly swept back. It had been taken near the Lincoln Memorial, during the fall. Her favorite season. He put the photograph away in a drawer. Trying to remember her face, the edges kept getting whited out, leaving only a fuzzy glow.

He decided that the time had come to try and force himself not to think of her last thing at night and first thing in the morning and every time he sat down alone for a meal.

He lay down, his Thai-grown belly partly occluding his view of his six-foot frame, though he could still see the outline of his calves, thick and dark. He sank deeper into the hot mattress as masses of torpid air began to swirl around him, disturbed by the rattling table fan.

When he woke up it was half-past five, and he was drenched in sweat. It was unusual for him to sleep for so long during the day, but now he was rested. He went downstairs.

In the restaurant Win's deadbeat partner Kurt was sitting by the orchid stand, looking out at the street while drinking away his Austrian pension. Win wasn't there, otherwise there would be the usual kerfuffle about booze that always ended with Kurt being shooed out for the night.

Benton headed to the beach. He sat in a little burrow in the sand, feeling the cool particles tickle his toes and gazing at the white waves bobbing sheep-like to the shore. Beyond, he could see the green lights of squid boats, already on before sunset, and a lone kiteboarder arched across the water as he tacked upwind, his kite hovering above him like a candy-colored crescent moon as he gradually gathered speed and sailed smoothly up over the ocean.

The tide was now lapping and sucking at the beach, the back and forth calming him but also, as the evening sea often does to a man, making him melancholy.

He patted the sand, and a small crab scurried away. What a place to land up in, alone on a hot beach at the end of it all. With a narrow escape from who knows what.

He felt the sadness welling up as he remembered another beach, the one at Sandy Point in Maryland where he and Sylvia used to go for Sunday walks, and the little shack where they feasted on blue crabs and beer. And the winter nights when they would cozy up in the den under a quilt munching Doritos and watching *Spencer for Hire* reruns. And then he reached farther back in time, to a fainter memory of Baltimore, snuggling next to his Aunt Zora under a pile of frayed and mothball-scented blankets, and later sitting next to the ruddy hearth that warmed him from the toes up, his aunt muttering prayers while raking the coals.

"You smart enough to be a preacher, Ben," his aunt would say after he talked to her about his future.

She half-expected him to end up, like other black youngsters in Baltimore, in the armed forces or else working as a factory hand. Or even digging ditches, like his blues-playing buddy Daniel Thigpen. For a while, he and Daniel dreamed of working as bouncers in a jazz club somewhere far away in Chicago or New York. But his grades and exemplary behavior earned him the attention of Jim Ruff, the school counselor who took him out now and then for a plate of ribs. Ruff was a graduate of Fisk, and he helped Benton with his application to gain the Cravath scholarship there. After that, he became an academic star, winning prizes and scholarships right through graduate school.

He patted the sand again, and then scooped some up and poured it out, watching it fall like gentle rain. His aunt would have a fit if she saw him settled in a faraway Thai beach town, among folks who seemed so utterly different from him. Exiled in the Land of Smiles, where nothing was quite what it seemed.

He realized that whenever he felt he was settling down, things suddenly became unsettled. It had been the same way in Adams-Morgan and in Vienna when the fire happened, just as he and Sylvia thought they finally had it all, at least in terms of home life.

"Trouble sure will find us, Ben." How right Sylvia had been about that.

The Thais seemed so friendly and hospitable, with welcoming bars at every corner, but visitors didn't realize that someone could be poisoned at the drop of a hat. The view of Thailand seen in the tabloid *farang* news, with its balcony falls and bloody bar fights, the hangings in *wats* and bludgeonings on deserted beaches, now seemed much closer to the truth.

And now Thailand's best and brightest were disappearing because of what was happening up in the Golden Triangle among the Palin, a hill tribe that had once relied on growing and smuggling opium. The Palin had become guinea pigs in experiments being run by the pharmaceutical giants, due to their somehow being unique and protected by elf-like sous. If that wasn't a weird historical turn, he didn't know what was. It was indeed a fantastically fucked-up place for a retiree to call home.

But home was wherever one settled; that was the best way to think of it.

When Benton returned to Win's, she told him the Thai police wanted to speak to him urgently. She handed him a business card. It had the sword-and-shield crest of the Royal Thai Tourist Police.

Its owner, Captain Wirachon, met him at Win's the next day, a short wiry man in plainclothes with well-oiled hair and a pudgy nose. Benton asked for a photo ID, and the captain provided it. It said he was fifty-one years old, but the Captain looked not a day over thirty.

The restaurant had Win's partner Kurt sitting there, so Wirachon suggested the beach. They crossed the road to find a phalanx of pink-shirted matrons crouched beside reclining chairs, massaging the semi-comatose *farangs* lying within. Farther out, Thai families in pink were wading into the water. It was Tuesday, pink-shirt day in Thailand, and Benton was in green, wearing a paisley shirt and cargo shorts.

"Why is everyone decked out in pink?"

"It's the color of Mars. Each of our heavenly bodies has an auspicious color."

Wirachon pointed to a small fitness park near the changing rooms, where *qi gongers* were doing their drills.

He stopped to lift with a stick a condom discarded on the beach.

"Brassiere Beach is off the tourist track. May I ask what you were doing there?"

"Checking out the scenery," he said, watching Wirachon extract a plastic bag from his back pocket and pop the specimen in.

"Someone took you there?"

"Toy. D'you know where she is?"

Wirachon smiled, showing white, evenly spaced teeth. "What about a description?"

"Tall woman, about thirty."

"You're going to have to do better."

"Long hair, wears tons of makeup. Played in a band called Exploding Heads. Highly educated and fluent in English. Ask over at the Irish Pub."

Wirachon stopped at a vendor's stall. The lady was selling little blackish-green packets.

"Try one?"

"No thanks. I'm off Thai food for a while."

"Trust me." Wirachon handed Benton a packet, as the vendor watched with a grin. "Just the thing for your stomach. It'll pick you up."

It felt warm to the touch. Benton removed the little wooden stick to unlock one end of the packet. Opening it, he saw white rice tinged with purple.

"The purple stuff?"

"*Khao niao pheuak,*" the vendor said.

"Sticky rice with coconut milk and taro," Wirachon explained. "Grilled in a banana leaf. Simple and clean, like the good things in life."

Benton ate, a few bits of banana leaf getting into his mouth. The vendor was waiting to see Benton's reaction. It was sweet, gooey and delicious, and he couldn't help smiling.

"I knew you'd like it," Wirachon said as he paid. "It's on me. A gift from Thailand."

"Thanks."

"Ours is a safe country. Not like America, where everyone carries a gun."

"Safety is a state of mind," Benton said.

"The Kingdom wants all tourists to feel comfortable."

Wirachon stopped to look out at the sea, where a screaming couple bounced along on a jet ski.

"While the investigation is ongoing, it's important that you don't speak about this to anyone."

"Too late. I blabbed to Roussel at the hospital. And the nurses. And of course Noi knows since she brought me there."

"I meant about your friend, Toy. Your poisoning was an unfortunate accident."

"Is that so?"

"Yes. Noi has already been visited by our food inspectors. It won't happen again. Meanwhile, please report to the station at nine on Monday morning so we can take down the details of the missing person's case."

Wirachon offered his hand, and Benton shook it. He was glad that the interview was over.

Benton hoped Toy was all right. If she was okay but had joined Siri underground, why wouldn't she have said goodbye first? The *farang* whom Noi had earlier said she had gone off with remained a mystery, with Noi unwilling to offer any further information. He wondered if it were only the foreigners who were left in the dark about such matters, or whether keeping things quiet and behind the scenes was a Thai cultural norm. Either way, it did not seem like Wirachon would be of much help.

The recent events were enough to make a retiree's head spin. Benton hadn't had a drink since the evening of his poisoning, so he stepped into a 7-Eleven. He treated himself to a nice fat donut. Instead of a six-pack of Singha, he decided to save and buy a bottle of Sang Som. As he came out, he took a swig. It tasted like watered-down Jamaican rum with a mysterious whiff of industrial solvents.

Then he felt a vigorous clap on the back.

7. Ballade

Little John was seated in a four-wheel pushcart piled high with vegetables and yoked on one side to a motorcycle driven by Nellie.

"*Sawadee khrab, Khun* Nellie," Benton said, waving to her.

Nellie gave him a broad smile, waving in turn. She had shed much of the fat from her pregnancy.

Little John was in a snazzy white suit with blue pinstripes, sitting on a white plastic chair between a heap of green leaves and an ice chest.

"Off to a gentleman's club?"

"Musical evenin'," Little John said, mysteriously. "Chopin an' all."

He was surprised at that. "Where's Nora?"

Nellie smiled. "With my mother."

"Bike's in the fuckin' shop, so we're ridin' the chariot," Little John explained. He pointed to a place beside him. "Hop on."

Benton had avoided listening to classical music since Sylvia's passing. He wondered if he would be able to handle it.

"How much are tickets?"

He grinned. "Forget tha'! Fuckin' freebees from the Klub."

Benton climbed onto the pushcart, abandoning his 7-Eleven bag on the sidewalk. Little John opened the ice chest, handing him a beer.

"Outta town fer a bit?" Little John asked, as Nellie drove them through the evening bazaar.

"I was at San Paulo's. Stomach issues." He took a long sip of his beer.

"Welcome to Thailand." He lit a cigarette. "Shited me arse off when I first got here."

The lane became narrow, and the vehicle had to slow to a crawl as it made its way through a mélange of humans, vehicles and loitering dogs. There was the expected ribbon of pink, but also bemedaled white government uniforms. People were in an evening mood, laughing, some of the young ones poking each other in the ribs, the infants and the old ones wheeled along, the entire town out to snack in the bazaars on sticks of satay and fried chicken and a beetle or two before bearing plastic bagfuls home for dinner. He spotted the nurse from the San Paulo ER reception. She was in high heels and waved, welcoming him back to the world. Benton waved back from the pushcart.

"Didn't know you were into classical."

"Mum sang. Verdi and Puccini."

They turned to the left before a sign for the beach and came to a glass building set in an untended garden, with tall palms lining the driveway. It was the Center for the Arts. They got down. Nellie waved goodbye and drove off, and the men walked to the entrance. Police officers holding walkie-talkies swarmed about, hurrying passengers out of their chauffeured vehicles. After passing through the metal detector, they entered the lobby.

Thai men were gathering under the chandeliers in summer suits. Their ladies wore glittering eye shadow, while the expats were attired more casually, parading their potbellies and sagging flesh.

An elderly bull-necked man nodded at them, his bald pate emblazoned with a green serpent tattoo.

"The Shark's on Top," the man's T-shirt said.

So that was Sharky D'Alosio, the Australian owner of the Kit Kat Klub with its many freebies. His gangster life had been all over the expat news two months earlier after the shuttered Klub was reopened. Close on his heels was a light-skinned Thai girl in a black netted top and stiletto heels, sporting gold bracelets and an oversized watch. She looked dazzling, the chatter dropping as she passed. She looked young enough to be the man's granddaughter.

A man approached, clad in a black jacket with a clergy collar attached to a purple rabat.

"Father Dennis, meet me wee man Benton," Little John said. "Semi-retired, shall we say?"

"Wonderful to meet you," Father Dennis said, clasping Benton's proffered hand in both his hands. "And welcome to our community."

A tall, well-built man in cowboy boots was standing quietly beside him, eyeing Benton.

"Allow me to introduce my good friend, Pierre," Father Dennis said. "Doctor and polymath."

"You are too kind, Father," Pierre said, smiling quickly. Benton felt a sudden chill looking at his face. The man's eyes were black yolks dissolving into green pools, calm and watchful like those of a tiger.

"Fuckin' scumbag," Little John whispered as Pierre went over to talk to Sharky. "But rollin' in it."

The bell rang thrice, and the crowd, including several men with matching crew cuts and polyester suits who looked like plainclothes cops, started to head into the theater. There was a quick scavenging for seats, with open seating in all but the first two rows, which had been reserved for dignitaries. Benton found himself seated between Little John and Pierre, whose long legs were extended with his boots all the way under the seat in front.

People stood up and bowed to a brilliantly bejeweled Thai woman in the front row, who waved her fan back at them.

"It's a bloomin' princess," Little John said. "Git yerself upright."

Benton slowly stood up, but by then everyone else had sat down.

An orchestra was being set up, and soon they had launched into something that sounded like Gershwin. Benton couldn't place it, but it didn't matter, for the orchestra soon segued to a different pop tune the name of which he couldn't remember.

The audience clapped to show that they had recognized it. When the song ended a few minutes later, they clapped even louder, standing up again to bow to the princess.

"What the heck?"

"*Lion King*," Little John said.

"Elton John? But you said Chopin!"

They checked the program. Chopin came after the break.

The drinks had made him woozy. As he dozed off, the image of Sharky's companion floated up before his eyes. She was standing in front of him with very little on. A part of him was hoping she would approach, but she didn't. She swayed to the left, creating a slight breeze which made him realize that she was swinging from on high. Then the camera in the dream panned to the left, showing two other women swiveling from meat hooks beside her, their skins partly flayed with the flaps of their throats exposed. Their heads lay limply to the side, like that of Jesus on the cross. Peering closer, he recognized their faces as those of Siri and Toy.

When he woke up, the intermission was on already, and Pierre was asking him to make way so he could get up and stretch his legs. Benton wanted to pee, but he was too drowsy and stayed put. He dozed again and awoke just in time to see a woman striding onto the stage dressed in a black jumper and black slacks. She wore no jewelry or makeup and had her hair tied simply in a ponytail in the back. After vigorous clapping, she bowed and then strode up to the piano and launched into her program.

Benton recognized the opening notes of the *Nocturne in C-sharp Minor*. Sylvia had played it the day she returned from her first bronchoscopy, a follow-up to her complaints of chest pain. The CT scan had revealed nodules in her lung. He could smell her sweating as she sat at the piano after that first verdict, and he had tried to be understanding.

"They'll zap it off and you'll be fine, honey... just wait and see."

Sylvia glared at him, her shoulders trembling.

"Cancer won't get you, my love. We've still got time. It's lack of exercise that'll kill us."

She looked up, angrier now. "It's not about *you* Ben. Ain't you ever gonna understand?"

He grew angry then. He had loved her truly and cleanly and as best as a man could. She had become sick, and he would do anything for her, give her a kidney or whatever she damn well needed, but here she was, rejecting his care.

He could hear leaves rustling on the lawn outside, and he got up and went out, raking them violently from all over the lawn until he filled up the lawn bag, all the while dreading what was to come. To both of them. And then to him alone.

When he came back in, Sylvia was still at the piano, but in a better mood.

"Ben, come here." He stood behind her, hugging her awkwardly. If only she would turn around, he could make love to her then, fuck the cancer into oblivion.

"Ben, you can be a real doofus sometimes."

"Only sometimes though?" He squeezed her gently, and she coughed.

"You of all people know how I get, Ben." She stroked his fingers. "And now there's this shit."

"That's why I'm here, honey."

"I love you, Ben." Then her hand became stiffer. "But you're not in charge, and never gonna be in charge. So let me be *me*. Please!"

Let me be me. He hadn't, had he? He had screwed up that last segment of her life, the part when he should have made everything as beautiful as she wanted so she could cry and rage and tear things up and go blazing like a meteor into the night.

The pianist echoed the opening theme, then segued into a weepy melody that grew increasingly turbulent, the notes calling out hopelessly for a response before falling away in despair.

"Who's playing?" Benton asked.

"Marie de Villeneuve," Pierre murmured, leaning close enough for Benton to smell his aftershave. "Such sensitive rubato."

The nocturne morphed into a calm and thoughtful air before breaking into an animated mazurka that lowered to a pause. The pianist then resumed the tragic tone, the music becoming delicate and anguished, anger yielding to finality as the wind hissed curses to the dead.

They clapped again, the Thais bowing once more to the princess and then nodding appreciatively to each other. After waiting for the coughers in the audience to finish, Marie de Villeneuve hunched her shoulders and started the next piece.

Tristesse took him back to the time when Sylvia's playing had been a prayer. Given the swollen lymph nodes found in the bronchoscopy, it was likely that she had stage three lung cancer, though the radiologist thought it could be stage two. The surgeon was young and good-looking, with carefully styled hair, and he removed the middle lobe of her left lung as well as her lymph nodes, after which he confirmed that it was in fact stage four.

"I'm feelin' better, honey," she would say, lying when he woke her up with his morning kiss. Then she would start coughing, each cough ricocheting up through her excised chest, the pain driving her to tears all over again. "I've had enough, Lord," she would beg. "Let me go."

He had to hear that before heading off to work, cursing. She didn't want to die in a ward, so they had hired a day nurse. He would return early afternoon with flowers to place next to the medicines on her night table. He knew she loved roses and lilacs, and her face would light up, and she would raise her cheek for a kiss. As he held her hand all evening and late into the night, she reminded him about the early days, the walks and late-night sessions at Fisk, the picnics in Meridian Park, the sex in the Adams-Morgan kitchen. And his thing for knee-high boots, the ones she had worn when they first met.

"Remember those ridiculous kickers, Ben? Saying I was your sex machine!"

He touched her between her legs, promising they would do it again. She sighed, and though he was aroused, wondering what sex would be like in her present state, he had the good sense not to venture further.

He would order Chinese and Mexican takeout and would spoon little morsels into her mouth, opening his own lips while watching hers, like a mother feeding a recalcitrant child. But Sylvia's gums were sore from her chemo and her taste buds had started to go, and after a few swallows she would push his hand away. He would wait until she drifted off to sleep, devouring the remaining takeout by himself, sitting by the bed watching her snoring chest rise slightly up and down.

He had the habit of coming close to check if she was still breathing. She caught him doing that one night and slapped his wrist. "What you staring at, asshole?" He said nothing back, praying silently without believing, just like he used to with Aunt Zora, begging the universe to send her that special light that would turn the sick cells in her body into healthy ones. But later she asked, indirectly as always, for forgiveness, by begging him to hold her in his arms. He did, rocking her gently as if cradling an infant, and she fell asleep with a smile.

And then she started playing games with him. When her gum problems suddenly subsided, he grew worried and then suspicious and emptied out her plastic chemo prescription bottle. A mix of vitamin supplements popped out—Lutein for color vision, Lacprodan to rebuild cognitive health, and Proline for restoring collagen and skin texture. He was at first angry but couldn't argue. She wanted to look beautiful, be whole again. Then he sighed, realizing that during the day she had periods of energy where she was well enough to resume online shopping. She protested when he swept those noxious nostrums into the trash, but her week off chemo was all the freedom he could allow at this stage.

There were other times when her memories would flow instead of tears. She would remind him about how much fun they had together, and especially the time when she performed at lunchtime in the atrium of the Kennedy Center while he sat looking bored, stuffing his face with popcorn. He looked so funny then, like a giant chipmunk, she had said. They both liked to snack, but in those days he had his weight under control, while her belly stayed flat no matter how much cannoli she ate. She recalled their trips in their ancient and unpredictable Volvo into the Blue Ridge Mountains, with Smoky Robinson playing on the radio, when he would make her laugh all the time. He squeezed her cheek, promising her that there would be a time for laughter again.

Her brother Jess visited, a repulsively fat man with weeping toad-like eyes who left after one night, unable to bear the sight of her deterioration. Then came Daniel Thigpen. He was poor now, his career in shambles after a valiant battle with crack addiction. But he was still living in Adams-Morgan and played now and then. He said he had heard about Sylvia and had come to pay his respects. And to remind them of old times, though Benton wasn't in the mood.

He had wanted her to die then. But her body wasn't ready to let go. Seeing her suffer, his frustration had turned to rage, and now, listening to Chopin channeled through Marie de Villeneuve, he thought of the dull glow of Sylvia's face with the hair thin over her scalp and the spit drooling down her mottled cheek. Her other features, including the eyes, had been whited out by time.

"Shush," Little John said to him, his fingers to his lips.

There was a minute's gap while de Villeneuve composed herself. As the pianist launched into the fourth *Ballade*, the music started to soak in, its eddies and undertows dragging out slivers of half-buried feelings and memories. It was Sylvia whose emaciated wrists were floating over the keys, just as she had played in those last oxygen-starved days when she still believed she might be heading for remission. She could not have been more wrong; her cells had been dividing relentlessly, a sinister and conniving prolixity of nature designed to evade the best of therapies, a mad biology of destruction. Her spirit was there in the music, her fingers a blur on the keys except for the nails shining like cloves of garlic, while her face was obscured as she leaned low, her hair turned to twigs and straw.

Her stale, deathly breath was on his lips. He had smelled it that final night as she lay inert and gulping for air in his lap, as the pianist took the music to its apex before bringing it back down as though plunging into a dark well, for her trills were now giving way to the desperate moans of Sylvia's sickbed. The moans turned into cries, and now the girls from his dream were back, swinging faster, and he was pushing them as they shouted "Higher and higher, Mister Benton!" The dream started to accelerate, the swinging too fast for him to keep track of. Then he felt a firm, hard nudge, for he had been leaning his heavy frame hard on Little John's shoulder.

Benton left the hall towards the end of the "Funeral March." He stepped over Father Dennis's sandal-clad feet and several other people's toes and rushed towards the exit and into the men's room where he held onto the urinal, trembling like a child whose birthday present had just been snatched away. His sobs gathered force as he watched his golden flow hit the porcelain. While zipping up slowly he heard a faint sound; he looked around, seeing nobody, but the sound grew to a high-pitched whirring, like a fan belt about to tear. Then it stopped.

Drying his face with a towel, he caught sight of Pierre's eyes in the mirror. They had a chilly, piercing look that got his adrenalin pumping.

"Are you all right?" Pierre asked. He raised his hand to his chest and shook his head from side to side. "Chopin can weigh heavy on the heart."

Benton didn't answer. He flicked the paper towel towards the bin and missed. His hands were shaking.

As he headed for the exit, he felt a tap on his shoulder and saw the business card. He raised it closer to his glasses—*Pierre Montha Bulsani, MD, FACS, MPhil*. There was an address with a little map on the back. The doctor lived at the Peak condo complex, up on the hill above the monkey *wat*.

Benton stared at Pierre, whose smile remained inscrutably pleasant, though he could hear the faint fan belt sound again.

"Would you like to join us for dinner on Friday? Around seven thirty? You can meet my mother as well."

Then his dull brain finally recognized the fan belt sound. He had heard it before at the shack with Toy, when there was no car present. Now he realized that it was a human sound, coming from Pierre. So this was the *farang* who Noi said had left with Toy that evening.

"I'll come," he said, realizing that it was the only way forward. "But I'll have to pass on the Thai spices."

8. Specimens

Journal of
Dr. Pierre Montha Bulsani

Records of the most remarkable occurrences,
public as well as private.

To be published
after Dr. Bulsani's death
by the Executor of his estate,
Father Dennis Gillespie, S. J.

July 6

I was a child once.

One hand filled with grapes, the other dipped into a box of liqueur-filled *saukaulats* that an admirer had left for Maman, I would lounge in the gazebo of our home on Rue Romain Rolland. From time to time I would stroll over to our koi pond, fascinated by the carp flitting like flapping tongues through the dappled water. I was living amid waving palms, with the breeze carrying the sweet fragrance of the flowers known as cannonballs. Above us the sky blazed blue, and I could hear parakeets and cowbells and, in the distance, the Indian Ocean surf dashing against the rocks.

My Pondicherry childhood, living in that piece of paradise with Maman and my sister Sara, must seem idyllic. It was that, and also deeply disturbing.

Maman was born in Battambang, Cambodia, into grueling poverty, but she had the gift of a golden voice—a true nightingale. She came to Phnom Penh with a wave of other migrants, starting out with full-throated Khmer ballads in the streets and later finding work in the nightclubs. She soon fell under the scrutiny of the Cambodian military, and for a while she dated a general, while still scrounging around for food. But her true love, she always told me, was a fellow singer called Montha, who later rose to fame and was executed when the Khmer Rouge arrived in the capital in 1975.

I shudder to think what might have happened had Maman stayed on. All I can imagine is the bone fragments from the Killing Fields, or another terrified pair of eyes from the Tuol Sleng school of horrors, a black and battered mass chained to a bed. She might have starved, like her parents, or simply vanished, like my maternal aunts and uncles. But Maman was a survivor, par excellence, and she found her way out.

Maman knew quite a few French soldiers and several American advisers who frequented the nightclubs. She tried for months to convince them to take her away, without success. Then fate intervened in the form of an Indian doctor. He was attached to a World Health Organization team tending to an outbreak of cholera, but in between, he managed to find his way to the speakeasies and hoochie-coochie clubs. When Maman first met him, he was dressed in a Savile Row suit, with his hands carefully scrubbed after a long day with patients. The doctor toasted the beautiful chanteuse, inviting her to his table between songs and to his bed that night. He soon had Maman camping with him at the Hotel Le Royal instead of in her tenement room on sewage-filled Rue Romdeng where the cholera outbreak had begun. He ended up bringing her back to India at the end of his assignment. Her passport to freedom was the almost fully-formed child in her belly.

I was born on June 1, 1969, a month after she arrived in Pondicherry. Father chose a porticoed villa in the French Quarter, believing that she would feel less displaced in that once-Francophone milieu with its cobblestoned streets and decaying colonial mansions. It was also far enough away from his wife and child in Cuffe Parade, Bombay, where he had his home and surgical practice.

As a child, I accompanied Maman—protected with her sun umbrella—when she visited the patisserie on Rue La Bourdonnais, passing stately homes with high walls and gaily painted doorways framed by lovely arches and pediments. Heavily suited old Frenchmen and their powdered *madames* would come sweating out of those gates, which were then firmly shut by liveried Indian attendants. When we needed cuts of ham from the charcutier, we forayed farther west, along hot little streets where the air was filled with the scent of fish and fresh-cut jasmine, and where I could peer into the old Tamil mansions with their long, inviting verandahs. It would have been nice for us to join the residents for their decoctions of South Indian coffee, but our introduction to Indian high society never happened.

One morning, when I was five years old, Maman and I wandered up Rue Marine to catch sight of a local legend, a mysterious French-Jewish lady called "The Mother." She ran the ashram of her late companion Sri Aurobindo, who believed that biological evolution was not random but was directed towards a future where the spiritual destiny of humankind would finally be manifest. Such views had attracted a large following, and some of those disciples, Indians as well as Westerners, now stood gathered eagerly outside the ashram for her weekly blessing. A wizened old crone duly appeared on her terrace. The Mother spoke without a microphone, reciting a poem of sorts and then waved, drawing tremendous applause.

Encouraged that morning by that atmosphere of idiocy, optimism and good cheer, Maman made the foolish mistake of venturing farther east, taking me down Beach Road to stroll along the long promenade by the sea. There our path was blocked by a gang of Tamil rowdies who were lounging about with streaks of cow dung ash on their foreheads and beedis jutting from their lips. As they caught sight of Maman, the brutes called her *Miss Chinee* and untranslatable Tamil epithets. From their taunts, it was clear that in that small town someone had spread the news that I was a bastard.

Sensing our weakness, the rascals chased after us trying to get their hands on Maman, and it was only by a few vigorous strikes with her umbrella and the whistle of a kepi-capped policeman that we were saved from a much worse fate. After that, when Maman desired a view of the sea, she confined herself to the balcony, gazing out at glimpses of the Indian Ocean with a smoldering cigarette in her hand. She might as well have been in purdah. What a comedown for her, the gorgeous singer who loved the cosmopolitan culture of her nightclubs, her ears attuned to the clink of glasses and the compliments of spirited men.

Maman was trapped, with Cambodia in chaos and no money of her own and a child at her hip. But she was a plucky young woman who took on the roles of mother, memsahib and mistress. The household kept her busy, managing a team of servants that included our cook Akbar, the remote and untouchable sweeper Mary, Wilfred the driver, an anonymous and hernia-afflicted gardener, a dishwasher called Amma who banged and clanged away on our plates and vessels, and a succession of watchmen called Samuel or Selvan. There were also tradesmen calling out or simply hanging around at the back entrance, a succession of milkmen, breadmen, broom and mat men, junkmen, fish peddlers, masala pounders, and on occasion, bands of dancing transsexuals or *hijras*, purveyors of monkey shows, and gangs of distinguished-looking beggars. Maman would bargain with them or shoo them away in a mixture of American bar slang and broken Tamil, to their considerable amusement.

I stayed by her side, observing and helping out as needed. I was her companion, her little man, and also her burden. I was curious about everything and at the age of six could take apart a pocket radio and reassemble it in less than five minutes. The dusty grandfather clock took an afternoon. A baby squirrel, much to my chagrin, could not be reconstituted. But I made do with lesser conquests. I remember asking Maman for glue so I could replace the eyes of a fat cockroach. Maman was clueless and pointed me to Akbar, who provided tapioca starch. Stuck back, the eyes looked like aviator glasses on a dark face. At my insistence, Maman came to see it, her own eyes tender yet disapproving, a look that persists in every picture I took of her.

It was natural for a child to be attracted to eyes, including the honest licorice-like oculi of geckos and the fearless teardrop-shaped ones of the green scarab beetle. But I soon graduated to other targets after witnessing superb dissections by Akbar. I must have been seven or eight then, but he made such an impression! I would stand at the kitchen table while he spread chicken and lamb parts out on the previous day's *Deccan Herald*, the masala and stomach juices staining the faces of notables and the recently departed. Thanks to Akbar, I boasted among my initial collection several fine chicken crowns and some early origami-like experiments with entrails.

Maman was puzzled and then annoyed by my attempts to reconfigure the natural world right in my bedroom, but her lack of education and Father's lack of concern kept her from interfering. She must have sensed from the very first tugs of my little fingers and the lustiness of my suckles a curiosity that was unstoppable.

"Nobody knows, *kaun proh*," she would say with a sigh in response to yet another query as to why nature was put together the way it was.

Had Maman known better, choosing to intervene during the earliest stages of the young Pierre's wing-pulling and tail-swinging activities, the beneficiaries of which included dozens of anonymous dragonflies and our dachshund Sherry, the world might have seen a different outcome. But as things turned out, my innocent urge, so common among children to poke away into biological matter, was left unchecked and evolved into a passion that resulted in a far more intimate knowledge of the body than most, and even though I could not sidestep the evils of our world, it culminated in a vocation that has now changed it for the better.

My education was that of an autodidact. School was boring, as I was tolerated well only by the teachers, while being subjected to ridicule by my fellow students. They despised me for being bright as well as quirky and conducting myself with European manners that they found peculiar in someone who looked half Indian. So, life centered on the safety of home.

I grew up among books and toys, the earliest of which included a hairy and noticeably androgynous teddy bear with fragile glass eyes, and then, if I can remember correctly, a sexless rocking horse with a tasseled saddle which transformed me much to Maman's amusement into a whooping, bronco-riding Genghis. But soon the playthings became more educational. Over the years I came into possession of a stethoscope, a View-Master with slide packs of colorful capitals including a fabulous shot of the Rome Colosseum with the famous Nero statue visible behind, Ali's illustrated *Guide to Indian Birds*, a Daisy air rifle that fetched drongos and barbets out of the blazing sky, a succession of Meccanos and Erector sets, a collection of lightweight Time-Life books with color photos of scientists and industrial processes, a microscope that revealed lively bacteria swimming in the eviscerated guts of Sambo, Sherry's still-born pup, an accordion, adventure novels by Haggard and Hope, a bamboo flute, a pair of perpetually mating garden lizards, recordings of Fats Waller and Sinatra, along with 60s-era Cambodian pop, a monogrammed lab coat, two flicked library volumes of Grolier's *The Book of Knowledge*, and, eventually, a projector to display home movies.

Meanwhile, my sister Sara had arrived. She cried nonstop at first, spitting out her teething rings in disgust, but soon broke out of the cage of infancy and grew into a capable playmate. She was rebellious, given to pouting and answering back, and also dreamy, flighty, intuitive, and fond of experimentation. She spurned dolls and cooking sets in favor of roller skates, silly putty, false teeth and fake fingers. And a crossbow, a pogo stick and darts. Middle for diddle, my little one! As she grew up, I started bartering toys with her, handing over my

View-Master in exchange for the crossbow. I let her caress my squirrel skulls and rub her fingers gently on my moldy birdwings as she watched my lizards, fascinated by the male's blood-red bobbing throat. She begged for my flute and I gifted it to her, and she was a happy piper as she played. I also read her stories before bedtime, even interesting her, for a while, in the *Book of Knowledge*. She was particularly intrigued by the sections on tricks, including the instructions for creating, using matchsticks, General Waxvestas and his family, with their heads synthesized, along with swords, umbrellas and other accessories, from blobs of freshly melted sealing wax.

Living alone, a singer isolated from her Khmer culture, Maman had few means of dispelling despair. Luckily, she still had her share of admirers, some of whom she eventually allowed into her life.

I would wake up to hear creaks and whispers. Tiptoeing to the keyhole one night, I spotted Maman's fair legs wrapped around the waist of a Southern businessman, his black buttocks clasped by Maman's long fingernails. The room was filled with incense that coiled in the pale light that came through the curtains. Then the jambs of arms and legs jumbled together, reminding me, for I was too young to understand, of the mess of chicken parts on the kitchen newspaper.

The next morning she was up and humming a Khmer tune as she served us Akbar's breakfast pancakes soaked in coconut milk. I remember Sara making a mess, letting the *appam* get all sticky on her fingers and face, though she was old enough by then and should have known better.

Children notice early on their parents' failings, and like it or not, are drawn into their petty intrigues. And so it was that while still a youngster I began opening the door for Maman's lovers, and eventually, when I became aware of the rules of human mating, secretly cheering at the thought of how Father was being deceived.

Father. We called him that, not Papa, Appa, or Dad. I wonder why he bothered to come, for though he was generous with his money, he ignored Maman. She would be waiting for his arrival, arranging the house frantically, only to have him arrive, wash, eat, and then drive out to the club, coming back late, rejecting all her pleas for attention. All in all, he treated her no better than a whore, providing her cash but little else.

In those early days, although he did not strike Maman or me, it was Sara who got it in the neck and the behind. I am certain that Father did not consider her his own. Indeed, he was tall and fair with thin lips, a strong and silent man with a calm and cunning mien, while Sara was dark with a thick, heavy mouth and a gentle roll of belly fat—a spontaneous and excitable being. Their differences were enough to set him off. The tiniest infraction on her part, the slightest surliness or disobedience, even the mellifluous sound of her flute, made him seethe and then explode, slapping her cheek and slamming her head against hard surfaces and carrying out methodical buttock lashings with a donkey stick. The latter he called *putting*, for he was a golfer with an under-ten handicap, and he carried out the whippings while holding a classic one o'clock swing pose.

The thrashings went on and after each one Sara trembled, wept profusely and loudly, sustaining, we learned later, irreparable injuries. Maman did nothing, out of fear mainly, but also because she owed everything to him. I tried mightily to snatch my sister away from Father, but it never worked, for he was strong enough to bar my then feeble intrusions with his knee or with a fierce swipe of his fist. Afterward, Maman would wrap Sara close, and they would refuse to speak to Father for the rest of his stay, and even the canine Sherry kept her distance. The servants knew better than to intervene. I remember, after Sara received a particularly vicious thrashing, stepping out to find Akbar and Mary nonchalantly playing Parcheesi in the dust.

Was it Father's Indian upbringing, with that culture's well-known fear of strong women, that made him behave so terribly? Or was it the hint of Maman's infidelity, a smile in the sway of her hips, a whiff of a stranger's aftershave on her pillow? The causes didn't matter—the end result was the pain inflicted on us all. He was a horrible man, and like many such, managed to live his life without being punished for his sins.

As for me, I kept promising my little sister that Father would never lay his filthy hands on her, only to see her thrashed again.

Then Nature intervened, apparently unable to witness the prolonged horror of my sister's existence. Sara was wrenched away at the age of eight with a fatal dose of cancer, leaving me bereft for life.

I have tried to make amends, Sara, so that no one will have to suffer like you did. If only I had possessed the moral strength when I was younger to save you, my little sister.

With Sara's passing, my childhood ended. The games were over, and life became a serious, competitive endeavor. The next year flew by in darkness and mourning, the saddest year of my existence. Then, when I turned sixteen, Nature intervened again, giving me an intimation of my true vocation.

It happened in class, where a frog lay calmly on its back, prepped with sweet-smelling formaldehyde, its thighs, trim and supple, spread apart as if in skin-colored tights, waiting for me to finger the marvelously multi-use cloaca before deftly snipping from there all the way up through the abdominal muscles via the breast plate to the mouth with its front-tethered tongue, pinning the skin flaps aside to reveal the prized internal organs. It was hard not to become excited at the sight of that enormous meaty mushroom-like liver, the three-chambered heart, the ventricle white and shiny, the stomach bloated with fresh insects, with the creature's winter fat stored separately in yellow, lettuce-like shreds, the intestines neatly packed and unraveling at my touch like a festive ribbon, and then the ovaries bustling with thousands of eggs and budding spawn!

While I had explored frogs, birds and several little mammals at home, this dissection was supervised by an oily-haired bespectacled teacher called Mrs. Kunkuma Poo and carried out alongside a dozen eager dullards all of whom dreamed of becoming doctors, each one learning to handle his specimen carefully so as not to make a mess. I was thrilled to be using proper equipment, including German stainless steel forceps, scissors, scalpels with excellent blades, teasing needles and T-pins. They were a far cry from Akbar's kitchen knives or my garden shears, though nothing like the surgical curettes, tenaculums, pessaries, punches, rongeurs and trocars that I would later come to know and love.

I felt reassured, even vindicated, to discover that there was a community of like-minded scientists who shared my interest in anatomy. Once the school reports came in, Maman also realized that I was headed in Father's footsteps, and she did what she could to support my budding interest in medicine. She gave me the freedom to pursue my interests in peace, ignoring the noises from the creatures trapped in my room. As I started putting extracted parts together to form increasingly complex wholes, I realized that a human being could be viewed as a giant jigsaw, though I had no inkling then of the distance mankind had to travel to put that puzzle together.

9. Banquet

Benton arrived at the Peak just as the sun was setting. The security guard checked his name and then rolled a squeaky gate open. He walked across the driveway to a glass door where he had to speak his name to be buzzed through. He passed a sequence of terraces, each one with a swimming pool surrounded by waving palms and rows of peculiar, bird-shaped flowers. At the second tower, he was buzzed in once more, into a glass box that ascended speedily into the greying light causing the pools and their surrounds to shrink with each higher floor until it glided to a halt on the thirty-fourth floor. The doors slid open to reveal a private entrance with a hand-shaped brass knocker.

Pierre was dressed in jeans and a tight kurta, his chest muscles bulging and his boots shining.

"So glad you could come, Benton!" Pierre greeted him with a beatific smile. "What will you have?"

"A Singha is fine, thanks."

The guests were standing in the living room drinking champagne. He spotted an old lady in a velvet waistcoat and jeans wearing a cap with sequins. She was swaying in time to "Voodoo Child." The guitar god's immortal lick made Benton feel reassured, though he reminded himself to remain alert. He took in the walls, adorned with paintings and fantastic rock-cut Buddha faces illuminated by a blue floodlight. His host had created a polychrome mini-Angkor Wat in his living room.

The woman smiled and extended her arms up to him.

"Jack! *Mon petit filou!*"

He was neither Jack nor her *filou*, but he exchanged kisses with her anyway.

"Why didn't you write, Jack?" Her breath smelled of champagne and ganja, and her face seemed familiar.

She was swaying faster, and he looked away to the Cambodian Buddha on the wall. Its eyes were bathed in the dream of some faraway time and place.

"You spoke at the National Geographic Society in Washington," Benton said, finally remembering. "I'm sorry, but I'm drawing a blank for your name."

"Machteld Megumi Tollendal," she said, leaning on his arm. "Memory is a fickle friend!"

Pierre handed Benton the beer. "Megumi is a dear friend and a distinguished scholar of hill tribes," he said, then hurried off to greet a new arrival.

"My grandfather was French—a caoutchouc planter in Trang province." She tapped her feet, as Hendrix reached a crescendo. "He married a geisha."

"MM, I can't believe you're still around." An elderly man came limping towards them. He wore a solar topi and sported a handlebar mustache and a beer belly larger than Benton's. In place of a left ear, there was a circular white scar with pink edges.

"Heyho, Harry—what a lovely surprise!" They kissed.

"I'm Harry Oldes. With an ee-ess." The handshake was old-school and vigorous.

"Harry's a spy, aren't you, my love?" Megumi said.

Harry laughed heartily, spittle forming at the corner of his lips.

Father Dennis greeted them with a tray. "Canapés, anyone?"

Megumi stuffed her mouth with one. "Mmm! Noix de Saint Jacques."

Benton tried some *foie gras*. "Thanks, Father."

"Thank our host," Father Dennis said, beaming and bearing the empty tray away.

A woman walked past without seeing him, accompanied by a huge Thai man. It was Noi.

"Hold on," Benton said. He followed her to the kitchen. She turned at the entrance as if she were expecting him.

Benton grabbed her arm. The skin felt crinkled, like cellophane.

She bowed, her head quivering with emotion. "I very sorry, *ka*."

He held on to her arm and then drew her closer. Her mouth opened in alarm. Her tongue was crooked, falling to one side.

"I go help Pierre," she said. She withdrew her arm quickly and then shut the kitchen door behind her.

He returned to the living room, prepared for the worst.

Harry pointed a finger at Benton. "Allow me to guess. You were at the Fort?"

"Wow."

Harry laughed. "I worked for years with SIGINT guys—can spot the regulars a mile away."

"You were USGC?"

"CIA SOG. Training our tribal commandos in the Plain of Jars."

"So you took on the Pathet Lao," Benton said. "While we shit-bombed their country to smithereens."

"I fought the good fight," Harry said quietly, pointing to his missing ear. "And resigned in protest once we started bombing."

"Hats off to you for that," Benton said. "I hear ordnance is still exploding all over Laos. Embarrassing, to say the least."

After more chitchat, a gong rang thrice, announcing dinner.

The guests were ushered into the dining room. He found his seat between Father Dennis and a young beauty in a black and red tessellated waistcoat.

"Benton, meet Mimi," Pierre said, indicating the woman beside him. He realized he had seen her before—at the Chopin concert.

"Where's Sharky?" he asked, quietly.

"Touring Cambodia," Mimi said. She wore diamond earrings that sparkled under the chandelier lights. "Back soon, *ka*."

Noi came over. She had white gloves on and carried a bottle of wine, which she poured for everyone.

"I'm Surry, by the way," the big Thai man said. His accent was Singaporean, or maybe Burmese.

Benton nodded and took an initial sip from his wine glass. The golden drink fell like clear nectar into his mouth. It sat there blissfully on the palate, waiting to be congratulated.

His hand shook as he caught Noi's eye and asked for a refill. The bottle label said Domain Leflaive. He didn't know that much about wine, but it was clearly the expensive kind.

"I thought it was just a private dinner," Benton said.

"I got carried away with cooking," Pierre said. "So I decided to have the crew over."

"The crew?"

"Some of the Foundation staff and well-wishers," he said, indicating the guests.

Benton had checked out ChantouBulsaniFoundation.org before coming. It was a research institution, registered as a charity in the US, Thailand and Australia. Their basic pitch was simple—gene therapy offered cures that people considered miraculous for diseases that included hemophilia, thalassemia and certain cases of leukemia. But drugs like Glybera cost a million dollars, which was outrageous and an insult to ordinary people. The Foundation was going to make genetic medicine affordable for the masses. Their targets were cancers of the stomach, liver and colon, and they had been carrying out trials since 2005. In some cases the drugs had been able to extend life by several months. In addition to studies of the effects on sick patients, the Foundation was also testing drugs for cancer prevention.

The site provided details of the Foundation's pharmaceutical sponsors, funding recipients and the annual reports. There were links to scholarships, summer camps for kids, beach cleanups and teaming up with a French medical outreach outfit that ran community clinics among hill tribes in the North, particularly the Palin. There they focused on ear and eye health, hygiene, safe drinking water and subsidies for healthy school lunches. The results from all their clinical trials over the past decade were also online, indicating that in over three hundred and sixty subjects, they had found only four instances of side effects that involved anything other than drowsiness, sore throats and temporary changes to taste buds.

All in all, it seemed like an exemplary site. And the webmaster was Pierre himself.

"Your verdict on the catfish?" Pierre asked.

Benton prodded the peanut-encrusted flesh, feeling the fine white segments coming away soft on the fork. He lifted the fork into his mouth, finding that the flesh had coagulated into a substance with the meaty flavor of jackfruit. It had a garlicky tang and wasn't at all spicy.

"Like mousse," Megumi said. "What is that fragrant paste?"

"*Kroeung*," Pierre replied. "Mainly shallots, lemongrass, kaffir lime and lots of fresh garlic."

"Mainly?" Father Dennis asked. He rubbed a finger under his clerical collar.

"I've added my own finishing touches," Pierre said, his incisors sparkling.

Noi nudged Benton as she served the second course, a golden cabbage-like substance with grated coconut. It lay basking in a bed of basmati rice decorated with fried potatoes that were still crackling.

"Careful, *ka*," she whispered.

Benton found himself tasting a small morsel against his best instincts. It felt as if an electric current had struck his tongue, and then it was melting in his mouth, filling it with the fragrance of aniseed. He swilled it against his palate as if it were wine.

"Any guesses?" Pierre asked.

"Pomfret?" Mimi wondered aloud, wrinkling her tiny nostrils.

"Shark?" The voice was that of a Thai boy sitting at the corner of the table.

"Bravo!" Pierre said. "*Fricassée de requin aux aubergines*. A Vieux Pondicherry specialty."

"I would never have guessed," Megumi said. "Somchai, you clever boy!"

"Caught near the Similan islands," Somchai said, using his phone to scan his plate. "Off the west coast."

"How can you tell?" Father Dennis asked.

"The barcode is a tell-all," Pierre said.

Surry nudged Somchai. "Go on, son. It's your baby."

Somchai smiled. "You inject the fish with a chemical that provides a unique signature when you run a light mask from your phone over it. Each time you scan it, the fish's history gets updated."

"So you can track," Pierre added, "the fishy journey from its home to yours. Somchai's invention is now in beta test. For Thailand's new catch certification system."

"It'll be humans next," Surry said. "Luckily, the additive is safe and biodegradable."

Father Dennis shrugged. "About as safe as those humongous Shanghai eggplants."

"I spotted them at the supermarket," Megumi said. "Aren't they grown from seeds germinated in space?"

"No worries," Pierre said. "I get mine from village markets."

The conversation sounded muffled to Benton as he helped himself to more food. He sniffed the heap of shark and rice on his plate before tucking in and gulping down more wine. His mind was soon tangled like the genetic material that lay coiled in his cells as he nosed deeper, grunting softly, his tongue clicking against his teeth. Until a meaty, mottled ball spun softly out, a black-and-gray truffle with swirls and spirals and tiny reflecting windows, like the childhood marbles at Shulkins', the second-hand furniture store on Baltimore's Orleans Street. He leaned low over the tablecloth, following the glass balls with their shiny blades and vanes, their milky sheens glistening under his nose as he observed shards of mysterious crystals within. He sniffed a miniscule green peewee that looked luscious enough to be swallowed and pawed a giant bumboozer that trotted heavily along, scattering obstacles in its path. Then he started to doze off.

Someone was talking to him. "You'll sleep it off, Jack."

Minutes or even hours later, he was awake enough to recall a dessert of lemon posset with fresh strawberries and wild honey. All that was left on his plate were the berries' green calyxes, glowing like radioactive plants.

"Somchai," Pierre was saying, "here is a problem for you. Two savages are sitting on a log, a big savage and a little one. The little savage is the son of the big savage, but the big savage is not the father of the little savage. How come?"

Somchai's head perked up. "The big savage is not the father?"

"Not the father," Benton murmured.

Somchai's fingers, long for a fat boy, darted across the back of his neck, scratching his opposite ear. "His Mummy?"

"Somchai, that's excellent," Pierre said.

"We have a genius among us," Father Dennis said.

"He's twelve, and enrolling in college next year," Surry said. "Did you know that our boy is also a poet?"

"Oh, a poem please!" Megumi said. She took off her waistcoat, revealing pale, rounded shoulders.

"Black don't crack," Aunt Zora said, her teeth clicking. "Brown don't frown."

She was suddenly seated behind Mimi in a polka-dotted dress, her osteoporotic back straightened out by the comforts of her heavenly abode. She had puffs of fat under her eyelids, and her cheeks seemed chubbier than when Benton had last seen her. The rest of her face, including her seedy grin, was formed from hard, yellow bone.

Benton's heart beat faster, and the hair on his back was standing up. He knew he was wide awake and that he wanted to scream WHATTHAFUCK! and flee from the cackling puppet mocking the memory of the aunt who had loved and raised him. But his mind refused to follow up, bolting him in silence to the chair.

He belched, the golden flecks of food scattering on the tablecloth. He lapped at the spillage, feeling lightheaded, almost buoyant in the presence of danger. Harry stood up in consternation. Noi rushed in to clean up, as Pierre frowned, swirling his brandy, its amber eddies glinting under the chandelier.

"My poetry is not that good," Somchai said, trying to break the tension. "I'm still learning about meter."

"Then recite something from our Asian anthology," Surry suggested, looking away from Benton.

Somchai cleared his throat and then began.

The wind of change forever blows

Across the tumult of our way
Tomorrow's unborn griefs depose
The sorrows of our yesterday.

"Bravissimo!" Harry said. "Though a tad morbid for such a festive evening."

Aunt Zora now began to sing in her deep contralto.

Whenever I am tempted
Whenever clouds arise
When song gives place to sighing
When hope within me dies.

Time dragged its feet as Benton gazed at the guests at the table. Somchai doodled on his napkin. Harry fumbled around for a cigarette in his pockets, finding a crushed one that he examined curiously between his fingers. Mimi came around the table and perched on the corner of Harry's knee, lighting his cigarette.

"More brandy, anyone?"

Surry got up as if on cue and went out, the heat of his body leaving a shock wave as he passed. Somchai followed him. Noi poured. Aunt Zora was snoring now, her teeth bared. Mimi took a puff and then returned the cigarette to Harry. Her waistcoat lifted up, revealing a six pack and a navel ring. She sported a swirling tattoo on her right side that vanished into her slacks. Benton stared thoughtfully, his nostrils twitching, trying to imagine her mating with Sharky. Harry started to tell a story. A fly landed on a napkin. Father Dennis excused himself, saying he had to be up early for a service. Pierre went to see him off. Benton's body was changing, with a pink protuberance sprouting from his person. And then another hairy grey one. The fly flew away. Mimi was kneeling before Harry. Then she was on her stomach with her slacks torn off, and now Benton had shoved Harry aside and was trying hopelessly to mount her, his pink protuberance stabbing her behind while he grasped a table knife that felt tiny between his trotters and brought it down on her neck. The blade flashed along with her diamonds as he grunted and thrust in time to the music. Mimi was kicking him in the chest and screaming her head off and then with a flurry of hooves it was all over and he was back in his seat.

71

"Cain hur yer naaaaaooooooow."

He was in the presence of Siri, hearing her render Smith and Springsteen's immortal anthem "Because the Night." Siri's punkness had gone as if it had been boiled out. Her hair was now straggly, her lips vulpine, her skin bark. Her head was now rising like a mirage below his hands, her flayed neck still visible above the dangling entrails. He turned her head around, and her face thrust itself lewdly towards him, the crucifix clinking against the table.

"Say yer wan me stay?"

You bet, he cried out in his mind, his iron protuberance lunging at the entrails that dangled before him. There was a muttony smell, and then someone's mouth was on his, gulping at his bloody lips like a fish. It was Sylvia, still lingering in memory. He wanted to touch her, but there was nothing there so he rode faster, hissing with soft squeals. But his mount was now ill-equipped for action, no more than an elbow and hip.

"Higher and higher, Mister Benton!"

He pushed harder until he came in a medley of grunts and snorts, his semen a mix of blood and piss. Someone started to clap as Megumi recited a haiku in Japanese, while the room rotated by ninety degrees, first clockwise, then in reverse, then back again like a pendulum.

The clapping grew louder, and his ears perked up. He could hear someone singing in the living room. He felt the urge to pee and vomit at the same time. Summoning all his energy, he slid off his chair and staggered out.

He kept it all inside until he got to the bathroom, where he vomited a mess of food and booze. Running the tap, he heard the water gurgling and swishing about before realizing that the drain was blocked. He peed as best as he could, observing as the piss splashed about on the floor that his prick had thankfully reverted back to its normal proportions.

He had been drugged, he knew that much, but now his brain seemed to have turned into putty, Play-Doh twisted by spirits. *Goddammit, Lord*, he tried to scream, *free me from my fate*, but the words only caught in his throat.

When his mind cleared, he stepped out. He turned right and walked down a long corridor drawn by the light from a partially open door.

The room had a desk with computers, several cabinets, work tables and toolboxes.

"My oh my, it's Jack the Knave," Surry said. He was draped in a white lab coat. "Welcome to our man cave."

On one of the work tables, under a lamp, Surry was carefully laying out an arrangement of white and yellow pieces.

"Wthefubarfucksit?" Benton had tried to speak, but what came out didn't sound at all like what he meant. He would shut his mouth rather than humiliate himself further.

Surry laughed. "This one arrived a few days back from Phnom Penh."

Somchai, who had been kneeling over a wooden crate, picked out an ear-shaped bone from it and deftly carried it over to his father, placing it near the pelvis.

"It's a challenge," Surry said gently. "A fractured tibia here, a smashed ischium there. Thank goodness Somchai is here to help."

"It's all the same person," Somchai said. "Dr. Pierre has already matched the mitochondrial DNA."

"We will know who," Surry added, "as more information builds up—size, age, gender, injuries, etcetera."

Benton watched the father and son for a while, as the body began to take its full form. They worked silently, together fusing a pattern out of bone hunks and chips. There were numerous gaps, but the skull was in one piece. When it was done, Surry took pictures, adjusting the lamp and taking shots from different angles.

"We are in the presence of a young lady," Surry said. "What sort of dress would go well for the museum?"

He pranced about as if in drag, to Somchai's pealing laughter.

"In a sarong?" Surry asked. "Or evening attire, like the boss's Maman?"

"Stop it, Dad!" Somchai was almost hysterical.

"Enter the dragon," Surry said quickly, as Pierre came in.

Pierre smiled at Benton. "I see you've calmed down. Though I think you owe us an apology."

Benton grunted an attempted reply.

"Never mind. I am glad that you are enjoying the puzzle. Surry and Son have a real flair for it."

"The museum is to honor Dr. Pierre's mother," Somchai explained.

"Yes. I promised that we would gather together her friends from the old days in Cambodia." He turned to a figure in the corner. "*Ne vous inquiétez pas, Maman. C'est un invité enivré.*"

Benton stared, and then he saw her, illuminated by track lights in the ceiling. She was wearing a lace blouse and a gold-embroidered Cambodian silk skirt, and to top it all, a beret. He recoiled at first as if he had suddenly realized he had gatecrashed into the wrong sort of party. Then he couldn't help shuffling closer.

She was real. Yellow, all bone, her skeleton small and squat, facing them propped against the side of a grandfather clock. The vestige of a person. It made him tremble, the tremor shaking him down to his hooves.

Pierre pointed a finger, with a flame flickering at the tip.

"Benton, as we discussed over dinner, you are now on your first Phase Zero cancer prevention trial." He spoke in a deep voice as if he were explaining the basics to a dopey undergraduate.

Benton was still reacting to the skeleton. He wanted to ask Pierre what kind of son would turn his own mother into a relic for his fantasies, but the words wouldn't come.

Pierre's eyes were now a pair of gleaming leaves floating on blood-red waters. "The Foundation is grateful, my friend. And I promise to work together with you on your fitness goals. Because in your present state…"

"Oops," Somchai interrupted. "The guest's gonna hurl again!"

Benton felt as if he had been violated. This was how it was going to end, falling prey to the schemes of a madman and his followers. He tried cursing, then screaming, but remained silent, his vocal cords trapped by a viscous membrane. Meanwhile, to compound his humiliation, a mass of gas was traveling swiftly through his caecum. He managed to stand up and raise his leg and look away.

"Wake up and smell the sausage," Surry said.

"Pee-you," Somchai said, holding his nose and laughing at the same time.

Pierre hurried out.

Benton lurched forward in a half-hearted attempt at pursuit, but he lacked the energy. He managed to make his way into the living room, where Megumi was swaying next to the stereo. A mournful Thai song was playing, of which he could make out only two words—*rak*, meaning love, and *khitung*, meaning miss. Those words now seemed the basis for all love songs and of life's own trajectory from love to death.

"To die is your grandfather's custom," Megumi said. "And you must follow it. That's what the song says."

She was facing him, her ancient shoulders gleaming in the track lighting. "May the sky take your strength, may the earth take your bones."

The Bayon Buddhas remained in their meditative trance.

He inhaled. Alive still. And exhaled.

Inhale. Voices of the ancients. Snatches of song. Exhale.

"Jack," Megumi said. "You're not making sense. Come outside to get some fresh air." She dragged him to the balcony, and he followed her like a zombie on a leash. The deck was narrow and damp, the sea and sky uniformly black except for a sliver of moon.

Megumi stood at the corner, blowing out a column of smoke that hovered like a question mark above the blackness. The railing was vibrating as if it were being shaken.

"Darling, Pierre is a man on a mission. There's no stopping him now."

"Badass." He was cursing now, his nose wet, though the words were now forming. "Bum. Boozer."

"Crazy and egotistic," Megumi continued. "But which Richie-rich entrepreneur isn't? At least he puts his money where his mouth is. Did you know that his life savings have been willed to the Foundation?"

The wind rose from the sea, hissing. Crying in shame. As he begged on his hind legs.

"*Mon méchant*," she whispered with her ganja breath. "What will you give me?"

"Two... Sir... Cur... Woo... Woolly...," he said, amazed at his speaking passable French. Even as he wondered what poison it was that had coursed through his veins.

"You will be meeting Toy," Megumi said quietly. "But it's too little, too late for Siri."

The night was now spinning like a top around him, and he collapsed.

10. Hill Country

Stop the car," Nadine said. "It's nine a.m., and I'm thirsty already."

Bert Passelsky pulled up near a stall presided over by a girl in an enormous hat.

It had been a terrific tour of Thailand. They had gone snorkeling off the island of Ko Tao, where they had glided among shimmering swarms of bluefin trevallies and parrotfish draped in silvery cocoons. When they tired of the life by the reefs they had kayaked, lazed about, and climbed the limestone cliffs that sprouted like monuments on tiny outcrops in the middle of the sea. Bert had gone boating in a mangrove swamp while Nadine had taken a cooking course where she learned how to carve watermelons into roses and turn daikon radishes into orchids. They had cycled together in a historical park, climbing in and out of ruined temples and posing for pictures in their safari outfits. In the evenings they had themselves massaged side-by-side until their brains turned to mush.

"What are those?" Nadine said, pointing to an array of beakers with drinks in different colors.

"The blue one is butterfly pea juice," Bert said. "The pink is roselle."

He asked the vendor about the pee-colored one.

"*Nam mathuam*," the girl said, stirring her ladle.

"Bael juice," he translated. "I remember now. Cleans out the insides."

They ordered the beverage, and then he started the car and they drove slowly on amid a crush of other Chiang Mai vehicles.

"Sweet enough for you?"

She crunched her ice and then grinned. "Not after what you did this morning."

They had made no friends on the trip, but Nadine didn't seem to mind that at all, for she was delightful and lovable and feisty. She also seemed in tune with all his moods, able to sense when he was in favor of banter and foreplay and when he needed to be alone with his thoughts. That morning, it had been the former, with Nadine becoming so rambunctious that they had toppled off the bed laughing.

"Must be an accident ahead," she said.

They were stalled near a fruit market. People were getting out of their cars and buying fruits. They followed them, drifting amid nature's bounty, inspecting fruits of all sizes, shapes and colors. He saw clusters of pimpled red *lichees* whose insides he remembered as soft and translucent, tangy-sweet and throat-tickling, and next to them were their scrumptious cousins the dumpling-like *longans*, and then bunches of thorny *rambutans*, their flavor acrid like over-ripened grapes, and over at the next stand, clusters of malty-sweet *lamut* or Mexican zapotas whose seeds sometimes lodged in his throat, and *mafuang* or star fruit, their crunchy yellow ridges tasting of tangerine and pear, and maroon *mangkhud*, or mangosteens, whose melt-in-the-mouth white cloves tasted like an exquisite pair of lips, and stubbled green *noi-na* or custard-apples, with their fragrant heart-shaped interiors concealing a succulent pulp that reminded him of Nadine's tongue that morning. He squeezed her hand tight, surrounded now by other fruits, clumps of the tiny yellow finger bananas favored by pregnant women.

"What's that?" he asked the vendor, pointing to one of the banana bunches.

"Twenty baht, mister."

"*Riak wa arai?* What is it called?"

"*Gluai jun,*" he heard another vendor say. "Sandalwood banana."

"I thought you were the Thai expert," Nadine said, laughing.

"I've forgotten, okay? It's been thirty years."

Bert had arrived for the first time in Thailand after a longish journey from the prison camp at Nelspruit where he had been awaiting his court-martial. His trip had started out easy, for his crime was not against his own kind. A military boetie posted to guard him agreed to be tied up after drinking himself silly, and then a hapless kaffir sweeper was deprived of his rags, and so it was that blackfaced Robert Bardeski had made it out in the night into the wilderness of the southern Kruger and then over the border into Mozambique. He had purchased a passport in the harbor at Lourenço Marques, and then in no time the newly-minted Bert Passelsky was on a flight to Nairobi and thence to Dubai and Bangkok.

Bangkok dazed him, the blasts of humid air leaving him drenched in sweat. The river was dappled with shadows, with tiny men in enormous hats plying swift boats. Occasionally a barge swept by, pulled by oarsmen wearing triangular caps, with a passenger sitting on a small chair in the middle. Bert boarded a skiff and cruised from one jetty to another visiting the pagodas, stepping barefoot on sun-scorched stones. He dropped into the Grand Palace where a male figurine was meditating in an expensive gold cloak.

"Emerald Lord Buddha," the guard said. "No touch please."

He wondered what the fuss was all about. Examining the statue while the guard was distracted, he observed that it lacked the glassy translucence of beryl. It was in fact jasper, common in the Northern Cape. Not worth flicking.

There were plenty of other pastimes to occupy him. He got himself tattooed. And massaged. Lying on his back, a pair of Asian hands and sometimes a firm leg would press on his thighs, and then his foot would be resting on a shoulder or lap. It left him relaxed, *sabay sabay*, a bit woozy. After that he was toned and ready for a night of drinking, following which, his inhibitions loosened, he would allow himself to be shagged for all he was worth, for he was shallow enough then to think of intercourse as a cash pleasure like beer.

He made few friends in the bars, as the men there held things close and did not share much. They were soldiers, sailors, deserters, small-time crooks and lamsters like him. He got into scrapes and gave better than he got. Once he broke the nose of a pimp who demanded extra after a busy buttfuck with a whore. He had meant no more than a tap, but when his fist landed he heard a grating sound and then blood spurted from the pimp's nostrils. Meanwhile the lady was bawling her head off.

He regretted his actions even then, but nothing could kill his youthful drive. It had been the same in Africa, where he had been punished for using excessive force. He had not hated the blacks and even admired some of the Zulu and Xhosa men for their fighting spirit. But because he was young and fit he didn't mind getting in a hard scrap, and with the kaffirs he and his fellow soldiers always had the upper hand. And once he had tasted the pleasure of seeing a strong man broken and driven to his limits, he had wanted more, even though he knew it was wrong and cowardly of him.

Now he was in Thailand, with nobody to lord it over. So he fished, got stoned, drank himself silly, ate sizzling street food and took watery dumps in the greasy river. He watched the boats, worked on his tan, and sweated through some of his old workouts. Then his money started to run out, and a fellow in a bar told him of the cheap living in the mountains of the Golden Triangle.

It was in May Tai that he finally came of age. The village was a cluster of bamboo huts on either side of an unpaved road, at the end of which stood a colorful little market with stalls selling wilted fruits and vegetables. The people there dressed differently from the lowlands, in colorful blouses, embroidered waistcoats and loose pajama pants, with some of the women wearing bright turbans and pinafores.

He left his backpack at a vendor's shack opposite the bus stand and then set off to explore the village. Some of the homes were bamboo structures mounted up on stilts, the ground floor home to pigs and chickens and scraps of lumber. Others were barely thatched holes in the ground. People stared at him as he passed, and some of the children playing in the dust hurried away. He spotted a pair of women conversing at their doorstep, with one picking lice from her child's hair. They looked stunning in their matching red blouses but turned away as he stopped and stared. Their speech did not sound like Thai.

A man was walking past with two mud-encrusted pigs. He decided to ask what language it was. "*Khotord, phasa arai?*"

"Palin," the man said, showing off a tooth he was wearing on his neck. He had scars on his jaw.

Bert pointed to the tooth. "Tiger?"

"Palin," the man repeated, looking at him sternly with bloodshot eyes. He had the look of a warrior fallen on hard times. The man reminded him of the Xhosa, handsome and dignified in meetings but capable of savagery when baited.

He didn't know much about the Palin, but it didn't matter as the place was affordable with rents at two hundred baht a month and good beer to be had at twenty baht a glass. Even cheaper was the Thai whisky; its bitter burn as it went down brought to mind the rugged red earth of his native land, the jagged cliffs, the herds of eland and gemsbok. He had loved that southern land where he could run free on foot and horseback and Harley over hill and plain with the thrill of living a physical life close to the land, looking up into those azure skies knowing they promised untold possibilities if only he could grasp them.

He knew he would never set eyes on his country, nor see his strong and silent pa who had taught him so many things, including, in his last summer of high school, how to hunt a leopard and skin it. The pelt, for all he knew, was still up on the bedroom wall at their farmhouse in Ixopo. Nor would he kiss the worn but sweet-smelling cheek of his ma, who always raised him up no matter how hard he fell.

There was boggerall to be done but to live among dark-skinned strangers. And he was content to do that, a fugitive sitting and gazing out at his particular patch of the planet. From his shack he could see hills striped with terraced farms, their rib-like ruts coursing down to the Burmese border. In the evening the valleys were filled with smoke from the hamlets, each one a ramshackle arrangement of huts and beds adjacent to a field or pond. And along the paths, coffee pickers returning home with baskets of berries. Sometimes he saw women climbing high towards a forest. He later explored it, discovering, in the valley beyond, a field of purple poppies.

He was a different person then, a young man who had made a few mistakes and was glad to be out of the reach of his homeland. He had never dreamed then of becoming a doctor. Soldier of fortune was more likely.

Now here he was in Thailand again, blessed with his beautiful young Nadine who was soon to be his wife, whom he had promised to care for until death, thinking of the young man he once was, who had never imagined he would be scrutinized from the future by his now totally altered persona. His intellect was no longer a half-baked mélange of rebellious thoughts but one that could truly be called a mind, skilled in the knowledge of medical practice and all the diagnostic methods and healing efforts that medicine entailed. It was his moral compass that had changed the most, for it was now inclined forever towards a distant pole where trust and reconciliation marked the way forward. He had started out on the wrong foot, and then in the village of May Tai his rind of hardness had peeled off to reveal the healing light that lay within.

The traffic eased, and the horns were sounding. They got back in, driving in silence till they were speeding into the countryside. As the land glided by, he felt grateful. He was heading back to the place that had rescued him, given him a second wind.

"Oh look," Nadine said, as they passed the iron gates of a long cypress-lined driveway that culminated in a glimpse of a splendid Italianate villa.

"Jade kings," Bert said. "They run their Burmese mines from here."

As they drove farther, there were carved signs for orchid farms and butterfly farms, and elephant camps. They passed the Queen Sirikit botanical gardens and a Dutch cottage with a windmill restaurant offering home-style pancakes.

"Home-style! Shall we try?"

"On the way back," Bert said.

Nadine was wearing a traditional Thai petticoat with swirling patterns and a pink blouse with pleats. She looked lovely, and he kissed her as well as he could while driving with one finger guiding the wheel.

They came to a village, the lanes edged with well-tended hedgerows and orchids sprouting at every gate, before heading west towards the Burmese border. The slopes here were gentle, furrowed with paddy and *lamyai* orchards. The roadside stalls were now manned by hill tribes, the Akha in black trousers and shirts, with the men decked out in smart hats and the women wearing white beaded necklaces. He rolled the window down and smelled the piney scent of Australian eucalyptus. They passed terraced farms where people were plucking tea, and old ladies bent over their patches of carrots and cabbages. And women standing on the back of pickups amid sacks of vegetables, wearing Palin blouses under blue pinafores, the cool breezes ruffling their frayed violet sleeves.

He spotted a sign for the turnoff towards the mountain of Doi Angkang. The road was now paved, unlike the dirt track he had been used to. He noticed other symbols of development, including electric poles and wires, satellite dishes, and numerous motorcycles and pickups parked in front of homes. There were signboards for homestay, for trekking trips, rafting and Bikram yoga. He saw a tall church with a slanting roof, its steeple like a white scar against the steel-blue sky.

"Hey, what's up with those kids with brass things on their neck?" Nadine asked.

"It's an ad for the Karen long-neck camp," Bert said. "You pay to photograph the twisted clavicles of abducted tribal kids."

"Bert, you are so cynical at times."

It was eleven thirty in the morning before the familiar sights of the village of May Tai began to come back, the old bamboo-and-thatch huts, the hill road barely wide enough for the car, and the herd of cows crossing with their tails swishing and the cowherd ambling behind. One of the calves licked the windshield with its purple tongue, and they had to wait until its mother nudged it away.

As they pulled up around the bend, a pair of snot-nosed children ran up to them, banging on the window and begging for candy.

"Hey, cutie," Nadine said, opening the door.

The child, a girl in black pants and a ragged jacket that might have once been pink, grabbed Nadine's hand.

"*Paw!*" the child shouted. "*Farang ma leeaow!*"

Hearing the cries, a short, dumpy man emerged from the gate of a brick villa whose top floor was still under construction. The man's face was wrinkled and gnome-like. The child ran to him, and he *waie*d to the visitors. The man smiled at Nadine and escorted them into the compound. The verandah had cane reclining chairs, and he beckoned to them to sit down.

Bert hesitated, for the man was a complete stranger, but Nadine graciously accepted a seat. Behind the munchkin owner was a dark room in which there was a faint glimmer of old photographs and a long red scroll with Chinese lettering.

The man served them tea in antique cups and home-brewed whisky in tiny glasses. From the size of the house and the quality of the china, it was clear that their host was a man of substance. Bert asked about his job, and the man explained that his name was Michael and that he was the headman.

Nadine was captivated by the girl. "How old are you, sweetie?"

The child smiled and showed four fingers. Her father grabbed her waist, and she twirled around.

The whisky was smooth and sweet, burning as it went down. Bert could feel his legs suddenly wanting to move, and his head kept turning away, towards the top of the hill.

"*Khun Nok u ti nai?*" Bert asked, his Thai tongue coming back to him suddenly as he demanded to know where Nok was.

The munchkin looked puzzled.

"Which Nok?"

Bert pointed up the hill. "Nok who lived by the big spirit house," he added.

Michael stared hard, then scratched his head.

"We have only church now, and the old *wat*."

Bert smiled.

The father said something to the child, who ran down the street.

A few minutes later a scooter arrived, screeching to a halt. The rider took off her helmet and dismounted, along with the child. The newcomer was fair and had long, wavy hair and was wearing high heels and tight jeans with stars on them. A cross swung jauntily over her chest.

The headman greeted her effusively. After a quick assessment of Nadine, she turned her attention to Bert.

"My name is Fai," she said, sliding a plastic seat out from under the table and sitting down.

"Meaning fire," Bert said, returning her gaze, his arousal tinged with admiration of her youth and vitality. She smiled back.

"Fai is niece of old Nok," Michael said. "Nifah's girlfriend." He laughed, his munchkin head bobbing.

"You knew Nok?" Fai's voice was silvery, like that of a karaoke singer.

Knew—the word was inadequate to express the ultimate gratitude of one human to another.

"Nok was my friend," he said, trying to hide the emotion in his voice. "It was she who first taught me about healing."

11. Lifesaver

One evening a group of men and women came and gathered in the clearing outside Bert's hut. They wore full tribal regalia except for their rubber slippers. Two of the men were carrying staves. They stamped in turn, pointed their hands to the earth, and then raised them to the sky, while one played on a bottle gourd flute and another strummed a simple lute. Their music was high-pitched and plaintive, their songs as they stepped back and forth made up of sharp cries and invocations as they speared some ancient beast. He did not know the words but their gestures spoke of a cycle, taking something forcefully before giving it back to the earth. When they were done, he clapped, and they smiled at him, staring hard.

Later he sat and drank their sake-like homebrew in a hut lit up by kerosene lanterns, sharing his smokes with them as the wind rose over the hills bringing with it the sad cries of peacocks and hoopoes.

He dined most evenings at a shack run by an old Chinese woman who served him fresh vegetables and *larb dip*, the salad of thinly sliced raw pork mixed with mint and lime, and chilies galore. He liked to rest there in front of the miniature spirit house. Inside were a plastic man and woman seated at a small table. One evening, feeling frustrated, he wanted to smash something and decided to pull the man out and crush him in his fist. He had just reached in when he felt a hand on his arm.

It was one of the poppy pickers, a grubby young woman, her face pink under her bonnet. Her teeth had been blackened to enhance her beauty.

"Please do not disturb," she said. "Okay, mister?"

"Because of your Lord Buddha?"

"It's a guardian spirit house. Disturb him and bad stuff will happen."

He laughed cockily. "I've had enough bad luck for two lifetimes."

"Time to bring good luck," the woman said, smiling.

She said her name was Nok. She had worked in a factory in the south. Then she had to come back to the village when her mother fell sick.

Dining together that night, she asked him where he was from.

"England."

"Have any children?"

"No."

"Why?"

"No time for marriage," he said. "I was in the military."

"You fight a lot?" she asked, looking him over.

"Just peacetime service."

She shook her head. "You're not English. Your accent is German or maybe Dutch."

"*Jou poes,*" he said, cursing as he finished his whisky. "Nok means what?"

"Bird. I want to fly away."

He laughed. "Me too." He ordered more whisky, and she poured it expertly, using her fingers to plop in a couple of ice cubes.

He had to pursue her for three long weeks before she agreed to sleep with him. He had never waited that long, even back home on the Cape. And then she taught him a pure kind of fucking. Like fish frothing in fresh foam, golden scales twitching in sunlight, with no holes barred, and even fingers becoming suckable. It was blissful, beyond happiness, and it brought them peace. A feeling beyond words or understanding. Oneness with nature and all living things. There was that and there was his memory, the past that he could neither reach nor escape.

Bliss and remembrance. The twin pillars of the art of living.

Nok said that was what Buddha taught. Accept the past, and be in peace with other living things. She was trying to live like that, though it wasn't easy.

He couldn't get enough of her. But she was distant at times. Absorbed in her thoughts. He felt he did not understand her needs. And it bothered him because it was the first time he had really cared.

On the night of the November *Loi Krathong* festival, everyone seemed happier and drunker than usual, dancing under a sky splattered with stars and fireworks, their music drowned out by bangs and explosions. He and Nok walked together to the stream to make an offering, the fireworks reflected in the fast-flowing water. She took a turtle-shaped basket out of her bag, along with a pair of candles that she stuck in the middle. It was a bread *krathong*, a floating raft offering to the river goddess. She lit it with his lighter, and as the flame caught he helped her place it in the stream where it bobbed quickly away.

Her face was aglow in the starlight, her sunburned cheeks carefully smoothed with powder and beads of perspiration on her neck.

The float was stuck against a rock, and he stepped in a few feet to push it away. The black water swirled around his ankles as a long, silvery fish chased after the bread.

"I made a wish," he said, coming back. "For us to find peace."

"I prayed for you," she said, with a sad smile. Her eyes glistened as she gazed at the float, which was now speeding away downstream towards the village, the candles snuffed by the breeze.

He was drunk and started to pull off his clothes, inviting her for a swim in the buff, but she pulled him back, her mouth wide open in alarm.

"You can't swim here! These waters are full of Yidosi."

"Yidosi?"

They were spirits, she explained, that lurked about in streams and stagnant pools. When someone swam where they were not supposed to, a Yidosi would appear in the guise of a whirlpool that sucked the swimmer down to his grave.

Over the next few days, she taught him the key dos and dont's of the Palin, all of which concerned the Ni, or spirits. A Ni would enter the body of a person, devouring his Ha.

"Who is Ha?" He was lying on a hammock with Nok spooned beside him.

"Ha," she said, stroking the tattoo on his bicep with a calloused finger. "It leaves the body when the person dies. But it can also return and make mischief."

"Ha's the soul, then?"

"Mamisu is also the soul. It leaves the body each night when you sleep."

"I have more than one soul?"

"You have five."

"And woman?" His fingers made an S shape on her back.

She held up her hands. "Ten." She laughed. "Because we do twice as much work."

The Palin world was unlike any he had known. Everything depended on the goodwill of nature. Upset the spirits and the wells dried up. Fruit withered on the vine. Babies were stillborn or came with extra fingers. Lovers broke up. The whisky turned rancid.

Nok explained that the spirits were there for a purpose. Musini, the spirit of the forest, would cause birth defects in the offspring of anyone who dared cut down the sacred *yang na* tree. She had been with them from the beginning, before the flood.

"A flood? Like in the story of Noah?"

She explained that the flood inundated the entire earth. The Palin had been nearly wiped out, but a brother and sister saved themselves by turning into maggots, living off the meat inside a giant bottle gourd. They were the parents from whom the tribe was reborn.

"Who's the mightiest Ni of all? I'd like to have a word with him."

"Jorani," she said. He was the Siamese crocodile that visited the wicked on their deathbed. He would place his jaws over your head, crunching down as he made you recount your sins.

But there were others, she said, with similar power. Himana was a giant bamboo rat who punished with stomach troubles those who ate forbidden fruits and plants. To make him happy one had to kill a black dog and eat its gallbladder. And then there was Nigandu.

"Nigandu?"

Nigandu was invisible but smelled like a leopard, tearing the heart out of people who trampled on hallowed ground. And Hagani was a blue wasp that entered through the ear and swelled up after burrowing into the wax inside, its buzzing driving the faithless mad.

"Would you like to learn more? We should go meet the Nifah."

On top of the hill, next to a paltry ancestor shrine that served as a Palin temple, sat the hut of the shaman. It was he who restored health and order, performed sacrifices, exorcised spirits and separated the souls of the living from the dead. Bert went in expecting nothing, driven by curiosity, not remorse.

The Nifah was a wizened, mouse-like fellow whose beady eyes exuded a lizard-like calm as he sat chewing on a toothpick. Nok introduced him, and then he was invited to a purification ceremony. Soon Bert was sitting next to the shaman with a wad of kratom stuffed into his cheeks. He knew it then as a miracle drug, with few adverse effects. It was only years later as a medical student that he understood that mitragynine, the alkaloid in kratom, was a potent analgesic which, unlike morphine, did not cause respiratory depression and thus did not carry a high risk of death.

The other substances supplied by the shaman during the ceremony could have killed him. Instead, they left him paralyzed. For a week. It was part of the treatment.

Nok cared for him, sponging him and making him sip bitter potions and anointing his limbs with stinking salves that cooled his fevers. She coaxed him to swallow one more spoon of rice gruel while he felt nauseous, fed him sauces with chunks of fatty pork to build up his strength.

In the end he was able to sit up, take a few steps. And eventually visit the squat toilet on his own. But those were the least of the changes. When he looked at her, with her hair tied behind her head with a green rubber band, he was overcome with gratitude. And when he was able to stand up and look at himself in the mirror, shaving his straggly beard, the old Robert had vanished.

He asked Nok what the shaman had fed him, beyond the kratom and opium. They were lying together in a hammock, swaying in the afternoon breeze.

To clear his head, a rat's entrails had been boiled, and the water was mixed with whisky to kill the bacteria.

"Yecch, disgusting," he said, holding his nose.

She grinned. "And sometime he adds turtle *tap*."

"Tap?"

"It's the Palin word for liver." She pointed to the upper right of her stomach.

"Turtle liver tastes like chicken?"

She laughed. "It tastes like human *tap*."

"You little cannibal!"

"In the old days they served it after battles. In a salad with sticky rice."

He decided to believe her.

Then there was the Asian bitter yam, which the Palin called *kloi*. Its tubers were crushed and cooked with sticky rice. The shaman had given it to him twice to clean him out, for it was used as a multipurpose oral antiseptic, for leprosy, syphilitic sores, abdominal spasms and colic. It was also packed into arrowheads and could kill an enemy within six hours, Nok told him, cuffing her hand around his neck. Through asphyxia. Its toxic ingredient, which he now knew to be dioscorine, never affected the Palin. His own survival had been a miracle.

There were hundreds of other helpful plants, Nok had explained as she walked with him in the forest above the village. She pointed to a bamboo thicket, where he saw a cluster of glossy, lobe-shaped leaves. He leaned down to examine them, his fingers rubbing the roots of shining filaments. It was goldthread, Nok said, and could kill germs on contact. Children drank it with tea to arrest hiccups. It was dying out. A lady from Europe who looked Japanese had come and spent time with the shaman, trying to get him to name the plants before they vanished from human memory.

As he walked with Nok that day, it started to rain, first a drizzle with a pleasant pitter-patter, then a timpani of sizzle and splash and crackle until, with the first thunderclaps, sheets of slanting water came battering down through the forest canopy. The jungle became a crescendo of thunderous peals and giant cracking sounds as the storm sprang at the trees, twisting the branches and flinging them from side to side. They fled for shelter as the ground turned to fast streams of mud tumbling down the inclines towards the poppy fields.

"Wait," he said.

He tore off a long banana leaf and wrapped it around her. She shivered, hugging him close so they were wrapped together inside their leaf papoose. Water droplets glistened on the leaf and like jewels on Nok's arm. A little slug crawled up their shelter, raising its antlers before sloughing off.

"Oi. Oiiii!"

"What is it?"

She lifted her ankle, hopping on the other. A layer of skin had puffed up like a water blister, with a red halo around it.

"*Maengpong!*"

He saw the scorpion, a brown rustle of armor scurrying away into the undergrowth.

He took off his T-shirt and started pressing it against the wound.

"Stop," she said. She pointed to the thick oval leaves of a green plant whose pink fruits resembled miniature mangosteens. He reached out and snapped off a leaf for her. She smoothed it between her fingers, then bent down and rubbed it on her ankle.

"Does it hurt?" His fingernail grazed lightly over the wound. The sap from the leaf felt oily.

"We call it *manpla*. Lifesaver."

12. Axenfeld

Bert's lip was still stinging as he sat in Michael's place with Nadine and Nok's niece Fai. He was beginning to put two and two together, and the answer was getting closer to four. What did not kill the Palin had helped them survive. Like Nok's lifesaver *manpla,* which he had come across again at UCLA's Mildred Mathias Herbarium, while doing his pre-meds. It was glochidion sphaerogynum. Highly cytotoxic, so much so that it could never be used in American hospitals, but it must have worked well as chemotherapy for the Palin. Thanks to evolution, the genes of the Palin had evolved to allow them to benefit in certain cases from plants potent enough to kill a Westerner.

Fai smiled as she stood up. "You can follow my scooter," she said. "And after that Michael has invited you to lunch."

Bert and Nadine got into their car and followed her scooter uphill for about two hundred yards, turning into one of the old footpaths that had been turned into a road. They were driving up the hill he used to climb. It was in the forest on top that Nok had taught him about plants, and where she had been bitten by the scorpion. He rolled his window down and peered up. He could see a row of tall homes with solar panels on their roofs, but the forest was nowhere to be seen. It had vanished along with the field of purple poppies that once lay beckoning in the valley beyond.

"*Voking* scumbags! How could they?" He banged the steering wheel twice with his palm, making Nadine bounce up in alarm.

"What happened?"

"They cleared the forest. All the beautiful and priceless plant treasures destroyed!"

Fai turned off just then into a narrower lane, and they followed her, passing a pigsty and a cluster of small mud huts. Several dazed men stared at them from the roadside, apparently unaware of their surroundings. A rooster scurried away at their approach.

Fai's scooter pulled up at a run-down dwelling, and Bert parked the car behind her. They got out. An old woman sat spread-eagled on the porch, a bong in hand. Two lean, younger women sat facing her, one smoking a cigarette.

The old lady smiled briefly at Fai and then stared at the newcomers through glazed yellow eyes. She stood up, swaying slightly, her silvery hair falling to her shoulders. The resemblance was unmistakable, from the eyes down to the long slightly freckled nose, but Bert knew it wasn't Nok. His friend would still have a gentle air and would not be wearing a rosary under a necklace studded with gold coins.

"Hello, mister, how arerrrr you, mister?"

Her eyes and speech showed all the classic symptoms of opium addiction. Her teeth had been blackened to hide the stains of betel nut use. Yet her gaze looked somehow different.

"This is my mother," Fai said, with a sigh. "Nok was her older sister."

"*Gkin kao rue yang?*" one of her companions asked. Had they eaten?

The companion stood up, pointing to the outdoor stove. She too had blackened teeth, but there was something about her gaze. He took a step closer. The woman paused, then offered her hand. He took it, found it cold, and then noticed that her pupils were not only distended but had a distinctly elliptical shape. The dilation was clearly induced by an anticholinergic, but the change in ocular morphology was highly unusual. The slit-like pupil seemed reminiscent of a disease he had come across in medical school called Axenfeld syndrome.

But here the pupil was also rotated to be vertical, the preferred orientation for spotting the movement of low-lying prey. The gaze was not cute like a cat's, but blank and vigilant like that of a viper or crocodile.

"Her eyes. Were they always like this?"

"My aunt has been sick," Fai said. "Luckily there is a doctor who gives us medicines."

"I'm also a doctor. May I see the medicines?"

Fai smiled, a charming Thai smile of refusal.

He asked about Nok. She became old, one of the women explained to Fai, who translated—and then her Ha left and flew over the village.

The woman moved her hands, in the shape of a bird.

"What's Ha?" Nadine asked.

"Ha is the soul," Bert said.

Fai touched the old lady's hand. "She couldn't even move her fingers earlier," she said. "We thought we would lose her to cancer."

"What kind of cancer?"

Fai shrugged. "Nobody knew. But she had severe stomach pains."

"Had they all been taking the same medicine?" Bert wanted to know.

"They get injections," Fai said.

"*Jep muk muk!*" The old woman pointed to her leg.

They were painful injections, administered intramuscularly. For cancers of the digestive system? What sort of medicine could that be?

The old woman was asking for money now, and Nadine handed her a one-hundred-baht bill.

Before returning to Chiang Mai, they stopped for lunch at Michael's. Bert couldn't help noticing something was amiss. It wasn't the company, which included Michael, along with his wife Nit, their four-year-old child, and a burly man who may have been the munchkin's older son. Nor was it the food, which was freshly made by Nit and prepared with locally grown fennel, tender yams and cured pork that was salty and flavorful. It was Michael's curious munchkin look.

He was staring hard at Bert, asking him questions about where he was from. Was Vienna in Germany? Bert seemed lost in thought, so Nadine explained that her husband was a doctor at a hospital in Fairfax, Virginia. Not far from the White House, where President Obama sat.

The slit eyes of the old lady flickered briefly at the mention of the famous man.

"Where does the Nifah live?" Bert asked.

"No Nifah," the headman said, with a smirk. "Last one left to run a *somtom* stand in Bangkok."

Bert shook his head. So the age of sorcerers was gone forever, with the shaman now selling papaya salad. But without them, what was left? Who would be there to repair the broken trust with the spirits, to restore the sanctity of the tribe? Not the religions of the Bible thumpers and merit makers, for he knew they had long lost their souls.

"Nok died of cancer? Like the others?"

The headman did not reply. He stared at Fai.

"Nok grew opium," Fai said slowly. "Then Prime Minister Thaksin launched his drug war, and she got caught."

"Caught?" Bert held his breath.

"Yes," Fai said, with a fleeting sad smile. "Shot by police. While working in the poppy fields on top of the mountain."

"Your lip," Nadine said. She handed Bert a paper napkin, for he had bitten it.

He didn't eat after that. He closed his eyes, wondering about poor Nok's last moments. Did she have time to say a prayer to the spirits?

"Are you all right, Bert?"

He wasn't paying attention.

"Bert are you all right?"

"I'm fine. It's them I'm worried about." He lowered his voice. "Looks like they've been given gene therapy injections. The aim being to target cancer cells without hurting normal tissues. Unlike your typical chemo."

Nadine nodded. "I see. But highly experimental, right?"

"Yup. They wrap the genes in a virus envelope to zap it straight into the patients' cancer cells."

"Like the herpes virus? Sounds awful!"

"The virus is sort of castrated first, so it won't replicate. But you might still hurt normal tissues. Or more likely, the therapy could cause unforeseen side effects."

The headman had noticed the couple's private discussion, and he summoned his wife to clear the table.

"Thai people say thinking too much make you sick."

It was what the Thais would say, but Bert sensed that it was a warning.

"I wish for the Palin to be healthy," Bert said, dabbing his lip one last time. "That's what every doctor wants."

"I will ask *farangs* to write you," the munchkin said. "What is the address?"

Nadine carefully wrote down DR. BERT PASSELSKY, 351 MAPLE AVE., VIENNA, VA 22180, USA.

"We look forward to more information," Bert said, though he was doubtful they would send any. Once he got back to Washington, he would have to get in touch with his friend Cathy Wu at the Food and Drug Administration. If the trials involved FDA fast-track clearances, Cathy would know.

When they left with Fai, the munchkin shook his hand. Bert was surprised at the strength of the little man's grip.

13. Spa

Benton woke and sat up in bed, noticing that he was naked. He grabbed a sheet, which carried a faint trace of ganja. He couldn't remember a thing from the previous evening.

He was sitting on a high bed with a bedside table and a wall mirror next to it. There was a window to the far left, and to the right, a door.

He had to jump to get to the floor. He took a few shaky steps to the right towards the door and found it locked.

The bedside table had a photograph on it. Looking at it closely, he realized it was Sylvia. The swine Pierre must have stolen it from his room! He knocked the photo over so it lay face down. He felt for his watch and saw that it was gone. His glasses were nowhere to be seen. And his wallet and phone were also missing. There were no cupboards and no sign of his clothes.

In the mirror all he could see was a pig-like form, and it was totally fucked-up. Benton the immaculate analyst had turned into a creature from a bestiary. A deranged quilboar, a haunted oinker. A dumb porky pigman.

He staggered to the window and, with a quick jerk of his arms, drew the curtains. The full force of sun hit his face. A beach lay far below, and then a set of pillars extending into a sea that was indistinct except for a fuzzy brown mass in the distance that resembled an island and a few squiggles which he myopically took for boats.

Under the window was a desk with a vase on it, depicting a repulsive creature that had a croc's head, a man's muscular body and a long, lizard-like tail. He was about to turn away, nearly tripping on the chair underneath, when he noticed that next to the vase was a clean-smelling laptop.

He flipped it open, hoping he could reach the world outside.

Bonjour, BENTON! Welcome to THE SPA!

Turning the WiFi on revealed no network. So much for that. He was about to shut it when he found on the Desktop a folder marked "Foundation." It had obviously been left there for him to see.

He drew out the chair and sat down. He was glad that his brain cells were still active, allowing him to work his way out of any situation, even when the shit had finally hit the fan and pieces of his normal world had come tumbling down.

Most of the Foundation subfolders were copies of what was on the Bulsani Foundation website, which Benton had scrutinized carefully before coming to the party. The only unfamiliar file was a video lecture by Dr. Tollendal on the use of medicinal plants among the Palin. He decided to watch it later.

The Trash bin was empty, but he searched a step further. He examined the console command history and found some *git* commands from two days earlier. Nearly a hundred files had been uploaded to a server. Right before that, a local copy of data from the server at ChantouBulsaniFoundation.org had been cloned, though the data had since been deleted.

His old analytical skills were back, which proved that the mind could survive anything, even though his fingers felt knotted together into two clumps, with only his thumbs able to flex properly. He started thumb-typing, inspecting the log files.

The laptop's activities were all unremarkable, records of accessing a wireless network named CHUMPS, messages from various software update demons, and numerous actions including the system waking up, alerting on various signals, talking to other machines on the network, and then going back to sleep. It was a day-to-day log as dull as life itself. The browser was anonymized and history-less, devoid of any meaningful identity.

He needed to search further, back along the timeline. It was hard going with his fingers all messed up. He found several accesses to files on a server named Journal. Nothing striking there either, except for a muddled message from the last week of July:

Failed to composit image for binding
VariantBinding [0x27d] flags: 0x8 binding:
FileInfoBinding [0x1c5] - extension: aln, fileType:
????.

The gobbledygook computer sentence was poorly constructed. Thanks to his years of staring at such nonsense, he understood that the operating system had trouble creating the right icon for a file with an .aln suffix that had been moved temporarily to the desktop. The movement was one of those trivial events that only the mechanical brain of an operating system would keep track of.

The wifi network CHUMPS was now connected, miraculously allowing him access to the world outside. His first impulse was to sign on to one of his accounts and send out an SOS, but then he stopped. Where were his years of training? He needed to operate stealthily if he was going to find out anything. Even if it meant staying around, if it came to that, in the Spa.

He checked the git logs again, and indeed one of the files that had been uploaded carried the .aln suffix. Scanning the file system, he soon found it via File Salvage. It was encrypted. He thought for a minute and then downloaded a program that his former DAO boss Chad, the genius hacker known as @pr8d8tor, had taught him about years ago. With the help of this miracle program—called cachegames—he managed to crack the key in under three minutes.

He scrolled down the .aln file, and the contents were in a kind of alphabet soup.

#P35001_PSEUDO_HUMAN AND Q12948_HUMAN	
P35001	LPGST**S**NAKEDGEF**G**WALLPPPQPPLQF**QSSR**DAPPLETADELFTHQVGDPFPVALVE**S**Y
Q12948	LPGS**A**PNAKEDGEF**S**WALLPPPQPPLQF**QTSQ**DAPPLETADELFTHQVGDPFPVALVE**N**Y
....	

He guessed that he was looking at a pattern involving an alignment between sequences of letters. Each pair of lines indicated subsequences that had been compared. He traced his fingers across the screen, pointing in two places. So in this case T, the element in position five, had been replaced by A. And S in position six had become P, and so forth.

What were those sequences? Not DNA, which had only four letters. He scratched his nose. Nor were they the names of atoms. He scratched his head with his trotter-fist. They could be proteins, could they not?

Proteins were made up of amino acids, so if a sequence was a protein, each letter might stand for an amino acid. He couldn't remember anything about amino acids, except for the fact that they were an ingredient in the medicines on Sylvia's bedside table.

In that case, S, he guessed, might be Serine, for he remembered it as a key ingredient in Sylvia's Lacprodan energy supplement. So Serine had been replaced by an amino acid with a different structure, namely P. P for what? He was playing Jeopardy now and guessed Proline, another supplement abused by Sylvia in her desperate last days.

"Sayerwonmistay?"

It was Siri. It was as if his thoughts were being amplified, made external and exposed.

He looked away from the laptop screen towards the window. A gull was sitting there. It was fat and white all over except for its grey wings. It tapped on the window with a pink beak.

The gull gazed at him sideways. Its retina was a shining crimson disk as if it were made of plastic. He could hear its shrill *kreega*, half-quack, half-screech. The poor thing was hungry, and he felt like letting it in.

"Try 'n understand," Siri said. He realized she was trying to help, though it was probably too late for him to return the favor.

He needed to backtrack. There was no point trying to figure out letters in the sequences. Not with his rudimentary grasp of biology. He needed Toy for that. He suddenly realized he had forgotten all about her. Where was Toy? Vacationing in the Spa like him? Or worse?

The Palin. He needed to concentrate on them. And their health. He looked at the file again, and then a buzzer went off in his pigman head.

The first protein being compared, P35001, was encoded, according to the comment line in the file, by a pseudogene. The *sous* Toy had discussed that fateful night when he was poisoned at the shack.

A part of the conversation he must have forgotten, in his fog of zinc phosphide, came rushing back to him. The part that had to do with nice elves and putting two and two together.

Toy had explained how in the old days the Palin and other tribal people had lived short lives. For their potions and poultices, they had to rely on medicinal plants and fungi growing wild in their homelands. Some were beneficial and others toxic, as they discovered through trial and error, and death. Over time, their genome became smarter and learned to coexist with some of the toxic plants, granting the Palin an immunity that allowed them to survive and thrive. Then, over thousands of years, as the tribe migrated to other environments, some of the genes for those protective capabilities had transitioned to sous. In most of the ones who moved, the sous had vanished out of irrelevance from their genome. But a few of the sous were still lurking around. And some still had part of their functionality intact.

"Wait—don't tell me there are Palins still blessed with elf sous? That protect them from cancer?"

"You're a smart man, Bento! I only found out when Siri told me. You see, quite a few Palins were tested by the local boss running the trials. They found only a handful of elderly individuals with sous that had the elf power. They were harvested right away, and then the collection was expanded using PCR."

"Which is?"

"Polymerase chain reaction. A standard tool to copy DNA. A bit like a Xerox machine."

Now, leaning back in his chair with his trotters clasped above his head, a brain-damaged prisoner at the Spa, the picture seemed obvious. The drug companies had resurrected the sous, blending them into potentially cancer-treating and cancer-preventing gene tonics. All made from pure Palin pseudogenes. They would naturally try them out first on Palin subjects, the sous preferring to mix with their own kind. And then they would inflict them on the rest of the population. That included, of course, "volunteers" like him.

It was one thing to be concerned about the impacts of GMO agriculture. But here was the whole nine yards, gene therapy coming home to roost. And it was now up close and personal.

He examined the laptop again, scrutinizing the file. What was P35001? He keyed it into Google, but couldn't find it.

What about the other protein being compared? Q12948. He typed that in and watched the results swim up from the internet. Q12948 was the Forkhead box C1 protein that encoded the FOXC1 gene. It was involved in the regulation of the development of the human embryo, in particular, eyes. Mutations in the gene caused a variety of problems, including optical irregularities, characterized in some cases by slit eyes and blurred corneas.

Slam dunk, Bento!

He smiled. It seemed likely that one of the drugs might have unleashed a mutation in the FOXC1 gene. The subjects who were victims of that mutation would undergo horrible changes in their eyes, among other problems. The mutation would probably affect their offspring too. And that was what Siri had probably discovered and protested mightily about.

"Money fer nothin'," Siri said, her voice fading.

"Siri," he said. "You need to hear this loud and clear. They fucked up your relatives. And now they're trying to undo the damage. Or at least mask any signs of it."

The boss and his gang would try to tinker with the sous, once they understood what caused the mutations in FOXC1. Or else they would try to come up with a method to mask the symptoms. But these would be no more than duct tape.

The problem was that the environment had changed. One didn't have to be a highly trained intelligence analyst to grasp that.

What had once been sous, had thousands of years earlier been genes. Evolution would have made sure those genes played nice with

103

the other genes in the genome at the time. But the snapshot of the genome then was different from the snapshot today.

Which was why the comparisons he had glimpsed in the file might have been carried out. Pierre and company were probably reconstructing the Palin phylogenetic tree. They were in damage control mode, trying to wind the clock back to a time when P35001 was a full-fledged gene. So that Pierre's pharma pals could try to synthesize the right cocktail. It was like reviving an ancient, half-dead language and then trying to alter it to accommodate the chatter of the modern world.

He heard a click at the door. The gull on the windowsill flapped its wings and fled.

14. Toy

Morning. Did you sleep well?" Megumi asked. She was dressed in slippers, sun hat and a green bikini, and she handed him the room key.

"Can't remember." He was naked but didn't care. "Been hearing voices."

"I think you owe us an apology," Megumi said.

"Me? For what?"

"You misbehaved with Mimi. Barfed all over the tablecloth. And then messed up the toilet."

"I was poisoned," Benton said. "For the second time!"

"The first was just a non-lethal pinch to test your immune system."

"Administered without my consent, thank you. It nearly fucking killed me."

"You need not have gone to the hospital, Jack. Your gut microbiome would have taken care of it. And Toy was fine after a toilet trip at the shack."

"What shit did they feed me last night?" He examined his hands.

"These are double-blinds, Benton, so I don't know. But it's safe. I think Noi and I are both on it."

"Is it derived from P35001?"

She shook her head. "Ask Dr. Tollendal about tribal cultures and medicinal plants. Not molecular biology. Did you view my tutorial?"

"Haven't had the time."

She smiled. "There's no need to expose your lovely *roubignoles.*" She pressed a button under the desk, and the headboard slid open to reveal an array of Hawaiian shirts and shorts with button flap pockets that looked just the right size for Benton.

It was then that he noticed his bedside drawer. In which were his watch, his wallet, his glasses, his pen and a few coins.

"Have you seen my phone anywhere? I had it with me when I came to Pierre's."

"If it's not here, I don't know," she said. "Was it expensive?"

"A cheapo Thai model. Must have dropped it somewhere."

"Pierre sometimes stays here overnight," Megumi said, as she watched him dress. "He left you a laptop stocked with your favorite acts. Hendrix, Miles, etcetera. And even a few of Thigpen's licks. But Pierre said no Chopin!"

He put on a shirt. It had swirling color patterns, with shapes that resembled geometric insects, birds and fish. Like a surrealist painting by Miró.

"For such a smart and sexy man, you stayed in the agency a long time, Jack." She fingered the sleeve of his shirt. "Mucking around with the lives of innocents. Until you were unceremoniously demoted."

"So?"

"You betrayed Paul Tetrault."

"I didn't." He started buttoning his shirt. "The agency asked who else was in our SNCC chapter at Fisk, and I gave them the fucking names."

Paul had been a point guard for the Fisk Bulldogs and had been Sylvia's first love. He was later arrested after an FBI investigation into black antiwar activists.

"It was part of the full disclosure required," he went on. "And I reached out to him when Sylvia died."

"Yes, you returned all his *billets-doux.* She had treasured them, hadn't she?"

He stared hard at the half-naked old woman. "And you know these thrilling details how?"

"TAENIA."

He stopped buttoning.

After Chad had shown him how to hack into TAENIA, Benton had deleted the fields related to his marital life. He had been careful to remove all traces of his intrusion, but he had not realized at the time that the entries might get refilled by updates from other servers. He would have to ask Chad, aka @pr8d8tor, how to address that.

"All and sundry are now using TAENIA?"

"The University of Maryland is a Foundation grantee," Megumi said. "One of the grad students was up at the Fort for a summer internship. Pierre has had him look up everyone and their friends. Would you like some coffee?"

"I'd love it," Benton said. "But I'll wait till I get to a 7-Eleven."

"Do you like this vase?" Megumi touched it with a fingernail. "The Palin call her Jorani. The spirit of retribution, embodied in our ancient crocodile."

"You're really into this shit, aren't you?"

"Jorani waits at your deathbed, meting out punishment if you're wicked."

"Luckily, none of us believes in that," Benton said. "So humans can run wild."

Megumi sighed. "We must run wild, Jack, for the rules have all changed. We are living in a time of great disturbances."

She gestured to the open door, and Benton followed her out of the small cottage. They were on the cliffs now, walking with the sun bearing down hard on them and glaring off the rocky beach below. A row of small cookie-cutter cottages lay ahead, and as they approached he saw a woman in sunglasses sitting on a deck chair, facing the sea, with a cigarette dangling from her fingers. Benton tapped her on the shoulder.

There was no response.

"Toy, it's me. Benton." He felt so happy to see her that he was almost shouting.

She reached her free hand out without turning her head.

"She's still in a daze," Megumi said.

"Toy, what's happening?" He squeezed her hand, which felt clammy. She gave him a brief smile. He could not see her eyes, but

107

her forehead seemed to be protruding, and her nose had changed—it looked flatter.

"Bento, my eyes are fucked," she said with a funny laugh. Her voice was husky. "I can hardly see."

"She's on a beta-blocker for that," Megumi said quickly.

"Yup. It makes me tired," Toy said. "And my asshole has constricted!" She blew out a column of smoke.

He leaned closer, lowering his voice. "Pierre forced you? Submit or dangle from a meat hook?"

"I did it for Siri," Toy said, her voice almost cracking. "I have to go through the prevention trial."

"Preventing cancer? How long is the trial?"

"The study is looking at ten years. With thousands of subjects—if possible."

"Wow."

"But the meds are taken only in short bursts. Anyway, once I feel stronger, I'm going to fucking raise hell."

"I'll help with the hell raising. Do you know what you're on?"

She shrugged, the exhaustion rising in her voice. "Ask Pierre. I'm pretty sure he put me on a FOXC1 antibody combo."

They would have had to inject an animal with the warped version of FOXC1 to harvest the antibodies that would have risen up to attack it.

"The mice went gaga," Toy said. "So they used pigs."

Benton could smell the acrid odor of a fire, but this time it came with the reassuring odor of a soup or an infusion of some kind being prepared.

"The Foundation has a farm," Megumi added. "They've been horsing around with the sows. And now chickens."

"But don't they have to humanize the pig antibodies?" Benton asked. "Otherwise, our immune systems will turn on them and reject the drug."

"Of course," Toy said. "They would have replaced as much as possible of the pig molecule with corresponding Palin antibodies." She paused to catch her breath. "After removing the one pig gene that humans can't stomach. Called gal-transferase."

"Wow," Benton said. "That's quite a fucking concoction you're on."

Toy touched his arm. "Enough about Toy! How's Bento doing? You're sniffing a lot."

"Must be my allergies."

Megumi patted his shoulder. "Jack's a tough old bird. Now you two darlings keep chatting. I'm off to fetch some Arabica for us."

Benton stared at her.

Megumi laughed. "Trust me, Jack. It's Pierre who spikes stuff, not me."

"You two...?" Toy asked after Megumi left. She laughed. "Dr. Tollendal calls all her lovers Jack."

"Nothing like that," Benton said quickly. "She's not my type. More to the point, where's the nearest exit? You can hitch a ride back with me."

"I have to stay," Toy said. "Otherwise my outlook isn't great."

He looked out at the sea, its shimmering essence forever changing. "And Siri?"

"Pierre told me about it."

"What happened?"

"Drug overdose. She was rushed to the ICU." Toy's voice was now cracking. "But it was too late."

"I'm sorry." He squeezed her hand.

She smiled sadly. "She lived a great life, Bento. Until the shit hit the fan."

He changed the subject. "What's it like inside?"

"If I wasn't so sick, it would be a fucking vacation. Up early, meditate, walk, then gym. Labs in the morning. Veggie lunch with meds. Afternoons are yours, unless there's a doctor's visit. You also have a game room, library, massage center, etcetera. And in the evenings a snack and then walk and meditate again. Cigarettes are fine but no beer."

"Sounds like torture. By the way, what is P35001?"

"Calpastatin, from pigs. It's there in humans too, as U31345."

"How come you know these crazy identifiers by heart?"

"At the MRC Lab, I spent long nights practically living inside the UNIPROT database." She sighed. "Give me five minutes, Bento. To catch my breath."

Y ou slept for a whole hour," Benton said. He had watched her as she slept, hoping she was breathing fine, caring and worrying about her as if she were one of his own.

"Hey, Bento." Toy rubbed her eyes under her glasses.

He served her coffee from the thermos.

"Where's Megumi?"

"She had to run off to visit Pierre. Something urgent." He took a long sip. The coffee tasted good, with not a hint of toxins. "I guess I too have to help with the trials?"

"Do you have a choice? Though I think he's taken a shine to you."

"No chance of being in a placebo group?"

"Not if you had the reaction you apparently had last night. Megumi was laughing her ass off about your piggish antics."

He didn't like her smirk. "So how come Megumi's involved?"

"Poor thing never had a retirement plan," Toy said.

"Who else is on the payroll?"

"You know, the gang you apparently met last night. And Sharky, a health ministry fellow, and a couple of others. Those are the execs. Then you have the worker bees, all contractors working remotely from India, helping out with the biotech. And of course the scientists back at US universities. Then there's the Thai contingent. Captain Wirachon, the staff at the Spa and tribal field workers at May Tai and maybe a few others."

"Wirachon? I met him one time, and that was once too many."

"A sad specimen," she said.

She sat up and slowly rose to her feet. "Feel like a walk?"

They strolled slowly along the cliffs as she leaned on his sweaty arm. A security guard stood up and saluted, before sitting to doze again. They could have been tourists, taking in the view. The sea, boatless for once, was flinging itself on the rocky beach below, causing white geysers to surge into the air. Seabirds swirled above the spray, shrieking. In the distance, he could see a line of waves advancing toward Brassiere Beach.

"Toy, what's Calpastatin?"

"What do you know about meat?"

"I like it when it tastes good. Assuming it's not poisoned."

"There's more to meat than meets the eye," she said, as she leaned harder on his large frame.

"Is that right?"

"Meat is mainly muscle, and muscles are made up of fibers, which are bundles of cells. Soon after death, proteins called calpains get busy, breaking down the protein bonds inside the fibers. They're essential to necrosis and decomposition."

"Yuck."

She shook her head. "Calpains are actually neat, for they are meat tenderizers. And Calpastatin inhibits that."

On the shimmering sea, a tourist was leaning out on his kiteboard, a purple sail jostling with the wind. Toy turned away, as the sun was now a glaring flash of gold.

"Why would Pierre be comparing a Calpastatin sou and FOXC1?"

"Hmmm. There's no such sou. What makes you think that?"

"He accidentally left an alignment file around on the room laptop."

She laughed. "Maybe he wants you to be de-tenderized?" She squeezed his bicep.

"My flesh is tough like old turkey," Benton said. "Wonder why the alignment file said it was a sou?"

"It could be a mistake."

That meant his line of thought that morning had been off. Instead of congratulating himself on his analysis, he deserved a lively kick in the rear.

"Toy, isn't it odd that you're part of the 1 percent who have side effects? Or are they under-reporting?"

"They aren't under-reporting. Things only approach their true proportions as the number of trials becomes large. That's a basic fact."

"I understand. But maybe Siri's concern over that 1 percent was overblown?"

"You mean Siri was delusional?" Her face was now flushed. "And risked her life for nothing?"

"No, nothing like that. I just wanted to get the whole picture."

"Do the math, Bento." She sounded tired now, even a tad irritated. "Let's say the risk of a younger person with a particular cancer dying of it within five years without treatment is 40 percent. And say the medicine, assuming it's affordable, reduces the risk by a quarter."

"I understand risk analysis," Benton said quickly. "By taking the drug, one out of a hundred gets severe side effects, but that compares against ten more out of hundred who will now survive."

"Right. Is it worth fucking up one person to save ten?"

"I get it now," Benton said. He had grown to love and admire this bright and strong woman, and now he needed to know something more. "Toy, do you mind if I ask you something?"

She eyed him through her dark glasses. "Fire away. Though I am ready for another nap."

"You and Siri. More than just girl pals into punk?"

She was silent and then sighed. "We lived together for seven years, Bento."

15. Check-up

At seven in the morning, a nurse showed up in a golf cart to take him to the clinic.

"For your physical," she explained. Her blond hair was tied with a purple bunny bowtie.

"Haven't I seen you before?"

"I'm Ning, on rotation from San Paulo," she said, smiling. "Your tummy Okay?"

"Fine, thanks." His rock-water rating was the least of his worries. "Who's shelling out for this?"

"You are lucky Dr. Pierre can help you, *ka.*"

She took him for an exercise stress test. After five long minutes on the treadmill, Benton stepped down, exhausted.

"Exercise intolerance," the Thai doctor noted, signing his form with a flourish.

"Bento need to run fast," Ning said with a smile, as she collected his chart.

He was brought to the lab, where he felt a brief stir of unneeded desire as Ning leaned over and pricked him with the needle, filling up five little bottles of blood.

He waited for the results in a small reception room, watching the Thai news on the military junta's NBX channel. He had left his glasses behind during the stress test, but he could see that Chow Hok Fuen, the serial gold-leaf-wrapping infant killer, had turned up again like a bad coin. This time he was in leg shackles, peering dully through the bars with a bizarre tattoo on his forehead.

Peering at the tattoo, he thought he recognized the face of Hank Hill, from the *King of the Hill* show. As if that wasn't bizarre enough, a pleasant Japanese-looking announcer provided a quick recap, including a fuzzy shot of the infant parcels and the handcuffing of the Bangkok temple abbot who had allowed the sacrifice to take place. Then, as the story moved to current political events, Benton started noticing lip-sync errors, due to the video lagging behind the audio, until he wondered if the announcer's lips were being artificially animated.

A news item came on showing the main gate of a hill-country school, where a line of young but surprisingly muscular two- and three-year-olds were shuffling together like zombies with their hands raised in front, with two men in lab coats standing to one side taking notes. The reporter's commentary was in Thai, which basically spoiled everything for him, though Benton knew that it was his own fault for not bothering to learn more than a few words of the language.

It was past noon when Ning returned and handed him his glasses. She carried a manila folder with his name on it, which he asked to see. She clutched it to her chest while opening it slightly to let him peek inside. His cholesterol and sugar were high, his liver fatty, his PSA above four. His BMI was at thirty-two, which merely confirmed the obvious. The only thing he seemed to be good at was peeing.

After a disappointing lunch of boiled carrots, spelt and Greek yogurt along with two pills, he met Pierre in his clinic office.

"Benton, would you mind holding onto the chair?"

He complied. He was asked to slide his shorts off and then his boxers. He felt the pressure as his prostate gland was squeezed firmly and deliberately, without his feeling much pain, though the fingers stayed in longer than he would have liked.

"You're all in the clear," Pierre said, discarding the stained gloves and then rinsing his hands. "The diet is just for a day or two, to give your body time to adapt."

"I'm free to go now?" He breathed out slowly, his sphincter relaxing as he visualized the glass of ice-cold beer waiting for him at Win's.

"You should be fine as long as you take your pills. But I would like you to remain our guest for a little longer. We need to work on your fitness."

"Fuck the fitness. I'm going to contact the US Embassy. And the cops."

Pierre sat down, his long legs stretched under the table. The boots appeared recently polished, and they had metal studs on the heels.

"May I ask about what? Has something inconvenienced you?"

"Coercion of subjects. Abduction of Toy. And who knows what happened to Siri."

"Excuse me." Pierre took a call, speaking in Thai, while Benton viewed the wall charts of the digestive and skeletal systems and then a multicolored map of human musculature. The figure with its exposed muscles looked like a bronzed warrior, all pecs and abs and the face tattooed with crimson stripes.

Pierre's voice rose, and then he stepped out of the room to talk more.

Benton was up and about ready to leave when Pierre came back, gesturing to the chair.

"You were saying? Oh, yes, Toy. Your friend is an excellent hands-on biologist. She's a key member of our Advisory Board."

Benton was shaken but kept standing.

Pierre sat down again. He studied the box of gloves that he had used earlier. "Humans are so hard to figure out sometimes."

"Meaning what exactly?"

"According to your agency's database, you spent four decades helping the American government fend off its enemies, real and imagined. With diminishing returns. Correct?"

"What the fuck does my job have to do with anything? And what about all your weirdness? Like your damn *mummy mia* museum."

The doctor didn't like that. He paused to crush a small cricket under his boot, grinding it like a cigarette stub.

"I invited you for dinner in a spirit of friendship," he said slowly, looking up into Benton's eyes. "And also to seek your help on a trial. In return, you tried raping a guest."

Benton's hands were clenched as he took a step back. "I never touched anyone! You drugged me."

"Are you suggesting it's acceptable to molest women while high?" He was trying on a glove again.

"I will apologize to the person involved. Not to you."

"There's no need to be rude," Pierre said. He examined his latex-draped fingers, which looked like shadows on an X-ray. "I'll talk to Mimi and see what she wants."

"Thanks. Meanwhile, may I remind you that the Nuremberg Code requires the voluntary consent of subjects?"

Pierre sighed, clicking a few times on his phone. "Isn't this yours?"

Benton took a look, leaning down close enough to smell Pierre's by now familiar aftershave. The document was a welter of inscrutable legal language. Benton skimmed over it, noting the permissions being granted for follow-ups and the collection of all pertinent information and for being tracked for years to check if the drug had managed to prevent cancer.

"The Palin must love the fine print. When most are barely literate."

"There's a Thai translation, and we have a spoken version as well." He stared at Benton's belly as if its floppiness offended him. "Suggestions for improvement are welcome."

The gloved finger scrolled to the bottom, where he saw the squiggle of his signature.

"Filched from where?"

"You signed at our dinner party."

"I was fucking drugged. I told you."

"Benton, your mind is going around in circles. By the way, there's something else you might want to know."

"What?"

He chuckled. "Someone has been around town looking for you. A bar girl known as Sugar Cane."

"Never heard of her."

"Ms. Oi says she's carrying your child."

"What! That's bullshit."

"Perhaps she was driven by desperation, impregnating herself with condom sperm?"

Benton became quiet.

"Anyway, I've asked Captain Wirachon to look into it. I was talking to him just a minute ago." Pierre got up, gently touching his arm with the gloved hand. "So no paternity test for now, *mon ami*."

Pierre pointed to a basket on a table beside the figure with the pecs. "As you leave, please help yourself to some of our protein bars."

The golf cart back to Benton's cottage was driven by a tight-lipped Thai man. As the cart descended the cliff road, Benton saw the sea hurling itself repeatedly on the rocks below. He could smell the burnt plastic odor of garbage burning. The wind had picked up, and birds were screeching as they always seemed to be doing of late.

He couldn't help letting fly a curse, loud enough for the driver to turn around with a perplexed look.

"*Mai bpen rai*," Benton said, waving the driver on.

He had fucked up, in the country only a few months and already balls-deep in the muck. And now he had to depend on the goodwill of his crazy captor.

It was his own fault. For accepting the dinner invitation. For getting mixed up with the fates of Siri and Toy. For his stubborn attempts to get at the truth—in a place where it didn't seem to matter.

He could taste bile on his tongue, and he swallowed hard. It was so unlike him to misbehave in public.

The Thais would make him pay. And he would have to remunerate Oi for that night of stolen pleasure. They were shaking him down, driving him penniless until he fled their goddamned country.

The golf cart lurched to a stop, and Benton got off, forgetting to thank the driver. He entered the cottage. His bed had been made, a fresh orchid on his pillow.

The cleaner had moved the vase next to the laptop. Jorani, still in profile, was now facing him.

16. Crocodile

It was evening, and the gull woke him—tapping on the window with its pink beak.

He felt in a better mood now, refreshed by his long nap. He walked over to the desk and opened the laptop. A notification popped up, reminding him that he had yet to watch Megumi's video. He hit Play and was transported to a garden at the Spa.

"*Eleuthero Senticosus*," Megumi said mysteriously, as she plucked a berry from a blackberry bush amidst a swarm of bumblebees. She rubbed the black pods between her fingertips and sniffed it. "Gifts of the Palin country."

In her gloves and sun hat, she seemed in her element. He decided to watch more.

She explained that the Golden Triangle was a special place, surrounded by mountains and bordered by the two great rivers that flowed down from Tibet, the Salween in the west and the Mekong in the east. Known to travelers since ancient times, it had once formed part of the Silk Road. The Palin were notorious for their bloodthirsty ways, but they were also gardeners and apothecaries. They had been lucky, she said, to have found in those mountains a natural homeland where some of their old plants could thrive, but now the plants were under threat, their medicinal uses forgotten by the tribe.

She tiptoed to another bush.

"This is bloodleaf, or *Irisene Herbstii*." The camera zoomed to a leaf, radish-red with translucent veins. "Common names are chicken gizzard and beefsteak plant." She placed it next to her cheek. "Grown from a rare shoot in May Tai."

As Benton looked at it, it felt familiar, as if he had smelled its tangy odor somewhere.

Then came the oblong red petals of *Ixora Coccinea* or jungle flame, which the Palin had been introduced to by the Akha tribe, and next, Dr. Tollendal was walking in a veritable jungle of plants, some taller than her. There was *Agyneia Coccinea* with its pink, garlic-like fruits, and *Coptis Teeta* with its lip-shaped leaves and roots like hair filaments, and *Cheirisophus Pontica*, with an enormous funnel-mouth like a lamprey that caressed her neck, and *Dioscorea Hispida*, or bitter yam, with its long and curling visceral tubers, and the cnidarian-like flowers of *Hieronymus Elegans,* straddled by a sun-spangling spider web, and then the leathery leaves and tomentose fruits of *Millettia Brandisiana*, and the morel *Agacea Xanthicles* from whose honeycomb cells Megumi rubbed out a green curd-like mucilage, and dozens of others whose names sounded like a roster of ancient Greek soldiers or hoplites, each carrying a secret weapon that could one day help bring about a major breakthrough and windfall in the fight against cancer.

Benton was impressed. Megumi clearly knew her botany.

The video segued to a discussion of the role of the warrior plants in the daily life of the Palin. Their medicinal use, Megumi explained, had to be understood in the context of their belief system, particularly the spirits or Ni. She was delving into the tribe's traumatic creation story when Benton decided he had enough ethnobotany for the day.

It was time to drill down and take stock of what he knew and didn't know, focusing on the facts, the well-known known knowns.

There were only a few clear ones, which he was about to put in the left column of a Word document, when he remembered that the laptop was Pierre's.

He went to the drawer and took out his wallet, looking for something to write on. The wallet had an odd leathery smell, a mixture of sweat and tanned hides that made him feel like throwing up. He shook the contents out on the bed, finding a thousand-baht bill and a couple of twenties. The coin purse was empty except for a USB stick from the office that had been there for years. His VISA and ATM cards were still tucked away in their slots, along with a plastic card with a hologram-like levitating Buddha on one side and on the other a Thai calendar for the current year, though it said 2557. It had been given to him by a monk at Wat Santisuk, and he hadn't had the heart to throw it away.

The only writing paper available, apart from the sacrosanct copy of the front page of his passport, was the one on which Apple had scrawled Toy's number. He sat down at the desk again. His notes would have to be extremely concise.

His handwriting looked awful, as his fingers were still partially closed together, but he managed to scrawl "business model?" in the right-hand column, and then lifted his pen off the paper.

Turning to the laptop, he examined the roster of biotech companies listed on the Foundation website. They included several well-known players with deep pockets. Everyone knew that big pharma invested huge amounts in research, hitting pay dirt on less than 5 percent of their investments. But Benton was well aware that they made up for it by enjoying the highest profit margins in the world. Congress also knew that they did not play by the rules, but the lobbies made sure the game went on, with a company occasionally paying a few billion in fines for malpractice.

The annual report on the Foundation website showed no net profit, with only two million dollars coming in for 2013. All of it was spent on the trials, administrative costs and research grants. The Spa was self-funding, thanks to an endowment. Pierre wasn't even mentioned. It was hard to believe that the physician-entrepreneur was living off his savings for the sake of a cure while his pharma buddies raked in the big bucks. There had to be a financial side that Benton was missing.

He steadied his pen and wrote "MONEY TRAIL?"

Next, the trials. First of all, Toy. The sou itself was unknown, though it might be P35001. It was highly likely, however, her side-effects involved mutations in the FOXC1 gene causing changes to the eyes. From the alignment file it appeared the antidote was a chemical responsible for modulating the post-mortem tenderization of meat. He recorded the abbreviations for Toy's drug regimen, with the unknown sou marked as ψx_1:

> toy: tx(1) / palin ψx_1 qd. se: mutn foxc1 via q12948.
> tx(2) / foxc1 ANTIBODY COMBO.
> tx(3) / BETA-BLOCKER.

It was one hell of a shitload to pump into poor Toy.

Turning to Siri, he knew little about her except that she was a Palin, and stunning, and that her gigs were great. She had gone back to May Tai for a visit, after years of being away, and had gotten wind of irregularities with the trials and had gone underground after speaking out.

He heard more tapping at the window. He clapped, then got up and banged on the glass, but the stupid bird refused to budge. He then wrote:

> benton: tx(4) / palin ψx_2 qd. se: mutn w. activn of
> ψx_3 pig sou.

So far, there were already three known unknown sous. Half an hour later, the right column of known unknowns was now four times as long as the left of known knowns, which was about right. He was pleased about that. But the left column was still too short.

He decided it was time for a break. He took a long shower, and through the thrumming of the miniature waterfall on his head, he heard a faint *Higher and higher, Mister Benton!*

After toweling himself dry, he sat down at the laptop and downloaded a tool called Off the Record that ensured encrypted messages would be sent without Pierre or Google or TAENIA or any other crazies getting hold of the key and reading them. He then sent a chat message to @pr8d8tor.

> Hi Chad. Benton here!

The reply that came back immediately verified that it was Chad.

> HAY, gramps! Whatcha doin in Thailand?
> Retired. I need some low-down from our fungus friend.

TAENIA's a different spelling, but shoot.

The folks at ChantouBulsaniFoundation.org. And a financial of the Founder.

Sure thing.

Plus any footage of Bert & Nadine Passelsky in Thailand. From early 2005. Need their details?

Nope, names sound uniquish. Just for fun?

Yes. One more favor?

Only if I can join you for R and R.

That afternoon with TAENIA. I tried deleting my fields after you left.

Didn't work, did it, gramps? You need to make a bunch of random changes to your fields and then replicate one thousand times. That way TAENIA's consistency checker will get its ass in a stir and drop all conflicting information.

Please do it, Chad.

It's three a.m. Consider it done tomorrow. TTYL.

In the evening he went for another walk with Toy. She seemed in a bleaker mood than the previous day. They talked about Siri. She had been very stressed in her last days. It turned out she and Toy had gotten into a spat. After which Siri had walked.

"I should never have spoken that way," Toy said.

"I know how it feels," Benton said. "I still regret all the things I said to my late wife."

"How long has it been?"

"Two years next Tuesday. Hard to believe that she's gone."

"I'm so sorry, Bento."

He asked her if she was working for the Foundation.

"What the fuck could I do? It was sign or die. He told me right there at Noi's shack. 'A chance to get at the truth from the inside,' he said."

"Is that right?"

"At least it'll pay off my credit card. Otherwise, my mom will be billed after I'm gone."

He wanted to talk more, to explain how she needed to collect inside information so they could figure out the entire program and expose its evils to the world, as Siri would have wanted. But Toy was too tired. He realized that she was getting weak, and he could no longer count on her active assistance.

He got back to his room and stared out of the window as the sun went down. The boats and even the beach would disappear one day, but the sea would presumably last much longer. On that time-scale there was only one thing that mattered—keeping nature going, allowing the world to survive. And everyone had their little part to play to make it happen.

It was now up to him, Benton solo against the Foundation and whomever else. He sighed. Why him, he wondered, when all he had wanted was to retire and be alone? Was this how he was supposed to atone for his sins?

His sins. There was no running away from them.

It was his career that had made him both proud and ashamed. He got into bed, breathing deeply as he contemplated the web of past transgressions.

He had carried out his work at the agency with the highest standards of integrity, but it had been morally compromised from the start. Soon after coming on board, and still thrilled to have been selected for a career of service, he had named Paul Tetrault as a left-wing radical. He had simply been honest in responding to questions under a polygraph. But it was a nice piece of treachery, for not only had they linked arms and sung songs of protest at Fisk, but it was Tetrault who had contributed some key ideas in Benton's prize-winning senior thesis on slavery and American idealism. Paul had spent a week in a Nashville lockup and then fought a long battle to clear his name, which had been further tainted by false accusations of membership in the Black Panther party. Benton could feel a bitter taste in his mouth as he thought about it, but the sad part was there was no way to undo it, or to ask Paul for forgiveness. So much for that. He heaved a long sigh, feeling relieved as all the air finally left him. Until he breathed in deeply again.

Mani

In Vietnam, his recommendations had led to successful ambushes of enemy units, and his contributions were recognized with a Meritorious Civilian Service award. He was the first black SIGINTer to get it. He was pleased as punch then, while knowing that his efforts at greasing the wheels of the American war machine had sullied him. He could never forget that it was his insightful analysis that had contributed to the Buffs and Thunderchiefs raining down hellfire on Vietnamese villages where the *mamasans* and *babysans* were blown sky high. He had always told himself that he was not directly responsible for those evils, but he also knew that he was.

As for his support of operations in Afghanistan and Iraq, the fact that everyone else in the Department of Defense was culpable along with the rabble-rousing politicians and media did not make it any less criminal.

To add to that undocumented catalog of sins, there were others of a more personal kind.

He had not been that great a husband. His departures from fidelity were in thought, not deed, but thought could be equally damaging. He had ogled and later fantasized about one of Sylvia's nubile piano students, a pink-cheeked Chinese girl with a name like Rose or Lily whose ass had grazed tantalizingly against him while being ushered into the patio for iced tea. He had flirted with sexy strangers in chat rooms. And he had wondered privately what the poor redhead Nadine Passelsky would look and feel like in bed.

He reined his thoughts in, concentrating on his breath, trying to be mindful. But soon they were back. He was being hard on himself, because those were just minor male misdeeds.

What was far more serious was allowing his romantic instincts to wither away over the years, which meant that in later life Sylvia was denied those little gifts that other women must have received, those frequent declarations of love, kisses, handholding and notes with hearts inscribed all over. When he did show affection, she glowed with energy and glided softly about for days after. But how often she had asked, before she fell sick, "Ben, why is it you never come to me," when all he could think of telling her through his mean-spirited silence was "Because, baby, your nagging has dried me out."

He was a cheapskate. He was willing to admit that. He could have offered more by way of tenderness. They could have gone to Alaska or Paris, or even to Nashville to revisit the chapel at Fisk where they first fell in love, but they vacationed instead in Virginia Beach. He remembered the little seaside cottage there, her hinting for a romantic evening indoors when he had insisted on going out for drinks, where they ended up socializing with another black couple, the wife being someone he knew in admin at the Fort. That night, when they got home, Sylvia had turned her back to him.

He knew he could have insisted on more intimate moments together, even if those, come to think of it, were mainly remembrances of other shared moments. And, worst of all, he could have coaxed her with all his cunning to linger on, if only for a little while longer, instead of letting her go as she did, those bluing lips gasping for their last breaths.

His throat felt choked up, and he noticed that his breathing had turned rapid and shallow. And now he was really upset.

Sylvia had wanted to adopt a child, but he was dead against it, for he feared he might fail as a father. He cited in his defense the Sardanians from work, who had gone to the trouble of adopting a boy from an orphanage in Ukraine and after a three-year struggle with the boy's unbridled shit-flinging autism had returned him. Sylvia had pointed out that they would be opting for one of their own kind in the US, where the odds were far better, but Benton was skeptical. They needed peace and quiet in the house, and time for each other, not the added demands of toddlers and teens romping and stomping about. And with her practicing piano constantly wouldn't he be the one stuck with orphan care? He proposed a puppy instead, as it would be equally cute with far less overhead, but the suggestion did not go down well.

"Ben you're one fuckin' selfish bastard. And a hypocrite. You're *never ever* gonna understand how a woman *feels*."

She harbored the grievance for years until Bev came along and the issue dropped away. And now the child was gone too. He wiped away a tear, realizing that he had been wanting to cry all along.

Had he been a Palin, Jorani would have reserved a special punishment for him.

He shook his head and took another deep breath in. As he exhaled, he knew it was time to stop the self-flagellation and get back to business. Regret and long whiskers were part of growing old, as were doubts about where things were heading. He had to accept what he was and had been.

He closed his eyes as the old Vienna neighborhood came tumbling back into mind on a Halloween evening, the quiet suburban lives devoted to work and lawn maintenance and extracurricular activities that together conjured up a picture of a peaceful hamlet that looked so soothing in the Fall light. He could almost hear the knocking on their front door, the shouts for tricks-or-treats, with Bev dressed as a witch with a broomstick and the still-intact Bert standing beside her in shorts though the weather had already turned chilly. He heard laughter, and giggles, with Sylvia and him watching at the door as the golden sounds of children's voices faded down the lane.

It was a distant world, the denizens now vanished or dead, and it was best to let them be. He yawned, and then after one last long inhalation and exhalation, fell asleep.

He awoke after midnight feeling something waving in the dark across his face. It was small and darted about like a butterfly, fanning his cheeks with a warm breeze. He tried to grab it, but it flitted just outside his reach, and then he realized it was his sheet of paper floating away. He got up to catch it, and then the breeze became a humid gust hissing on his face.

"It's mine! Give it back!"

He heard himself shouting, his heart racing as it had on the treadmill. He was sweating, panting, and the paper was right there, its cellophane protector touching his cheek. Except that it was soft and tongue-like, his voice smothered into doughy silence as the warm and wet appendage explored his nose and cheek. Then, with a yeasty stink, the tongue approached his lips. A green pool slid into view, the dark ellipse of a vertical pupil watching him with intense curiosity.

17. Healing

Journal of
Dr. Pierre Montha Bulsani

Records of the most remarkable occurrences,
public as well as private.

To be published
after Dr. Bulsani's death
by the Executor of his estate,
Father Dennis Gillespie, S. J.

August 2

A therapist suggested long ago that it was high time I confronted my demons, but it is only with this writing that I have truly embarked on the journey towards knowing myself.

I was a tender fifteen-year-old when I was tortured for the first time.

It happened during my sister's final illness. Sara had withstood chicken pox, malaria and dengue like the rest of us, but then she experienced a low-grade fever that stayed for weeks. It eventually soared, leveling off at a temperature of a hundred and three degrees. I remember Maman sponging her frantically from head to toe with ice water while Sara sobbed relentlessly. She who so loved the endless pranks she played on the Sisters at her Little Flowers Convent, causing her to be suspended once—bravo, my little princess!—remained confined to bed, groaning. And the hockey she had been getting so good at, scurrying on fast little legs with her stick scooping the ball straight into the goal! Now she lay complaining of pain in her ribs, due most probably to an enlarged spleen.

Maman tried to cheer her up as best she could with floral arrangements. She picked enormous orange sunflowers and meat-colored cannonballs from our garden, but the rare scarlet and yellow petals of *chaddachi*, or *grewia damine* made Sara's skin look dull and pale. When I turned her over there were fresh bruises on her bony back, even though Father had not visited us for months. She was exhausted, barely able to smile as I fed her some of her favorite toffees, her gums white as whalebone as she tried her best to chew.

Inhaling the sweet fragrance of the cannonballs with her brother sitting beside her, she must have dreamed of escape, of sprinting on soft turf with her hockey stick, or given her flighty imagination, soaring deep into the patch of sun-blessed blue that lingered at her window. While all the while she sank steadily into the miasma of a miserable death.

Father sent us to Aurobindo Hospital where the doctors informed us that her blood was teeming with white blood cells and blasts. They did a bone marrow aspiration and a spinal tap, which confirmed that Sara had acute lymphoblastic leukemia. She came home suspecting nothing, for Maman was in denial and believed that lying to the patient was the best way to keep her spirits up. But once our little eight-year-old got her chemo, she knew. The methotrexate and asparaginase mix left her disoriented with a fatty liver and severe jaundice. Weeks shaded into months, and she wasn't getting any better. Then Father finally arrived from Bombay.

Usually, Father would phone in advance, and the chauffeur Wilfred would prepare the Ambassador sedan and then drive to fetch him from the airport in Madras. This time, the household had no warning, and I didn't even hear the taxi. Maman was down in the kitchen when the front door banged. I was with my sister, hoping that my touch—an innocent hand soothing her forehead with a cool towel—would calm her down. And trying to steady myself as well, for I could not bear to see her suffer.

Father burst into the room and grabbed my shirt collar with one hand and sent me crashing to the floor. Startled, I tried to think quickly of what infraction I had committed, but none came to mind. Unless it was my experiments on the effects of strychnine versus zinc phosphide, which involved leaving rat remains around for a while. The wretched servants, seeking to curry favor for additional *baksheesh*, may have informed him about them.

But it wasn't the rats.

"Pierre!" He gazed scathingly at the damp towel.

"Yes, Father."

"Please wait."

Father listened carefully on his stethoscope. He palpated her stomach. He examined her skin, taking a careful look at her back. He checked her lymph nodes for swellings. He asked if it hurt here or there. He depressed her tongue so he could examine her oral cavity, where she had a large blister that was troubling her. He shone a light into her eyes. There was a rough edge to Father's movements. Sara, weak and clammy as she was, detected it and moaned a warning to me.

I was incensed to see Father beside her pretending to care. I had long suspected that in brutalizing my sister Father had caused irreparable changes to her immune system. The locket of hair that I preserved before we slid Sara into the cremation oven was recently analyzed by Mary Novak at Stanford and shown to have a spike in the number of unmethylated immune system genes. Those epigenetic changes, the genetic alterations due to severe external stresses, weakened my sister's immune response, leaving her with one less weapon to fight cancer. Father, in other words, was nothing less than a killer.

Maman rushed in then.

"*Bong proh,*" she said to him. "You surprised us!"

She had been hoping for a hug, a gesture of affection after calling him older brother as Khmer wives did, but none was forthcoming. And none ever would be. He merely shook his head. Maman looked like she was going to cry, when Father pointed to the door.

"*Va t'en,*" he said to her in his saloon French. And she left, for Maman knew where her bread was buttered. As for me, I remember vowing right then that I would kill him one day, but nothing came of it.

When he was done with his exam, Father left the bed and came towards me. My stridor, with its whirring sound, had started by then. I steeled my muscles for the blow, preparing to duck in case it was aimed at my head. Instead, I felt a sharp pain between my legs that dropped me to the floor like a stone. I started to gasp as the adrenalin began pumping. Father looked tired, his thin lips twitching as he bent down and kept up the pressure, squeezing my left testicle with all the strength in his surgeon's fingers. I could feel the lobule crumbing as I started to go into shock.

As a child, the driver Wilfred had often borne me on his shoulders up the ladder to our garage attic, sliding open the panel so I could heave myself up inside. The attic was a dumping ground for things that had outlived their usefulness, and amid the cobwebs and filth and rusting steel trunks, I had come across moldering Japanese dolls, empty Quality Street tins and frayed issues of *Punch* and *Strand*. But these had all been cleared out in the great spring cleaning that Maman had carried out the previous year, to the joy of the local *kabadiwala* ragpicker community. Now, as my eyes opened in that stuffy chamber, all I could see in the murky twilight was a gardener's pile of rakes, hosepipes and watering cans.

From the pain I knew I had a head wound, but I could not inspect it as my hands were immobile. I was able to turn slightly, only to discover that I was lying nude and spread-eagled on a pallet, my hands and ankles strapped to the rusty sidebars. I felt a dull throbbing down in my scrotum and could hear a chittering from the rafters. Motes of dust were dancing in the faint light, and I coughed, strafed by spasms of agony.

I heard footsteps on the ladder.

"Ish my fault," Father said. I peered through half-closed eyes, watching his long body slither in. His voice was gentle and apologetic as he came closer.

"She wanted a late-term, a bore, shun, at Shishowath hosh shpittle." I could smell his drunken breath, hot and stinking. "Ish my fault I shed no."

I had heard him slur like that only once before, after a particularly long session at the Club, before he slouched off slamming the bedroom door. But now he was coming straight at me.

"Doctor shuns a shesh shore fender," he said incoherently. "Wash the prescribed med shin?"

His face looked exhausted in that milky light, and he had the same frown he wore when explaining some trivial medical fact to a nurse or patient. I was now whimpering in terror, on top of the high-pitched whine of my stridor. It must have irritated him further.

"Cash tray shun," he whispered.

Kneeling on one of my thighs, he twisted my torso like a corkscrew. I let out a sharp cry as my body arched up, like an insect about to be broiled. It was only then that I realized he had inserted a hot poker into my backside.

"In shesh," he said, as if he couldn't quite fathom what it meant.

My asshole was now on fire, the attic filling with the stench of cauterized flesh.

I called out for him to stop, though I knew it meant arresting his own paternal urge to heal me once and for all.

"Shuns a bloody deejun rat," his voice continued, coming from the floorboards. The poker was now prodding at my prostate. "Ish my fault."

I yelled out a denial right then—that I had never touched my sister.

He stopped, as if he realized the truth of that statement. The poker came out. For a full minute, he listened carefully to my whimpering and groaning. My heart was pounding, ready to leap out of my chest.

"Shun, shtop wining and take der dam med shin." He turned me around and jabbed the poker hard against the silken sack that protected my gonads. There was a crackling, and the parchment yielded, and then I felt sparks! I was being grilled alive, the air escaping from my lips like the hiss of a lobster in a cauldron, as my already undone testicles were stabbed viciously by his flaming pitchfork. I begged for mercy. And wept.

Agony is tolerable for a few seconds, but several minutes of it are enough to change a young man forever. My asshole would heal slowly. I couldn't shit for long periods, and when the feces did emerge, the wounds tore. Then I had a bacterial infection, which spread to my prostate. The anal crypts were ruined, and I had to wait for two years experiencing intermittent constipation and incontinence before undergoing reconstructive surgery, which took place during my second term at Cambridge. After the operation at Addenbrooke's hospital, my rear end was repaired, normal functioning restored.

I am sorry to say that my testicles and perineum did not enjoy that happy ending. Father maimed me. He left me unmanned and infertile, my sperm factory in ruins, unavailable for use in the *in vitro* fertilization experiments I had planned. And from that moment on I have had to live with extreme sensitivity when I pee.

I had fainted by the time he took the poker away from my privates, but Father was not done with his medicine. He burned each of my toenails off. By then the poker had cooled, so the injuries were less extensive. I was left with deformed toes, the nails growing periodically only to turn black and die. Since the age of fifteen I have preferred to hide my feet.

I was rescued by Akbar soon after Father departed for Bombay. The old cook didn't say anything, though he handled me tenderly for he could see I was in great pain. It was Maman who cared for me, sponging my nethers and feeding me *bor bor* and other soups that she had prepared with her own hands. She was completely beside herself, for Sara was now beyond all hope. My sister had stopped recognizing anyone, though sometimes, when there was a great din in the street, she would frown, or move her little fingers. She slipped into a coma and died soon after. We never got to say goodbye properly.

I know, from deep meditations where I relive my past experience, that Father would have stopped at nothing. I have imagined him lingering on in that attic, slurring and grunting as he tears out my fast-beating heart.

I could never forgive him, for tormenting me, and for imagining that I had done something improper with Sara. It was my duty to take care of my little sister. How wrong he was, and how unfair to poor Sara and me!

August 3

I received several more beatings, none as wounding as the first, but they came to a halt when I turned eighteen. Perhaps it was too much effort for Father to raise a hand or poker on someone who was now almost twice his size. Or maybe he feared that I would hit back, which I never did.

I was so ashamed, and still am, for allowing myself to be humiliated by him. The shame was there whenever I thought of him, as if that initial beating, with its violent caress of my body, was a shameful bond we shared. It added to my mortification that I had not brought it up with him, and maybe he felt ashamed too... who knows? These dark emotions between victim and tormentor clouded all my further meetings with him, increasing my nervousness and stridor whenever I saw him. I still had to interact with him, remaining dependent on his footing the bill for an expensive education, and I forced myself to converse with him periodically for Maman's sake, pretending that everything was okay so we could remain in his good books. While all I harbored inside was the curling hiss of hate.

Hate. Rage. Shame. Revenge. These feelings can rise up like a great ocean wave, defying all therapeutic understanding. I would have liked to rip Father limb from limb, but I had neither the chance nor the guts to do it. Father lived his conceited, self-centered life to the full, surviving comfortably into a ripe old age in the midst of his family in Bombay. The swine left me nothing in his will, though it did come out that I had a half-brother Ali, a prominent Bombay stockbroker. I wrote the man a long and friendly letter, but he never bothered to send me a reply. It was all Father's doing, and who knows whether Ali Bulsani was spared the thrashings.

Like the patients of yesteryear who bore pain during surgery by clamping down on a stick, I have my own ways of dealing with pain. I have gnashed my teeth while scratching and scraping, thinking of gouging out flesh with my scalpel as if it were his. How often have I longed, while quietly performing abortions, to flay the fetus, plucking the blue skein of its face apart with my fingers and stuffing myself up to the eyeballs with it! All the while hearing the infernal refrain "Ish my fault. Ish my fault."

But I never yielded to such violence. I forced myself to remain calm, remembering to breathe deeply, trying so hard, while anger and hatred were suffocating me, to remind myself of Maman's boundless love for me and the promise of happier times. And so, to the rest of the world at work, I managed to remain the cool, impeccable surgeon and scientist.

That is far more than my terrible father could ever do. It is my karma to share genetic material with an ogre like him, and to have made the mistakes I did, but I have made amends in this lifetime. I have kept my promise to Maman, reminding the world of her people's suffering. And meditating for weeks on end at the feet of our revered abbot at Wat Santisuk, I have sought forgiveness for my personal failures, for the way I interfered with small and helpless animals in childhood, and for my inability to form healthy relationships. I have also confessed to struggling with continuing anger and self-hate, for I have been living these last few years at the extreme edge. I have spoken often to Father Dennis about the tensions I face. Sometimes they seem unbearable, and nowadays if I stand on my condo balcony overlooking the sea, I feel the overwhelming urge to leap.

As my executor, Father Dennis will have included this journal, with its hundreds of entries, among the papers of the Foundation. The journal will be available for future historians trying to understand the human story that lies behind the brilliant science that led to the prevention and cure for cancer. This record is also part of our intellectual property, an asset that along with our seed bank of GMO pseudogenes, will be of interest to pharmaceutical investors who might be seeking to acquire the company. Father Dennis, bless his Jesuit soul, has assured me there will be no censorship.

Though I am gone at the time of reading, I know I will be remembered for the difference I made to others' lives, for my key contributions to the fight against cancer and to furthering the health and genetic fitness of future generations. This is more than a doctor of my modest talents could ever hope for.

18. Fitness

Benton woke up to knocking. It was Pierre. He was in a Foundation vest and jogging shorts and carried a small backpack.

"What happened to your face?"

"Mosquitoes," Benton said. "Or maybe vampires."

Pierre handed Benton a gym bag containing a similar outfit to what he was wearing, along with a pair of Adidas sneakers.

"For our workout. Today is going to be a special day."

"I don't think I can lose any weight," Benton began.

"This is about fitness, not weight loss."

Benton was tempted to resist, but it was not in his best interests. He changed quickly. The Foundation T-shirt felt smooth and light like fine Egyptian cotton. Pierre was waiting outside, and he glanced quickly at Benton's belly as they started walking away from Toy's cottage.

A garden soon appeared on the left with a gazebo and a small nursery.

"That's Megumi's little piece of paradise," Pierre said. "Did you watch her video?"

"I did. But learned nothing about the plants and cancer."

"Megumi can't discuss that part. It's our partners' intellectual property."

After fifteen minutes, a row of jagged karst formations came into view on their right, looking like a miniature version of the Grand Tetons. The path began to ascend, and Benton could feel the pain mounting in his chest.

"Where to?"

Pierre pointed to one of the shorter rock towers, on which a shining Buddha was seated, gazing out to sea.

"Up there? I'm no spring chicken."

"It's a pleasant hike. At the end, you get to sit in the Lord Buddha's lap."

Neither the hike nor the idol's lap was at all enticing, but he followed Pierre onto a range of low hills, their thickly forested slopes marred by long white gashes. At the foot of one of the quarries he could see a backhoe and two trucks. The blaze and heat made him wonder if it was all a mirage.

They had been hiking for nearly two sweaty hours when they entered a wood. He heard the burbling of a stream, which appeared soon after, its clean water coursing busily over smooth stones. They crossed where it was narrow, the cool wetness seeping into his new sneakers. On the other side a line of monks stood before a pavilion in saffron robes, each carrying a brass begging bowl. He nodded politely to them, sidestepping the transparent bags of offerings strewn at their feet and only then grasping that they were statues.

He took a pee break, and when he returned he found Pierre sitting by the water. The doctor had taken a thin leather case from his pocket. As he snapped it open, a knife-blade flashed.

"Try some passion fruit." Pierre reached into his backpack. He sliced one and handed it to him.

The pulp with its black seeds was crunchy, and the nectar inside had a tangy-sweet and refreshing taste.

"Another?"

"Sure." He could have been a monkey, sucking away all day at the fruit. Except that the man who had cut them was sitting beside him.

Pierre opened a bottle of water that had traveled all the way from Fiji and drank without touching his lips to it. Then he handed it to Benton, who took a swig. As he stretched his legs out, Benton felt a soft squish in his back pocket. His sheet of paper was still there, carefully shielded from prying eyes.

"Pierre, what's the deal with the Calpastatin sou?"

Pierre smiled as he packed away the bottle. "Calpastatin slows muscle decomposition and necrosis. It's a functioning gene, even in humans."

Benton noticed a pair of blue-bottomed wasps, which seemed larger than any he had ever seen, inspecting the leftovers of his passion fruit.

"Yes, Toy explained that. I was wondering about its sou P35001. I couldn't find anything on it, though I checked all the public sou databases. Pseudogene, psiCube, etcetera. Are there others?"

"You need password access to our datasets, Benton. The Calpastatin sou not only delays decomposition but stimulates regeneration and growth in inactive muscle. Until, that is, rigor mortis sets in."

Benton looked at the wrinkles on his hands. "Wow. You mean it can revive the recently dead?"

"No doubt you've seen a headless chicken do a tango?"

"More like a frenzied death-dance."

Pierre fingered the knife, pretending to nick the tip of his index finger with it and then shaking his finger as if it were in pain.

"Removing its brain doesn't switch off a neural network in the spine, which keeps running for a bit, processing its internal inputs and responding appropriately. Likewise, the Calpastatin sou is able to stimulate a motor network to regenerate movement in certain dead muscles."

"Which muscles?"

"The ones that control the eye."

"And why is that relevant?"

"The Calpastatin sou made it into early humans. And survived in a few Palin... in one subject, in fact. Luckily, we managed to extract and copy it before he popped."

"Cool!" The knife was now hovering, and he wished Pierre would stop playing with it.

"Precisely. We're trying to see if the sou could nix the ophthalmic side effects of some of the other sous. The ones that fight tumors."

It was now coming together. "And the Calpastatin sou could be used to nuke FOXC1 mutations?"

"It's not that simple, my friend." Pierre used the tip of his shoe to draw in the dirt. "See here, FOXC1 regulates a growth factor called FGF-19 that represses expression of the CYP7A1 gene that in turn oversees the synthesis of bile from cholesterol. And this pathway is connected to numerous others forming one of the many biological networks inside your body."

Benton didn't understand all of that, but he had a key question. "I guess one has to tread carefully?"

"Of course. Otherwise the 1 percent of our subjects who suffer side effects might end up drowning in bile. Or get liver cancer."

Benton had never given much thought to bile beyond its revolting taste. But he had often wondered about what the vast bile-producing system was all about. And now he had an answer of sorts. Beneath his own familiar outward persona sat a marvel of nature, comprised of vast constellations of molecules, millions in each cell, with all their glittering elements swaying together to a mysterious chemical melody. And once that melody was heard clearly, new melodies could be created, perhaps even flawless ones that would allow humankind to finally sing, in a symphony of transformation or even transfiguration.

But not so fast. The mystery of a complex system like Benton Sims would only be partially understood, at best. But that hadn't stopped modern medicine, and those who would profit from it, from charging full-speed ahead.

Pierre nodded, apparently registering Benton's thoughts. "We can't just tweak things and hope it will work. The science needs to be understood better. Eventually, of course, the sous we've harvested from the Palin are going to have a huge impact."

"What sort of impact?"

"The genome we have today is the product of slow cooking over millions of years. But of late the environment has been pushed to the limits by climate change. It's all changing far too quickly for our species, like being thrown into a flash fry." He pointed with the knife to the giant wasps that were still hovering around Benton's head. "That's why we're seeing huge numbers of epigenetic mutations, as organisms desperately try to cope with environmental stress. Your friendly wasps are one example."

"I've read that we're now in our sixth mass extinction," Benton said. "And nobody has the guts to change things."

"That's right," Pierre said. "We're in a time of great disturbances. When we can't leave it to others anymore. We have to take it upon ourselves to plan for our survival. That's what the young have been trying to tell us."

"And you believe resurrecting the past with your sous will help humans survive as a species?"

"Just think of your increased fitness, Benton, and imagine these benefits percolating to the world at large, the diseased as well as the healthy."

"But it's only part of the solution, right?"

"Of course. It's best to think of our resurrected sous as a seed bank. As with seeds, one day this repository and the technology to exploit it will be in demand worldwide. The underlying vision goes way beyond cancer or the small pharma investments we have so far."

"This enterprise—will be run by you, Pierre?"

Pierre didn't reply, and Benton figured the man was on guard again. But he needed to keep the conversation going. He cleared his throat. "Once we learn more, will computing be able to figure out what evolution can't? Predicting which genetic modifications are likely to be the fittest?"

Pierre finally put away his knife, after examining the blade carefully.

"I would hope so. Mind you, a human is a huge search space with a vast number of genes, once you include the dark matter. And we have only a small number of examples from which to derive fitness functions. It's a hard computational problem. Our friends at UCLA are trying to figure out the algorithms."

"Good luck to them!"

"Thankfully, they're being helped by groups of volunteer biohackers."

"Biohackers?"

"People who are willing to alter their own biology by DIY experiments. Editing their own genes and such. They're brave souls, willing to venture where the pharma industry doesn't dare tread. Their service is a nice example of how humans can help optimize the fitness algorithms."

"But humans aren't programmed to be optimal," Benton said. "We are fucked up but manage to survive. Some more so than others."

"You're dead right, Benton," Pierre said, ignoring the intended insult. "We all have built-in imperfections, which we make up for with sophisticated error recovery. Whereas the goal of rationalism, embodied in all our engineering, is a kind of perfection. Once humans are engineered for fitness, they won't have to go through all the trial and error and make stupid mistakes."

"Perfection can be deadly," Benton said. "The search for it must be guided by values."

"Spoken like a preacher, my friend. But whose values?"

They started climbing again, leaving the woods, and Benton was moving faster now. The minutes of rest and the passion fruit had done him good, and he was glad they had had the conversation about sous. The big wasps were still buzzing around his ears, and he was thankful they hadn't stung him.

"Pierre, I've still got Calpastatin on my mind. Can't you use FOXC1 antibodies instead of the Calpastatin sou?"

"It's been tried. However, it can reduce the antioxidant effects of FOXC1, giving rise to other eye problems."

"Is that what Toy is on?"

"I can't say. These are double-blinds. Where neither subjects nor the experimenter knows who gets what."

But maybe he *could* say. "What about me? What am I being saved from?"

"The disease that claimed your aunt Zora Wright."

"Colon cancer? Am I prone to it?"

He turned, the tiger eyes glinting. "You don't know? Never asked TAENIA?"

"Why bother to learn what could kill you?"

"It won't kill you, my friend. Not if you take the right medicine. I can help you with that."

Benton touched his wallet. He now had several more knowns for the left column. He was grateful to Pierre for being so forthright.

They climbed on, the doctor humming a tune. Benton studied the man in all his complexity. What to call him? Logical, scientific, the paragon of reason. But delusional, his mind like that of an adolescent, stuffed with grandiose dreams and schemes. And perverted, a collector of bones and who knows what else. Dangerous and manipulative, and desperate for success, willing to ram his potions down the throats of innocent victims——though perhaps the science and pharma industry weren't that far behind. And also threatening and unpredictable. Capable of extreme violence, if given a chance. With a crocodile-like curiosity, willing to pursue, examine and tear apart anything, living or dead.

And yet so friendly and straightforward, even helpful, at times. Perhaps there really was a spark of goodness in everyone? He doubted it.

Pierre remained silent, perhaps aware of the ongoing scrutiny and judgment. They were now passing a tiny village of lean-tos and simple beds set out under the trees with garbage strewn about. Three men were sitting on their haunches around a smoking pile, waiting with plastic plates. A pack of dogs stood beside them, tails wagging. At first, all Benton could smell was burning plastic, but then the familiar odor of rat came sweeping into his nostrils. Peeping at the spit, he saw a row of little creatures lying on their backs with their heads flopped to one side and their insides slit open, baring a few glints of meat. Benton couldn't help stepping closer, drawn as he was to the meat. He nearly tripped.

"Watch your step!"

The dogs whined, cowering with their tails lowered, as the doctor approached to lend Benton his hand.

The path had become very steep, and soon the Buddha appeared beyond a high saddleback to the east, hundreds of feet above them on an adjacent hill, his gold-plated skin catching the sun.

"Prepare for a climb, my friend."

"Cross that ridge? Are you out of your mind?"

But he took it on. For something had taken control of his will. He couldn't put his finger on it, but it was as if his mind had decided to stop analyzing and instead geared itself up to cope with the challenge ahead, realizing that tiredness was simply an excuse to avoid exploring one's true capabilities.

They descended along the saddleback, traversing a smooth concourse. Then it was up a slope and a long and heart-thumping climb until they reached the ridge. Pierre darted on ahead, bounding giddily like a mountain goat across the rocks. Benton stopped once to catch his breath while waiting for the pounding in his chest to subside, but after that he was able to move smoothly without resting, until he came to a place where the path narrowed to eighteen inches. To the left below him was a scree slope sliding into a black void. It was best not to look at that.

Meanwhile, something was bothering his ear, buzzing inside it. He shook his head, tried to scratch, leaned his head down, then up, and tossed it from side to side. It was tickling now, then pinching and burning inside the ear canal, driving him crazy, making him shout and laugh hysterically. He felt the buzzing intensify and then saw a line of insects flying out of his ear, becoming successively larger, until one came and faced him.

Its face was that of an ancient idol, not Jesus or Brahma but a wasp-face, and on its forehead was blazed, in an odd Cyrillic-like script, the letters HAGANI! He screamed the word out loud, as the enormous eyes and glistening mouth approached, preparing to feed.

Then the scree slope heaved up. It was like a slow-motion earthquake, and he was stomping about like a madman when he became dizzy and lost his balance.

His arms flapped out, caught in a wave of panic as he went down. The buzzing stopped suddenly as the beach far below rushed towards him, the wind ripping at his eyes. Time slowed to a crawl to allow a few last thoughts to unspool from his mind. He tried to shriek but the words formed bubbles as he rocketed down, and the dark wall shot up beside him, its craggy face streaked with bird shit and fossilized remains.

He needed to focus, to reach out for any protrusion that would arrest his descent, but there was not a tree or bush in sight. He searched for a handhold, a ledge, anything, but all he could feel were cold, confused thoughts flitting away in the wind. He was freezing, his eyes burning, his eyelids about to peel off, his balls turned into icicles. As the glimmering disk where the beach met the sea grew steadily larger, he could see someone waiting on the sand, in a black blouse with her waist slim as never before in a snazzy yellow and black striped skirt.

His aunt waved to him with gossamer arms.

"Hunch your shoulders, Ben. No bits and pieces."

"Help me, Aunt Zora. Please. One more chance—I'm fucked!"

"Watch your tongue, boy. Any last regrets?"

"None. Except maybe that I didn't love enough."

"You didn't never, and even now you thinking of her."

"She was classy. Those boots!"

"Classy to monkey about with white tunes? Going *dan-ta-da-da* with no damn beat?"

"That was the life she chose."

"At least she got music. What your faith, boy?"

"Faith in reason."

"Don't fool wid me, Ben! You ain't got none. And never did no singing in church!"

"I'll be good, Aunt Zora. I promise."

"Only Truth gonna set you free, boy."

"Just give me one more day. I promise."

But it was too late. He was heading for a slab of black rock on which a long-tailed lizard was sunbathing. It raised its snout, the vertical pupil carefully eyeing his surprising descent.

Smack and then *thump*! But he didn't land, protected no doubt by the charms of his aunt. He was still on the cliff.

He tried taking a step forward. Then another, only to find that his left foot had crossed in front of the right one. He tried to again grab onto the rock, but his fingers kept slipping, with pebbles rolling off the limestone. He pressed hard against the rock with his palm and lifted his right foot, trying to get it ahead of the left. After hovering for a few seconds, he put it back where it had been and slid the left foot a few inches ahead. His hamstrings were now stretched, so he raised the right foot and tried to step forward. And tottered.

He was back at the edge, standing on the path with his back to the precipice while holding onto a boulder with both hands.

"Help!" He heard his voice echo down the ravine.

Out of the distance a figure came floating towards him, his feet flying over the rocks. It was Pierre.

"One step at a time, Benton."

"My foot slipped."

"Watch me. Place the next foot firmly forward. But first make sure you have traction. Watch it, step to your right!"

"I can't turn, and in front of my foot is a drop to hell."

"Take a deep breath, Benton! Don't let your stomach control your brain."

Benton managed that deep breath and then quickly hopped to his right, so the precipice was on his left, and then he tried to take a step forward. He lurched, clutching onto the boulder on his right with his arms, only to see stones roll off under his grip. Then his supporting boulder started to move. He flapped his arms, desperately trying to balance while standing still. He could feel bile welling up.

He knelt down, breathing heavily and then crouched on all fours while the world twirled around him.

Pierre cupped Benton's jaw in one hand and raised his face up.

"You have vertigo, my friend. Try to relax. Your eyes are flitting like crazy."

He grabbed hold of Benton's hand and pulled him firmly to his feet.

Pierre took one step, and then another, with Benton following behind like a pig to market. Pierre's grip was firm, his hand like a suction cup. When the cliff face on the right vanished and they were exposed on both sides, each step for Benton became a trust fall with his mad mentor. His heart hammered as he secretly begged Pierre, a good four inches taller and far more lithe of limb, to guide him safely across.

And then they had crossed the ridge and were ascending another slope. He could hear the shushing of a giant bathtub along with the shrieks of gulls, and soon they were climbing alongside a little irrigation pipe.

One more tug from Pierre, and with his heart pumping gratefully, Benton was finally on top.

19. Viewpoint

They came in near the monks' quarters, ducking past robes hung out to dry. A young novice was looking at the valley while smoking, and another had his earbuds on. Pierre went straight to the shrine hall where a trio of beefy Buddhas sat waiting, alongside a statue of the founding abbot. He pulled out an envelope from his backpack and slipped it into the donation box.

"From our staff," he said. "They pray that all living things be delivered from suffering."

Pierre knelt down and kowtowed three times before the idols, reciting a Buddhist stanza before sitting back in a full-lotus pose and meditating.

Benton rested with his bare feet stretched in front, his glasses off. His clothing was soaked with sweat, and he needed the time alone.

The hall was cool, with a high ceiling with crossbeams, and it felt quiet and peaceful with a live monk sitting at a desk watching them. Young couples were stepping carefully towards their gods, each one bearing a pair of joss sticks and a lotus flower sticking out of a cellophane packet. They lit the incense, then prostrated themselves as Pierre had, before sitting and mouthing prayers.

Their devotions and clean-cut looks made the Thais seem nice and decent. He didn't care for their culture and superstitions, but they seemed so much calmer than his compatriots, with far more robust traditions than those of the land he had grown up in. He could say, with certainty now, that he really appreciated Thailand, and he wasn't going to let Pierre and his gang blow his retirement home to pieces with their mad experiments.

Sweaty but surprisingly not that tired, Benton also felt strangely euphoric. He put his glasses back on and noticed the murals on the walls. With soft green trees and cool blue streams, the scenery was lush and calming, the elephants cute and cuddly with enormous heads, the deer like gentle lambs, the people light skinned and bare chested with simple oval faces. The royals were wreathed in jewels and wore elaborate tiaras, sitting or floating in curtained pavilions. The artists had tried to compensate for the lack of skill in perspective with rich colors and fine ornamentation. It called to mind a people who were drugged.

When Pierre was done with his prayers, he stood up and heaved a sigh as they walked back. "A beautiful *wat*, isn't it?"

"What's the deal with those giraffe-necked tigers?"

"It's from an old Jataka tale, imported from the Northern Buddhist tradition."

"Jataka?"

"Episodes from the previous lives of Lord Buddha."

"The tigers?"

"Would you like to hear the story?"

"I'm all ears."

"Once upon a time, the bodhisattva and his disciple Aditha are wandering in a forest. They come upon a tigress crouched behind a rock. Her ribs are showing, her fur is mangled and she is about to devour her newborn cubs. The bodhisattva sends Aditha away to fetch food from the village. When he returns, he finds his teacher's shredded and bloodstained robe. He heads farther into the bushes, and there he comes across his teacher's jaw and thighbones."

"He sacrificed himself?"

Pierre stared thoughtfully at Benton's shorts, his nostrils twitching. "Grudging neither his marrow nor brain to the beast."

Benton was relieved when they stepped out. The front gates of the *wat* opened onto a road lined with stalls. People were shopping for religious merchandise, sifting through talismans, amulets, medallions and jewelry, all of them stamped with buddha images. Farther along were second-hand clothing and gadget shops, staffed entirely by Burmese women, their faces streaked with *thanaka* paste. The air was thick with the smell of fried chicken and barbecued sausages, along with meatballs and other delicacies.

Benton bought himself an iced coffee and drank it in a few quick gulps, crunching vigorously on the ice as they strolled up towards the ledge to see the giant Buddha. People of all ages were carefully sticking small squares of gold leaf on his hands and legs. A child had climbed into his lap, with the mother taking pictures. A tourist was posing for selfies by his feet. The Buddha was at least fifty feet tall, and his eyes were wide open as he sat observing the glittering sea.

The viewpoint lay a few yards ahead of the edifice. People gathered by the stone wall, taking turns to peer through a telescope. Benton waited and then took a look. Two fishing boats gently rolled on the swells. A row of kite surfers arched in unison, their kidney-shaped sails flapping above. The waves spurted after them, their white crests lambent under a sun that now peeped between fast-moving grey clouds. Farther out were squads of fishing boats and what appeared to be a small naval vessel basking near the horizon. The sweep of the coast was visible for miles, quiet bays, gentle promontories and hills topped with the spires of golden *wats*, and beyond them, the cliffs of the Spa and the road into town, with its high-rise hotels and bars and the promise of freedom.

The wind was strong now. It ruffled his hair and beard, soothed his drenched neck and back and cooled his testicles. Benton took a deep breath, soaking in the sunshine and clean air with the minerals glinting on his skin.

"How are you feeling, Benton?"

"Fine. You do this often?"

"I usually swim for exercise." Pierre smiled, approaching closer. "But I promised to make you fitter. And you're doing great."

Benton was breathing deeply, raising his arms. He felt like banging his chest and shouting *Bundolo*!

"The Palin sous are giving you an extra boost," Pierre said into his ear, his voice low and calm.

Pierre's hand was now resting lightly on his shoulder. Like the claw of some repulsive prehistoric beast.

"You chose the right place to retire. Thailand is awesome, isn't it?"

"It is," Benton said. "And will remain so if we don't fuck it up."

Pierre was quiet for a minute. Benton remained tense, drinking in the view, wondering in which direction the hand was going to move. He was about six inches from an eight-hundred-foot drop.

"Benton, there's something I've been meaning to tell you."

"What?"

Pierre paused, the whirring of a fan belt the only sound.

"I know you think I've been over-aggressive in the way I recruit subjects. At the Spa the other day, you seemed confrontational about it."

"Really?"

"But you now understand why it's so urgent."

Benton nodded.

"And I'm sorry about the other night. When I invited you I was thinking only of a quiet dinner, chatting and listening to old hits. But our cancer work never stops, and you seemed an excellent subject. I couldn't control myself."

"No worries." Benton hesitated but decided to wing it. "You've helped me become fit. And that evening after the concert, I realized how similar we were."

"I'm glad you understand," Pierre said, looking relieved.

"While we're chatting about personal stuff, I want to ask you about Mimi."

He felt a squeeze on his shoulder. "She will not press charges."

"Great! I guess I should apologize in person."

"She's away in Pattaya. But Sharky will be visiting this weekend and would like to meet you."

"Will I have to pay?"

Pierre looked shocked. "You have it all wrong, Benton! She's not that kind of girl."

"What kind of girl is she?"

"Oh, I don't know. What kind do you like?" The eyes hovered curiously.

"I didn't mean it that way."

Pierre laughed. "*Mon ami*, you can do much better than Ms. Sugar Cane. After you talk to Sharky, who knows?"

Benton wiped his brow. "But I thought Sharky was Mimi's man."

"You have it wrong again," Pierre said. "He's her dad."

"Is that right!"

"He can be a bit overprotective, but then he may look kindly on you."

"My oh my," a voice said. "Jack's everywhere."

Benton turned around. It was Surry, with his son beside him.

"We drove here for a ceremony," Surry said. "Thought I'd show the young man how proper rituals are done."

"It was awesome," Somchai said. "The volunteers were really cool." He eyed Benton's Foundation shirt.

"What volunteers?" Benton asked.

"It was a *Lang Pa Cha*, a space-saving ritual," Surry said. "In Thai Buddhism, unclaimed bodies are buried, not cremated. But these village cemeteries can run out of space pretty fast. A crew of volunteers—mostly ER types—get to work digging up the bodies, stripping them down to the bone and then cremating the bones in a mass ceremony. We were lucky to be invited."

A raindrop fell on Benton's arm. More of it and the ridge could become even more slippery. Pierre brushed away the drop.

"Surry, I hope you can give us a ride back?"

"Of course, boss. But how about lunch first?"

They ate at a picnic table right by the viewpoint. Surry opened a bag of baguettes, stuffed with *sai ua*, a dark, curled sausage flavored with lemongrass and green chilies. Benton was delighted to find that the spice didn't bother him. Surry said they had already eaten a bit at the ceremony, but the leftovers were simply too good to throw away. They slaked their thirst with fresh coconut water, sipping it straight from the green shell.

Surry fancied himself as a raconteur, narrating tales of his father's survival at the hands of the Japanese. Major Robert Surry of the Fourteenth Army, Lushai Brigade, was captured by the enemy and put to work on the Death Railway at Hellfire Pass in Thailand. Pierre became very quiet as Surry waxed on about his father, who apparently not only bore no ill will towards his captors but remained an admirer of their warrior codes of *bushido* and *seppuku*. Surry explained the details of the *seppuku* procedure, and then the conversation turned to Cambodia and Sharky's work there on behalf of the museum. Eventually, Surry mentioned the Kit Kat Klub. Some of their lap dancers, he said, were superb.

"Dad, what's so great about a lap dance?"

Surry laughed. "Wait till we have a men's night out, son. You'll love every minute of it."

"Do the girls also have fun at the night out? Otherwise, it wouldn't be fair."

"Be patient, Somchai," Surry said. "It will all become crystal clear one day."

It was an unforgettable afternoon, the food excellent, the fury of the Thai sun tempered by clouds, with a fleeting shower creating a double rainbow across which a swarm of swifts lured by insects tossed up by the wind swooped and swirled and dive-bombed in a thrilling aerobatic display.

To top it all off, Pierre indicated that Benton was now no longer in need of monitoring at the Spa.

"As long as you take your pills and exercise regularly, you should be fit as a fiddle."

"That's super," Benton said. He breathed a long sigh of relief as he looked up at Pierre.

"But meanwhile, my friend, I hope you'll consider volunteering at the museum. Your analytical smarts could have a huge impact on the team."

"I'm sure Madame Choam would be delighted," Surry said, laughing. "If you're nice, she might even sing you one of her songs."

The laugh turned into a thigh-beating howl, and Somchai also joined in. Benton couldn't help smiling, though he had no idea who Madame Choam was.

20. Mimi

A droplet of sweat dripped onto the paper, smudging one of the knowns. Benton dabbed it off with a towel. It was a humid afternoon, and he had been back at Win's now for several weeks after being discharged from the Spa. The fan didn't help, and for once, he missed the comfort of his air-conditioned Spa room.

He had been working with his earbuds on, listening to the sound of a wistful Palin flute. It brought to mind a tired warrior or woodcutter sitting on an overlook piping to the valley below a melody from ancient times. Not for him the comforts of the hearth or the babbling of a joyful child, for the flutist was alone with the elements, playing a rustic mountain tune that had been handed down the generations. Benton hummed along, thinking of the quiet dead, the unruffled sleep of ancestors long gone.

His pleasure was marred by the fan blades rattling ominously inside their cage. He had complained about it twice to Win, and a handyman had been in to fix it, smiling afterward with his inhaler stuck ridiculously up his nose as he received his tip. The fan began rattling with renewed energy within an hour of the repairman's leaving. But it provided a percussion in time to the music, as did his breathing, which had grown heavy in the heat.

A ping interrupted his thoughts. Chad was chatting online.

"Got a USB stick?" he asked.

"Hang on… it's in my wallet."

"Remember how to set up GPG keys? From your first week here in DAO."

"Yup." It was a week from hell and not easily forgotten.

"Then boot up Tails, set up the keys, install the secure Dropbox and then pick up my tarball. Need any help?"

"Chad, I'm not a moron. I'm fully capable of doing this myself."

"Coolio. I'll wait."

Benton carried out the procedure in about seven minutes, without a typo, the system cooperating at every step.

"Wow. Gramps is now superuser!"

"Got it. I'll watch the videos later. What about Bulsani and Co?"

"Foundation is kosher. Their grantee Shepherd is a science star, working on computational modeling of dark matter in the genome. But tagged twice in your neighborhood."

"Where?"

"The Kit Kat Klub."

"The researcher at MIT?"

"Clean. McArthur Fellow."

"Dr. Bulsani himself?"

"His stock options made me throw up. Owns fat chunks of Pfizer and J and J. Ratings are five stars. 'Would do anything for his patients.'"

"I need the low-down, Chad."

"One infraction."

"Which was?"

"Missing specimens."

"What kind?"

"Four fetuses and a brain. Plus some chemicals. While summering as an RA in the UCLA Path Lab."

"Thanks, Chad. I owe you a beer."

"Ask Chad anytime. But one more thing, gramps."

"Yes?"

"Have a peek at this."

It was a YouTube video of a small building in an office park, with a Californian backdrop of desert palms, mountains and a sky of glowing blue. The sign said "CBX Women's Health." People were standing outside holding placards.

"Looks like an abortion clinic. What's the connection?"

"CBX is a healthcare conglomerate, based in the Cayman Islands. Privately owned. They run clinics in seven states."

"And Bulsani's involved?"

"Founding board member."

"Does TAENIA know more?"

"Not yet. But I'll keep you posted, dude."

It was clear that Pierre didn't need the Foundation to make ends meet. The abortions were presumably keeping the doctor afloat. Leaving him enough leeway to start sowing the seeds of empire.

Benton went back to his notes. His analytical smarts were in full force, and he wrote down more.

At a quarter to four he removed his earbuds, stood up and stretched. In the mirror a clean-shaven African warrior stared at him, with broad pecs and tattoos on his bulging biceps. He inhaled, drawing his stomach in, then raised his arms high. The pills had worked wonders, as had the dawn jogs and the weights at the gym, giving him a rejuvenated physique even stronger than the one he had as a youth. Even the *qi gong* at the beach seemed to help, the smooth Chinese movements generating and releasing subtle energies.

His pig-like symptoms had left him for the most part, though he was still hungry all the time. He had been staying off pork and had thankfully stopped seeing those little white worms in his shit. He had asked Pierre about them three days earlier, and the doctor substituted his usual gourmet concoctions with a plate of sticky rice mixed with bitter yam, which had done the trick.

On his last visit, Pierre had presented him with a tiger tooth to wear around his neck. It was from the *wat* of the Golden Buddha, to remind him of his fitness achievement. He was getting to like Pierre, despite everything that he was finding out.

He felt hungry and opened the fridge, finding only a bunch of tiny, finger-sized bananas that had turned black. He could have sworn they were yellow that morning in the bazaar. It was as if time had accelerated, causing the fruits' insides to swell up with hormones and rot before they could reach maturity.

He ate four bananas, all of which tasted good, and then stepped out to find it was cloudy, the westerly sun lurking behind a puffy black cloud.

He started his scooter, immediately feeling a wind gust on his back. Looking behind, he saw a flotilla of enormous clouds approaching from the north. A giant thunderhead appeared as a monstrous anvil and looming above it, a brilliant white skyscraper with puffs of vapor blowing from its top. He stopped the vehicle to watch a huge tower sweep over, topped by a flaming white mane. As the formation fanned out, it cast a liver-hued stain over the sea. Flocks of white-banded swifts took to the air, screeching as they soared and plunged giddily on the wind currents, while a convoy of little cormorants glided like sharks through the choppy waves, all moving purposefully in the hunt for prey. He could see blobs rising in the distance, possibly breaching dolphins, tritons or other sea creatures riding high above the waves. Then the shadows changed as the clouds headed out to sea, after which the sky once again reverted to eggshell blue and the sea to a bright foam-flecked green.

The afternoons of the rainy season always seemed like a stunning nature documentary. But now a pack of dogs was disrupting the picture, a canine cacophony that escalated with fresh snarls and yelps, and then he saw them approaching, their feet lifting off the ground in slow motion and then thundering down as they flew towards him.

He started back on his scooter, revving it up to max speed as he shot by the boardwalk. It was a blue 125 cc Yamaha, with a comfortable seat and a sleek front end whose twin side lights converged Cyclops-like in front. He was renting it at a hundred and fifty baht a day, having yielded to the urge as soon as he got back from the Spa. The only issue was the traffic, and now a big white pickup truck veered towards him, driving on the wrong side as it overtook another vehicle. There was no security lane, so he had to swerve onto the sidewalk, braking hard in order to avoid knocking into a noodle cart. He managed to keep his balance, with his feet planted firmly on the ground, but he couldn't help cursing.

The noodle lady smiled at him while holding tight to her stand.

"*Jai yen yen.*" He smiled back as he returned to the lane. He would go with the flow.

Mimi was waiting outside Wat Santisuk in her sun jacket, her face glowing as it did after prayers.

"You late ten minutes, Bento!"

She pecked his cheek and hopped on, sitting side-saddle as she worked on her phone.

"Did you pray for me, Mimi?"

She grinned. "I pray you become very rich, Bento!"

If she had her way, Buddha would have granted her all the nice things on her wish list. Like a scooter of her own. An upgraded phone. And all that bling and makeup that she never seemed to tire of wearing.

Now she had pulled a cigarette out of her jacket pocket and had the audacity to tap him on the back, asking for a light.

He had met Mimi after checking with her father, Sharky, who had accepted Benton's apologies with a solid clap on the back.

"No worries, mate." Sharky was at the Klub leaning against a pole, a cigarette stuck to his lower lip. "Mimi's been around drunks since she was yay hoi. Wiped their puke and all."

"Is that right?"

"But don't you forget one thing."

"What?"

Benton noticed a line of young women sitting on metal chairs, hypnotized by their vanity mirrors.

"She ain't ever hung out with your sort."

"What sort is that?" He felt a hot flash and instinctively reached for his belt.

Sharky clapped him more gently this time. "Don't get me wrong, mate! I've done time in the boneyard with your black brothers."

"I wasn't one of the brothers," Benton said. "I worked for the US government."

"I know," Sharky said. "Little John said you're a spook. No worries! But I'm tellin' you the little one ain't easy."

"How so?"

"Her mum died young," Sharky went on. "She's had it hard growin' up with my girls, everyone bawlin' for attention. And she'll be buggin' you for stuff."

"I only wanted to apologize," Benton said. "But I'll keep an eye on her."

"You do that, mate. The good news is I'm sendin' her back to Australia for schoolin'. She'll learn proper manners if I can help it."

It was not finishing school that would help Mimi. She needed a mentor who would steer her away from her parasitic view of other humans. And yet he could hardly blame her, for she had been born into an expat subculture where a pretty girl was either predator or prey.

When he met her to ask forgiveness, it was inside the *wat*, in the presence of the Buddha. Imitating Mimi, he bowed to the embalmed abbot. He sat down, but Mimi seemed uncomfortable, squirming as she squatted on her knees before seeking the abbot's silent blessings.

"Mimi, I'm so sorry."

"For what, *ka*?" she asked, her opal eyes staring at him.

"For behaving like an animal." He cleared his throat. "I was high, didn't know what came over me."

"*Mai bpen rai*." She sniffed, touching his arm and holding back a tear. "No worries. Dad explain already."

He knew that though he had not been entirely forgiven, he could not press further. It was as if she wanted respect but had, as a result of her family background, zero expectations of receiving it. Later, over coffee and donuts, she mentioned that he had torn her little waist chain. He bought her one the next day, presenting it to her at the Pub after a substantial dinner. She gave him a surprising smooch with Apple looking on, amused, and then Benton asked if he might put it on her. As they walked out together, Little John—who had been watching approvingly from a table nearby—gave him a double thumbs-up.

In his room that night, he kissed her as they sat on the bed, and her smooch this time was long and responsive. She asked if he wanted to fuck, and he hesitated, but by then she had pushed him gently down and was sitting astride him, pressing against him where it counted before they had any of their clothes off. That initial move led to several hours of shared pleasure, his born-again vigor raising his performance to an intensity and subtlety that he hadn't seen since the early days with Sylvia.

As he later lay back on the pillow, experiencing the satyr-like satisfaction of sexual conquest, with his nymph Mimi asleep naked beside him, her hair askance on his shoulder, he wondered why such a beautiful young woman had come to him. Surely she would be mocked by her friends for doing so. Like other Thai women—of all classes—she had dispensed with the formalities, with none of that *let's get to know each other first*. But why him? If she was desperate for an old-timer on his deathbed, why not a wealthy white groom? There were so many better-off studs who would have given anything to share her bed.

Money management was certainly a problem. She received an allowance from Sharky but ran through it within a week on clothes and accessories. She had already demanded a scooter, and Benton had promised her the rental money starting the following month. If they stayed together long enough, it might be a car or even a house, not that he could afford that.

It soon became clear, however, that her needs were more than financial. She was looking for someone she could count on, turn to for advice and reassurance, something her absent but doting dad and her series of stripper stepmoms could never provide. She was a needy child, and stability was what she was after.

She was a girl of many moods, easily excited and often tearful, especially in his arms. Sometimes after meeting up with her friends, she returned to him looking down in the dumps.

"What's wrong, Mimi?" he asked one day when she arrived while he was still in bed.

She shook her head and stared, like a Thai actress about to have a tantrum. "I feel life go on without me."

"What d'you mean? You're going back to school soon."

Sharky had pleaded with the principal to have her reinstated after being suspended for missing way too many classes. But the man had held his ground, saying he had seen many like her, entitled and obsessed with fashion and accessories, and though he acknowledged her brilliance and skill at acing tests, he was of the firm opinion that the child should be taught a lesson. A deal was finally made to have her back on a provisional basis after the October break.

"School suck, *ka*. English teachers who not speak English."

He sat up, covering his lower parts with a sheet.

"You're going back, Mimi, if I have anything to do with it. And Sharky's also promised to send you to Sydney."

"Australia suck, *ka*. Fon go there."

"Your friend Fon has been abroad?"

"She go holiday aller time. Meet so many interesting *farang*, *ka*. Girlfriend experience, *ka*."

"The bottom line is she dropped out of school and became a hooker, Mimi."

She propped herself up on an elbow and stared at him. "Bento, why you say bad stuff about Fon? She's from good family, work very hard for money."

"Well, work hard and get educated, and you could have a terrific life. Be patient."

After receiving that generous piece of advice, Mimi frowned and pretended to pout. That look, with her eyes turned up towards the ceiling, her lips slightly parted, brought back a memory that Benton cherished above all others. It was of Sylvia standing in the choir singing "Deep River."

> Oh, don't you want to go
> To the Gospel feast
> That Promised Land
> Where all is peace?

As she sang, the light from a stained-glass window fell on her face, giving her an unearthly, spiritual glow. And now that light had faded. He had wanted to seek Sylvia's permission to fall in love again, but memory's corrosive currents had dissolved all traces of her.

Mimi's lovely opals had become misty, and a tear had emerged, which he couldn't help brushing away.

"Lord Buddha love Fon. Give her good stuff."

"Mimi, stop comparing yourself to others. You're unique... remember that." He stroked her hair as she played with her phone, and even as a tent pole poked up through the sheet in the presence of the rest of Mimi's sexy young body, he couldn't help remembering how thin the hair could be at the end of a life.

He tried his best to cheer her up. He took her to dinners at the Pub, her feral eyes glinting as she attacked the ribs and mashed potatoes, flecks of sticky gunk clinging to her watchband. There he introduced her to Little John, who gave her a peck on the cheek, but she couldn't understand a word he said. She had better luck with Nellie, and was soon hanging out at her vegetable stall, getting advice, Mimi said, on their relationship. When Benton and Little John visited the gym to watch Mimi learn to kickbox, Nellie asked to come along. They all clapped and cheered at Mimi's *muay thai* moves and her lack of fear that her stunning face could be smashed up. Mimi's coach was a good-looking Thai man with a ponytail, and her sparring partners included a sinewy Thai boy who at first seemed loathe to hit her, and then gave up and sent a kick flying towards her jaw, which she blocked smartly with her knee, extending it to a kick right back to his solar plexus. And when she fought other girls, she became even more competitive, and the small group of onlookers cheered wildly.

Benton taught Mimi to appreciate the things he now loved about his new home, starting with the sea.

She had at first hesitated, being water-shy like her Thai mother, but he held her from behind and dragged her out screaming into the ocean before dunking her. Soon she was standing knee-deep, splashing his face with fistfuls of warm, briny sea. She laughed nervously as the tide plucked at her calves and then climbed up to her waistline as she raised her still-functioning smartphone high and took a crazy picture of him beating his chest while a flock of gulls swooped above. And no picture or video could capture the feeling of surf crashing on the beach with the sound of doors being banged and the fizzing and plunging and the pounding on their eardrums as they were carried like flotsam into the frenzy of churning water.

Mimi preferred the relative safety of Brassiere Beach, where she could troll for shells by evening wearing her sun hat and shirt on top of a straggly bikini. She had the sheller's sharp eye, finding amid scampering sand crabs and scurrying sandpipers disk-shaped limpets, smirking cowries and a pair of deep, dish-like shells with their brown snail bodies huddled inside. She presented him with a crunchy auger cone whose swirls reminded him of long-ago ice creams at Baskin's. She picked up mottled tuns that looked like woven baskets and a pair of purple sundials that wore their clockwise spirals like proud insignia. Once she dug up an enormous chocolate-colored horse conch.

"Big like you," she said, grinning as she rubbed her finger all over it.

He smiled back, more than a little embarrassed, but still pleased that Pierre's treatments had given his sex life such a massive boost.

Mimi enjoyed shelling, but she never arranged her collections, storing them instead in a garbage bag under her bed at home. He had been there once, a vast bungalow with an unkempt garden and a resident water monitor that he spotted scuttling across the lawn. A couple of skimpily clad Thai ladies were hanging around a soupy swimming pool drinking whisky. Her room was large with an AC unit and a vast flat-screen television that she kept tuned to a fashion channel, while her bed, unmade and springy with stuffed creatures sitting against the pillow, made him uncomfortable, reminding him she was still half a child.

She called him names, her favorite one being Wilbur.

"Meaning?"

"Forest pig."

"You mean wild boar."

"Because snort when sleep."

"Not snort, Mimi. S-N-O-R-E."

"No, I mean snort." She made a grunting sound. "Just like Wilbur. Stuff face too much haha!"

He wanted to share his favorite music with her, starting with blues and classic rock. But she found their coded messages too obscure and was soon yawning and fiddling with her phone. She saw his attempt to inflict his tastes on her as a game of one-upsmanship and resented the implication that she was lacking in sophistication compared to Mr. Know-it-all. She believed herself to be essentially Thai, though blessed with insights into *farang* mores, thanks to her dad. She was much happier humming along to Thai pop tunes, like Tata Young's "Sexy Naughty Bitchy," which he was unable to appreciate.

Then there was Chopin. Mimi had mentioned the concert one night, as they lay together, exhausted.

"So beautiful, Bento. You see princess diamonds?"

"And Chopin?"

"Mmm. Tired, honey. After what Wilbur do just now."

She fell promptly asleep. He watched her small chest rising and falling, still tasting her skin and feeling a strand of her hair on his tongue, his heart gradually slowing after soaring on sweaty trapezes. He inserted his earbuds and lay back listening to the master's first scherzo, the reflective ten minutes spent with Marie de Villeneuve's piano rendering a sober reminder, after their sex acts of near-annihilation, of the need to exercise one's freedom without flinching in the face of finitude.

He was far more successful learning from her. Mimi became his sleeping Thai dictionary. She taught him weather words, how to describe the sky when it had dry tears, when it flashed, when it split in two. She tested him on the vocabulary for rain and storms, for when it rumbled and wept, drizzled, sprinkled or spattered with fine drops, and gently remonstrated when he forgot. She explained about the seasons, for rice planting, and harvest, the dry season, the monsoon, the season of winds and high seas, and *naa dtit sat*, the season when the animals mated. In his arms she shared with him the celestial vocabulary, including the term for the short-lived white morning moon that coolly gazed down at them as they lay sweating after yet another night of Tarzanian lovemaking. And then she revealed her real name, *Sukonta*, which meant beautiful fragrance.

She had been given her nickname Mimi because at age seven she kept calling out "Mummy, Mummy" in the months after she had lost her mother a decade earlier. She said she still remembered her hug, the way she danced to karaoke beats, making her daughter wiggle beside her, and the makeup she put on every evening before work.

Mimi did special prayers on her mother's death anniversary, the sixth of September. She informed Benton that, for a week, she would eat only vegetarian food, and even worse, refrain from sex. When the day came, she dressed in white and walked softly beside him to offer prayers before the dead abbot at Wat Santisuk and make the donation. The priest on duty, a dark young man with wide-set red eyes, tied strings around their wrists while intoning mantras in a wasp-like hum. Mimi seemed in a trance, her eyes closed, listening carefully, nodding from time to time. He imagined then what he had dared not earlier, that she actually loved him.

Later she explained that she had been meditating. She had learned vipassana in high school, but she practiced it only when visiting the *wat*. It helped with the violence.

"What violence?"

"Mummy." She sobbed into her sleeve.

He managed to coax out the gory details. One of the johns had taken her mother to a fancy hotel. He claimed to be a Malaysian tourist, though the other girls at the Klub suspected he was a southern Thai. She was later found in the hotel bathroom bleeding to death. The hotel CCTV captured the man's picture, but he struck four more times before authorities caught him in Chiang Mai and confirmed a DNA match that ultimately linked him to decades of similar crimes. A broken beer bottle, the police said, was discovered in Mimi's mother's colon.

"I see him, *ka*."

"It's just a nightmare, Mimi." He held her close. "He's on death row, can't hurt you now."

"No, I see him in prison."

She had gone there with Sharky's mother Devona. The authorities only let her spend a few minutes with the man. He crawled towards her in his leg shackles when he heard her words of forgiveness, but the guards dragged him away.

Her early experience with death and forgiveness had made her wise beyond her years, but most of the time Mimi was a teen. He loved her for that, for feeling firm and yet soft in his arms. For the way her hair fell over her ear while he whispered nonsense into it. For the beads of sweat glistening on her cheek, her silly laugh as he tickled her, her sharp nails with their flecks of leftover polish, the faint peach fuzz down her forearm, the freshly mowed stubble of her armpits, her taut hips and toned abs, the ring of rebellion on her teeny navel, and the way she pouted or threatened a *muay* kick when he asked for favors.

He pried into her past as he had never done with Sylvia.

"Do you have a *fan*, Mimi? A young boyfriend?"

She said she still had one, and that he'd better watch out when he came for her. He laughed at that. Who was the first, he asked? She refused to say. Had she liked making love with them? She blushed and turned away, showing him her moon-shaped derrière, while he imagined her in the arms of a lithe and nubile Thai youth, the thought of her legs parted and the stripling's flame-red tongue lapping between them disturbing him while getting him hard. Which Mimi had readily anticipated, as Benton could tell as soon as he entered her.

It was uncanny how within a month of getting together he and Mimi had learned to sense each other's desires if not thoughts. Theirs was an intimacy limited to sex, food, trinkets and conversations about absurdities—and nothing like the many-splendored, wide-spectrum relationship he had with Sylvia. He had become a sugar daddy and mentor to a young woman with the mind of a preteen, but he was surprised by how much pleasure it gave him. He loved handing her gifts, which he had been loath to do with Sylvia, watching Mimi open the wrapping paper and getting overwhelmed even when it was just another lifeless panda.

He had become like a teenager, unable to tear his eyes or thoughts off her, dreaming when he was alone in bed of having her beside him and listening to her silliness. He was drawn by the same blind force that drove Little John to Nellie and many a hoary and unfit expat to an enchanting and seductive Thai damsel. For this blessing, he had to thank not only Mimi herself but Siri, for triggering the chain of events that had brought Mimi into his life. And finally, Pierre, for turning him into a new being, fit for love.

21. CBX

He had been visiting Toy daily. This time he thought bringing Mimi along might cheer her up.

"So, there you are, finally, Mimi. Well done, Bento!"

Mimi now had a little nick above her eye, a leftover from her last kickboxing practice. She *waied* casually, adopting the stylish hi-so mien she used with people she deemed classy. But then, sizing up Toy's sickly yellow look, her sisterly instincts kicked in. She touched Toy's hand.

Toy smiled. It was obvious, from the way her face was turned, that behind her dark glasses she saw nothing.

"Toy, how are you feeling?"

He shouldn't have asked that.

"Like a bat, I guess. Had to fucking pee in my pants yesterday when nobody came around."

"Are they changing the shitass drugs?"

"Nope. Pierre is worried about the bile buildup. I'm fucked either way. At least my mind is still there."

"Just give it time," Benton said. "That's how it's been for me."

"Yeah, you sound good, Bento!" She squeezed his arm. "Lean and mean or what!"

"Thanks to Mimi," Benton said.

"I hear you've been up at the Peak?"

"I went there a few times," he said. "Did some swimming and poked around at the museum."

"Volunteering, I think the man calls it." Toy scowled. "He's off his rocker."

Her attitude had definitely changed. "Have you resigned from the advisory board?"

"I should. He's going to kill me either way."

Mimi interrupted. "Why you say bad stuff about Pierre? He's good man, help me so much."

"Yes, and Hitler was into animal rights," Toy said.

"Who's Hitler?" Mimi asked, extracting a cigarette packet and lighter from the front pocket of her denim.

"Forget him," Toy said. "What about the crazy kid?"

Mimi lit up a cigarette, filling her cheeks and blowing smoke rings towards Toy, while Benton explained about the electromagnet Somchai had inserted between Madame Choam's jaws, making it clack in time to songs from the wireless speaker the little devil had hidden inside her thyroid cartilage.

"He's brilliant," Toy said, "but his gifts are misdirected. Mimi, *khotord ka*, the smoke is hurting my eyes."

"I think Pierre is planning to send him stateside."

"Where?" Mimi asked, as she stubbed out the cigarette in the grass.

"To college in the US."

"Boy suck, *ka*. No manners, talk nonsense aller time. Next time I tell Pierre send me instead."

They all became silent as the sun began its evening farewell. A band of gold shimmered across the graying water towards the dark line of the horizon where the sky was painted with matching flashes of ochre and saffron, complemented by clusters of low-lying clouds of violet and indigo with black undersides. In the far distance, heavier clouds were raining black spaghetti-like strands into the sea.

When darkness fell, Toy was tired and sad, and they had to head back home.

"Toy look like junkie," Mimi said, as they waved goodbye to her.

"She's not on those kinds of drugs."

"My stepmom is junkie. Same-same."

He dropped Mimi off at the gym for another training session and drove towards Win's. It didn't look good for Toy. He had hoped to be able to share his notes with her, but he knew she was getting feebler by the minute. It was clear she was part of that unfortunate 1 percent with irreversible side-effects. Nobody said that life was fair.

When he got home, Benton watched once more the footage Chad had sent him. The first video concerned the Passelskys. It began with a night shot of an opulent retreat, with Nadine parting the bed curtains and stepping towards an in-suite plunge pool. TAENIA seemed to know how to fuzz out body parts and what music went with what. As Nadine slid into the pool, the camera zoomed in invitingly, playing the "Girl from Ipanema."

The video featured a great deal of Nadine and included Bert's close-ups of her lying on a massage table wrapped in mud and another one of her holding a yoga pose that TAENIA had labeled as a handstand scorpion. There were night dives aplenty, off private boats and into seas shimmering with creamy moonlight and milky phosphorescence. The couple seemed to frequent only the finest spas, where exclusivity was guaranteed and where Thai beers were priced like champagne.

The second video that TAENIA had patched together had to do with CBX. It included a shaky segment set in the fabled Dusit Thani hotel in Bangkok that had clearly been filched from someone else's phone. Benton had examined it before, but knowing TAENIA and its voyeuristic propensities, had gone through it pretty fast. Now he ran it at half speed.

The event was a medical convention, with men and women standing in small groups networking and exchanging business cards. TAENIA had spliced in some highly inappropriate background music to go with it. The convention featured the usual signage with corporate logos, suggesting one of those continuing medical education seminars where drug companies rewarded high-prescribing physicians with generous speaking fees and other perks. CBX had a small booth, with a couple of guests leafing through brochures next to an arrangement of blood-red orchids. Later, there was a scene of a banquet in the Grand Hall, with a large portrait of the Thai Queen. A group of nattily-tuxed men sat at a table, apparently both well-heeled and pleased about it.

Wait, he said, aware that his brain had spotted something. He slowed the video down further to a quarter speed. Waiters had been flitting past, but now they moved in a pantomime, approaching their guests as if they were stalking them. It was painful to watch unless one was interested in the subtleties in the art of locomotion. Even worse was TAENIA's soundtrack, Shakira's "Hips Don't Lie," where the singer Wyclef Jean was now calling out the songstress's name in a terribly prolonged groan. A waiter finally made contact with a seated guest, bending down to offer a tray. Benton waited for the movement to complete and then tried to focus on the guest's face. There was something familiar, and then, when he froze it, the features became clear. There was no mistaking him, for the man now smiling in slow motion had a telltale gap-toothed grin. It was Bert.

Given the expensive vacations, he wondered if Bert had ended up moonlighting for CBX. He was thinking of asking Chad when he heard a familiar ping. It was @pr8d8tor himself, wanting to chat online.

"You there, gramps?"

"Chad? What's up?"

"TAENIA has been hacked. Insider job."

"Was it you?"

"Haha. Bits and pieces have landed in China. You need to be careful."

"Any other news?"

"Chad has it. Take a look."

Bert Passelsky, according to TAENIA, had contacted one Dr. Cathy Wu at the Food and Drug Administration. Bert's account of his trip to May Tai must have carried some weight, for she had initiated an on-site Clinical Investigator Inspection.

The pair had messaged each other off and on, but their latest session from 2010, the year of Bert's passing, was the most relevant.

BPrb999: Cath, any news on Thai pal?

Woozy8091: Minor protocol deviations. Inadequate informed consent.
BPrb999: No Axenfelds?
Woozy8091: Nope. Sure you saw it?
BPrb999: With my own eyes. Going for a VAI?
Woozy8091: Insufficient grounds. Investigator faced language barriers and Thai translator no good. Then fell ill with dengue fever.
BPrb999: Sounds like a wimp. You need real men, Cath.
Woozy8091: Got anything better?
BPrb999: Not yet. But soon. I've got Fire on my side.
Woozy8091: Fire?
BPrb999: My on-site informant.

After he finished chatting with Chad, Benton checked the FDA website. The classification VAI meant Voluntary Action Indicated, which was one level below Official Action Indicated. The latter could lead to shutting down of the project along with disqualification, once the principal investigator was given a hearing. Some of the institutions with official actions were prominent ones like Stanford and Penn. Pierre's name was not, however, on any list. He would no doubt have wined and dined the investigator before the man fell ill.

When he next visited the Peak, he decided to ask Pierre whether he knew Bert. As for Fire, the informant with a strange alias, he would have to look him or her up if he ever got to May Tai.

It was Noi who opened the door. She *waied* him and then hurried away to the kitchen, where he could hear her scolding Somchai.

Pierre was working on his laptop, staring at a long sequence of symbols.

"What's up?" Benton leaned down over the doctor's shoulder.

"Looking at MIAO-W. A peptide that breaks down neurotransmitters in the brain."

"Why is this particular thingamajig of interest?"

Pierre looked up, the tiger eyes alert, and shifty. "It may reduce a certain type of degenerative brain disease in children. It leaves them locked in, unable to communicate in words, though otherwise physically fit."

"But why work on that?"

"Because the disease may be a precursor to childhood cancer."

The approach seemed highly indirect and made no sense to Benton. He suspected from the doctor's eyes that he was lying.

Benton examined the sequence more closely. He was by now used to the long ciphers made up solely of the symbols A, C, T, and G. It was like reading a minimalist piano score that started out with ethereal footsteps but soon became a lively *danse macabre*.

"That GAGA pattern is showing up often."

"It's a short tandem two-repeat," Pierre explained. "It's as if in the middle of a sequence, the genome suddenly stutters."

"Is the pattern significant?"

"We don't know. The three-repeat variant is the so-called warrior gene."

"The one that's more prevalent among us blacks? Linked by racists to anti-social behavior?"

"Yes, though it's been found in East Asians as well. And Maoris. And it's role in violence is still a matter of debate."

"Pierre, does the name Bert Passelsky mean anything to you?"

"It seems somehow familiar."

He spoke to the Mac, and the press reviews of the incident floated up.

"Vienna. Looks like your neck of the woods. Was he a friend?"

"Yes."

"Shocking. Why did you ask?"

"He may have been with CBX. Aren't you still involved?"

"Once I moved here, I disengaged from day-to-day activities. Though I do attend board meetings."

"And you heard nothing about this?"

"He must have left CBX by the time it happened."

"How many doctors do they have?"

"More than eight hundred, and hats off to them. It's a dangerous job back home."

"For the patients?"

"For the doctors. Ever come across the Army of God? Google them."

He did. It turned out the AOG were far-right Christian terrorists involved in arson and bombings of abortion clinics, and, even worse, had been responsible for snuffing out several abortion doctors. Their website, with a heraldic eagle set against a blue field, showed photo mashups of fetuses, along with Old Testament verses defending the handful of members who had been incarcerated or executed. The rest operated freely under the cover of the First Amendment, with their headquarters in Chesapeake, Virginia.

"A vicious bunch," Benton said.

"They're well-connected, with ties to Operation Rescue and other activists around the world. And then you have the lone wolves inspired by their crap, who're even worse." Pierre examined his gloved hand. "That's why I left my country."

22. Wild Boars

H oney," Win said, "you have trouble."

Wirachon was standing in the guesthouse restaurant, wearing a smart uniform plastered with insignia. He seemed to have grown older in the two months since their last meeting on the day of the de Villeneuve concert.

"You missed your appointment, Mr. Benton."

"I was detained at the Bulsani Spa. I thought you knew, Captain."

Wirachon smiled. "I'm now a major. Shall we take a walk?"

They crossed the road to the beach. The morning sky was overcast, which made for a lot more activity, with hundreds of birds whirling low and diving into the shallows as if something large and delectable had been shipped in by the tide.

"The promotion has meant more administrative work. Not enough time for interesting cases."

He pointed to the fitness park, where a few oldsters were seated together catching up over tea. "You took my advice?"

"The *qi gong's* great."

Wirachon nodded and squared his shoulders. "You look like a young man now, very strong. And it's good that you're wearing our Monday color."

By sheer coincidence, Benton had on a yellow T-shirt, a gift from Mimi, with the name of a soccer star and the number "10" printed on the back.

"Why didn't you talk to us further about the missing person?"

"Toy's at the Spa," Benton said. "Not doing well."

"Hope she feels better," Wirachon said. "I should cancel her missing persons report."

They stopped at a vendor's stall, selling black-green banana-leaf packages. The lady recognized them, asking after their health.

"*Khao niao pheuak*," Benton said. "This one's on me. To celebrate your promotion."

"About your friend," Wirachon said, chewing slowly.

"Toy?"

"The young lady who collects shells."

"What about her?"

"What she's doing is illegal. Thailand does not permit rare shells to be removed from the beach."

Benton let out a long breath.

"You'll have to tell her to stop. People have been arrested for it."

"She'll be disappointed."

They were walking along the sea now, which was grey and seething under a canopy of storm clouds.

"She will be more disappointed by some other news," Wirachon said. "I've met the family, you know. The girl resembles her grandmother from Australia. What is her name again?"

"Mimi. The news?" The sky was growing darker by the minute.

"Patience, Mr. Benton. Have you visited the Kit Kat Klub?"

"Once or twice. To meet the old man."

Wirachon nodded. "Entertainment is just one of her father's businesses. Were you aware that your friend's father has a long criminal record in Australia? Swindling, drugs, motorcycle gangs."

"What does that shit have to do with me?"

Wirachon placed the branch down on the sand, covering the remains of a baby turtle that had been savaged by dogs. There was not much left, but the stench was rank enough to have attracted not only wasps and flies but a swarm of Paris peacock butterflies. Disturbed by the branch, their black bodies fluttered into the air, scarlet eyespots flashing on their wings.

"I thought you would like to know. If things go as planned, he may be deported soon. His Thai assets will be seized."

"Oh no. Fuck!"

That was indeed bad news. Sharky had set aside college money for Mimi. She was counting on it.

"You know our immigration policy—good guys in, bad guys out."

Benton felt a momentary panic, as his mind had conjured up an image of Mimi. She was in rags, looking as if she had been sleeping outdoors, her eyes forked with blood, about to perform a ceremony at Wat Santisuk. Sitting at the foot of the esteemed abbot, she was reading aloud from a funeral pamphlet full of black-and-white photos.

"What's Sharky done now? Trafficked in heroin?"

A low rumble had accompanied their discussion, but now they heard a bang and a series of loud thunderclaps that made them stop and look up. Within a few seconds, a jagged flash of lightning ripped across the sky, illuminating the roots of a vast celestial tree. The air crackled, making Benton's hair stand up. Wat Santisuk looked like a giant lantern, the shadows of its Buddhas quivering and bouncing about in the eerie morning light.

The thunder had frightened away the apparition of Mimi, but her appearance was a sufficient reminder that her future was now his responsibility. Benton had put aside nothing for her. After he was gone, she might be tempted by her hooker pal Fon in Pattaya. Then it would be downhill all the way.

"Bones," Wirachon said.

"Did I hear 'bones'?"

"He had them packed and transported by truck. But then the drivers got greedy."

"How so?"

"You ask questions like a detective, Mr. Benton. You worked for the US government?"

"I was just a low-level flunkey. What were the authorities after?"

"Charcoal. Our laws restrict its production. But imports from neighboring countries are allowed. Unfortunately, the kilns were in protected forests in Cambodia."

"The Cambodians cracked down?"

"Correct. That's when they found the bones, hidden under the charcoal."

"And my friend's father was using them for what? Rituals you said?"

"I didn't say that. He's in violation of Customs laws against organ smuggling."

"And you're hunting for more information about him?"

"That's where you can help. If you notice anything suspicious at his house or the Klub, please give us a call. It will make a stronger case for deportation."

The wind was now wet. The rain started, first as a drizzle, and then changed its mind and became a downpour. They hurried across the street towards the *wat*, but the gates were closed.

"Follow me," the major said. He turned down a *soi* and then started sprinting. Benton ran along, his feet moving swiftly, his yellow T-shirt hooded over his head as the rain slapped at his face. Wirachon pushed his way into a crowd waiting under a shop awning, and Benton joined him. He took off his spectacles to wipe them.

"*Sawadee-ka*," someone called from behind them. "How you doing, handsome?"

Wirachon's uniform was sopping wet. "I need to get dry," he said. "How about we stop in this restaurant?"

It was more bar than restaurant. Wirachon ordered two espressos. The waitress bowed respectfully, practically touching the floor as Wirachon walked past them to the bathroom.

Benton stared at the bar. He had been there before, the night after he first met Siri. He was reflecting on the events of that evening, culminating in his encounter with Oi, when Wirachon reappeared, carrying his shirt, his wet hair nicely combed. He draped the shirt over a chair, sitting down in his vest and khaki pants. His gun holster, Benton noticed, was now dry.

"That's much better," Wirachon said. He glanced at the girls, and the espressos magically appeared.

It was time. Benton could not remain passive when his heart was still yearning.

"Major Wirachon, I would like to share something with you."

"Speak your mind. The ladies won't bother us."

"While at the Spa, I heard stuff about the Foundation."

His notes were almost done, his painstaking analysis sitting snug and dry in his wallet. All he was missing was the final nugget, and then he didn't give a damn if it was Armageddon in Thailand. He was going to betray his betters. For the second time in his life. For the sake of what exactly? To save the world from evil? Or to save the young waif-girl he loved?

"Rumors?" Wirachon said.

Benton squeezed the bottom of his shorts, trying to wring them dry. "Things that will create a bad image of your beautiful Kingdom."

"Get to the point," Wirachon said.

"What if I were able to dig out more incriminating information?"

Wirachon nodded. "I'll need hard evidence. Something that will stand up in court. No wishy-washy allegations."

"Want me to wear a wire?"

"No. Translating the audio into Thai will be too much work for me."

"The Foundation is well regarded, isn't it?"

Wirachon remained silent.

Benton squeezed out more moisture from his shorts. "Is it something personal? With Pierre?"

Wirachon's face turned several shades of red, before settling on crimson. He pushed his cup away.

"Major Wirachon, I want to help you. And Thailand. But for that, I need you to share."

Wirachon looked as if he was about to explode. "That chickenshit foreign doctor messed with our kids in Mae Sa."

"Shit! What happened?"

"The little ones are now unable to speak. Half-paralyzed when they walk, using their arms as if they are legs. It is some neurological problem. Everyone is praying for a treatment, but so far nothing."

"Sounds awful!" He now remembered the zombie kids he had seen on television at the Spa clinic. "Where is that exactly?"

"It's the same district as May Tai, where the doctor has his trials. But their muscles have become strong. The doctors are calling it '*moo pa* syndrome.'"

"Wild boar?"

"Yes."

"The Palin children were hit first?"

"Yes, their parents took the medicine prescribed by Dr. Pierre. Now our Thai kids have it. They mix with the tribal savages in school, so maybe it's an infection."

"And none of the kids were on any clinical trials?"

"Certainly not! And please do not breathe a word of this to anyone. We don't want the whole world thinking Thais are running trials on children."

"Surely public awareness of the disease would help?"

"There were one or two news stories, but our government has since censored them. We can't afford to scare away tourists. And when tourists go down, Major Wirachon's job goes away."

"Sounds pretty bad," Benton said.

"The government may end up quarantining some of the hill districts."

"I'll get you the information," Benton said, draining his cup. "But I'll be taking a risk. You understand?"

"I don't know about the risk. I'm only a cop. A flunkey." He repeated the word twice, giving an odd laugh.

Things were becoming even clearer, an *aha* moment if there ever was one. Benton needed to put it all together before he forgot. He took out a piece of paper from his wallet and began writing in an odd shorthand and then drawing a diagram with circles and arrows, while Wirachon looked on approvingly.

The children were displaying similar symptoms to what he had experienced after the banquet with Pierre. Presumably, some May Tai subjects had received the same Palin sou cocktails as he had been given. The result seemed to involve a regression to an earlier stage in evolution. That would explain the increase in muscle mass, the sensitivity to odors, the loss of natural language and the pig-like characteristics. And none of that regression, as Benton had realized earlier, sat well with the rest of the twenty-first century environment.

Luckily, those regressed symptoms had proved temporary in his case, but who knew whether it would be the same for others?

What was far more worrying was the fact that the changes had been passed down through the parents' DNA to their offspring. Even more scary was the way the symptoms had spread to children in the general population. The vector for transmission would have to be identified right away, or else, if the condition persevered, Thailand's youth might end up completely brain damaged.

Wirachon was getting up to leave.

"There's one last thing," Benton said, standing up as well. "I would like Mimi's college funds to be set aside. So that she has a future."

Wirachon smiled. "Our friends in the Ministry of Education will take care of that."

They were shaking hands when Oi approached.

23. Museum

Time zipped by after that meeting with Wirachon. By September, the full force of the monsoon was evident, with the skies thundering, the seas heaving, the roads runny and muddy. Benton tried to devote all his spare moments to Mimi, but his days were now given over to the company of Pierre, preoccupied as he was with his mission. He knew he was neglecting Mimi, and she also sensed a tension in their evenings together. To give him some space and time to unwind, she started staying late at her *muay thai* gym.

Meanwhile, the museum had come a long way. Although still located in Pierre's flat, a diorama had been put together of the Killing Fields in Phnom Penh with a miniature model of the famous stupa containing thousands of skulls, each one represented by a shelled peanut. The mass graves were re-created with cardboard mounds littered with matchsticks. So far, none of Chantou Bulsani's friends had been found, but others had been recovered. Among them were three gaunt figures—Madame Choam in front of her blackboard, a young man named Rith Van with a fully-formed ribcage frozen in the pose of a traditional Apsara dancer, and a third, the writer Prey Son, standing before his desk contemplating a blank sheet of paper along with a pack of cigarettes and an ashtray. The floor lamps were arranged so that the figures' right sides were bathed in light, while the rest of the ghastly scene remained in shadow.

One morning in mid-September, Benton was at work early, helping Somchai out with a jigsaw. The boy had drilled several small holes in a set of severed finger phalanges, and now he was expertly inking in the holes with glue before threading the segments together with wire. The hand and other pieces in the jigsaw belonged to a male who was otherwise unknown with no matching DNA relatives, so they had christened him "Mr. Man." Pierre had informed them that Mr. Man was thirty-one when he died, judging by the remnants of his sternum, and he had suffered from arthritis, rare in such a young man.

Pierre came in just then in a smart leather waistcoat, accompanied by Surry, who was beaming.

"Ready, son, for your demo? Boss, you got to see this."

Somchai got up slowly from the floor, took out his phone from his pocket, and launched his app. It was all thanks to Pierre having ordered the boy a robotics kit from Denmark.

There was a brief whirring, and then Madame Choam's marble eyes spun energetically in time to music as she clicked her fingers. Prey remained standing at his desk but frantically waved a pen that he held between his tattered fingers, while the dancer Rith took a few cockroach-like steps forward. The tune was the classic Stevie Wonder hit.

Isn't she lovely
Isn't she wonderful
Isn't she precious.

"Shut the damn thing off," Benton said. "It's an insult to Cambodians."

Surry was chewing on a toothpick. "The young man can tell their life stories however he likes. They don't get a say."

"Madam Choam came to a horrible end," Benton said. "The least one can do is show respect to her remains."

According to the Cambodia War Crimes Tribunal, Choam was a teacher of English, accused of stealing rice, who underwent surgery at the Tuol Sleng prison to check for its presence in her stomach. The operation was carried out by the notorious Dr. Eak, known for his Nazi-like penchant for removing vital organs without anesthesia and documenting the results. The boy's animation completely dishonored her memory, and it was ironic that it was Somchai himself who had managed to identify Madam Choam, based on her cleft palate.

"Art is a matter of personal taste," Surry said. He took the phone from Somchai's hand and increased the dance speed on the app, making the three skeletons move grotesquely sideways as they wagged their hips. "Do you think it's not commercially viable?"

"I didn't say that. Body shows are very much in these days."

The public, Benton knew, had a thing for the grotesque, and shows featuring human bodies with their water and fats replaced by plastics had been runaway successes around the world. The Thais, not wishing to be left behind, had created the Death Exhibit Museum at a hospital in Bangkok, stuffed with mummies and deformed fetuses. It was a fair bet that the Survivors Museum, if handled properly, could catch on with tourists and even students.

"Or are you saying you don't like our taste?" Surry asked, staring hard at Benton. "Because if you are…"

Pierre grabbed the phone from Surry's hand and closed the app. "Everyone calm down, please."

Benton shrugged. If the museum were to go forward, a disclaimer was essential, stating that no disrespect to the living or dead was intended, clarifying that the show was no substitute for a study of the history of the Cambodian civil war. And that no reimaginings, however colorful, could re-create the essence of what it had been like to be Madame Choam. A sleazy simulacrum or a creepy skeleton could never capture what it had meant to live, to have loved and been loved.

But there was no point trying to convince Surry in particular of these subtleties. They had been arguing too much of late, and he didn't want to raise any alarms. So far, they had shared all the details of the museum with him, and he had scrupulously avoided showing any interest in the drug trials. Meanwhile, time was running out.

Somchai had returned to the hand he was touching up. "Dr. Pierre," he asked, "what about their rights?"

Pierre offered a sad smile. "Maman's friends had their rights taken away from them, Somchai. They were tortured horribly by the Khmer Rouge and then killed. Then they piled up everyone's bones together so you couldn't tell a Rith from a Vann. Leaving us with a problem of reverse engineering."

Somchai looked up from his work. "Does Mr. Man here have any rights? He isn't really a person. Or is he?"

Mr. Man's hand was good, but he stood there gaunt and woebegone with his jaw hanging and his skull partially smashed.

"Skeletons aren't people," Pierre said, tapping Mr. Man's hollow chest.

"Then we can fix them up as we like? And it's all entirely legal?"

"Respect for the dead..." Benton began. "It's pretty basic to all cultures—"

"It's legal," Pierre interrupted. "But not always ethical."

"What about the fetuses, the ones you took skins from?"

"What skins?" Benton asked.

Somchai was insistent. "Haven't we violated their rights, Dr. Pierre?"

"A fetus is only a grown blastocyst, Somchai. It's a body part, like a liver." His voice rose, until he was almost shouting. "How can a bloody liver have the same rights as a person?"

Somchai, unfazed by the outburst, scratched his distal ear. "But is it okay, Dr. Pierre, to kill a fetus?"

Pierre paused, and Benton heard a faint whining.

"In places where women's rights have advanced," Pierre explained, "a doctor can operate and terminate the pregnancy, in a procedure called an abortion. But only under certain conditions. For example, if it endangers the mother's health or if it is the product of rape or incest. The killing must take place in utero, though. It's illegal to extract the fetus and then kill it."

"Extracting before killing will be viewed as killing a person? Even though it's not?"

"Correct, Somchai. For that, the US government would send me to prison."

"Sounds like your government is confused," Somchai said. He twirled his hair, thinking hard again. "Do the doctors who abort fetuses cut open the stomach and scrape it all out?"

"It's more subtle than that, Somchai. It's a serious operation, one that doctors carry out with due respect to both mother and fetus. And the stomach isn't involved."

"How is it done?"

Pierre crouched next to one of the skeletons that was lying prone on the floor. "It's like this." He folded the knees back with a click. "We have the person lying on her back with her feet in stirrups." He pointed to a notch in the pelvis. "If it's early in the pregnancy, the doctor inserts a thin tube into the vagina here up through the cervix into the uterus and suctions it out in a few minutes."

"Eew! And if it's later in the pregnancy?"

"Then you have more material to extract. You first give it an injection to stop the thing's heart, then dilate the cervix, and finally vacuum it out."

"Pierre, does the boy really need this?" Benton was starting to feel queasy.

Somchai was persistent. "What about the head? Will it fit coming out?"

"A good question. There may be residual elements left behind."

Surry gave a loud chuckle, but his son was frowning. "So how do you fish that out?"

"You first need to scrape off the easy parts with a curette. Next, you make a small incision in the skull." He looked around, sliding his hand under a table. "Somchai—where have you put the bloody clamps? You must learn to keep everything in its proper place!"

Somchai, trembling suddenly, reached under a chair and found a clamp.

"You use this clamp to widen the incision. Then you pump the brains out. As for the skull, it collapses once brainless and then pops out easily."

Somchai was quiet and went back to work. But his thoughts wouldn't stop ticking, and soon he was at it again, with his eyes squinting. "Dr. Pierre. In the early-term procedure, doesn't the fetus feel pain?"

"It doesn't, young man. That is, not until the third trimester."

"Why not?"

"Because connections to the fetal cortex from the rest of its body only form at around twenty-four weeks."

"You mean," Benton asked, "that before that, there's no way to relay pain to the brain?"

"Precisely. And even after, any pain the thing's brain might feel will be slight compared to the pain it will feel after birth when it becomes a person." He stared hard at Benton. "For being a person means dealing with the trauma of living."

"Which will inevitably," Surry added, "include extreme pain. As you learned, son, from the Survivors' case histories."

"Dr. Pierre, have you performed abortions in the third trimester?"

"I have, Somchai. But even the early-stage ones are getting more dangerous day by day."

"For the mother?"

Pierre stood up. "No, for the doctor. Because of all the religious nutcases who are out to kill us. Now go and play outside, Somchai."

With that, Pierre ended the discussion and stepped over to the smartphone that protruded like a periscope from Rith Van's skull.

"Come here, Benton. I want to show you some new findings."

Pierre opened an app. The screen displayed a landscape with pairs of steep volcanoes laid out in strips. Below the landscape was a table of information. The dancer's bone counts and his bones' original geographical locations were all clearly specified, along with the information that he had died of starvation at twenty-five. He still had two teeth left after the others had been removed and decontaminated earlier by Pierre, who now clicked on the DNA Profile menu.

The volcanoes, Benton realized, were graphs, indicating counts of something at particular positions.

"What's Halod 99?"

"It's one of the thirty indels we amplified from Rith's DNA," Pierre said.

"What the heck are indels?"

"Short for insertions and deletions into our genetic code. At a molecular level, my friend, you and I are different by virtue of mutations or changes in our DNA. Indels are particular patterns of mutation."

"And we care about this because?"

Pierre's gloved finger pointed at a volcano with steep green slopes. "Rith's Halod 99 graph shows the counts of insertion of TGAT after ACTT and before CTCTTTGA. It peaks at 112 base pairs."

"I get it. It's a stutter, like the GAGA you showed me earlier."

"Precisely. Sometimes the genome goes ACTT-**TGAT**-CTCTTTGA."

"It reminds me of a verbal tic, saying *secre-ma-tary* or *fan-fucking-tastic*. But hardly that interesting."

"On the contrary. These idiosyncrasies are what distinguish us, Benton."

"Are you telling me these thirty DNA elements are enough to ID each Survivor?"

"Precisely."

"So indels could be useful in tracking down our Survivors' living relatives?"

"Certainly. And these few features can also help distinguish between you and me. Of course," Pierre said, with a smirk, "that's not all that makes Benton Sims unique, I hope."

"D'you really think a deep dive into his DNA will help visitors get what Rith Van was all about?"

"The visitors, particularly young people, will learn that what differentiates us is much less than we think. If people realize that, there would be far less hatred and war."

Pierre stepped over to Prey Son's screen, and Benton followed, trailed by Surry. There was no TAENIA to come to the rescue, so tidbits of information such as the Khmer Rouge's hacking off the writer's fingers had been put together by fusing data from the website of the Khmer Rouge Tribunal and an interview with one of Sharky's Cambodian informants, a survivor of the genocide carried out at the Tuol Sleng school in Phnom Penh.

The glistening makeup on Prey's face gave him the look of a catwalk zombie. "I thought we agreed," Benton said, "that greasepaint was over the top?"

"I know we did," Pierre said. "But Surry and I were worried that the sight of unvarnished skulls would have all the kids rushing home to shave their heads and eyebrows."

Hearing his name, Surry came over.

"The last thing we need," Surry said, "is a kind of Survivor Chic catching on. Remember the Bangkok school performing their dance pageant dressed in SS uniforms with Hitler mustaches? So we added makeup to humanize the figures."

"What did you use?" Benton asked.

"Skin," Pierre said.

"Calfskin?"

"No, human. It's strong and elastic."

Benton touched Prey's skull cheek lightly. "You're having me on. It's too thin for skin."

"It's second-trimester skin," Pierre said, with a smile. "We had to first scrape off the cheesy coating before patching it on, after which Noi layered a primer on top."

"Yikes! And you got this how?"

"The Palin have been known to strangle fetuses when inconvenient, claiming it's their worm spirit Niban. It's a waste to simply let them rot."

"What's next?" Benton asked. "The Elephant Man? This is getting to be a fucking freakshow."

"Enough discussion," Surry said, spitting out the remains of his toothpick into his palm. "The boss wanted it this way, and that's that."

Just then they heard a screeching sound.

"Surry, do you know why Mr. Man was screaming just now?"

"You ask so many questions, Benton." He shrugged. "Maybe he was hungry?"

"It's the balloons," Pierre said.

Somchai had earlier attached a pair of remotely inflatable balloons to Mr. Man's pubis, the gores on the upper one forming a furrowed blue shaft. It was the sudden inflation of the shaft that had set off the proximity sensor.

"The Cambodians don't really need this. Do they, Pierre? After all they've been through."

"Benton, you've made your point. Surry, don't you agree?"

"Yes, boss."

Surry stared thoughtfully at Benton before shuffling out to the balcony.

Somchai was dragged in by the ear, bringing with him a whiff of strong tobacco. Son, say sorry to Dr. Pierre and Mr. Benton.

"Sorry, sirs!" Somchai *waied* as well as he could manage from his position. "But I didn't do anything."

"You're grounded."

"What's that mean, Dad?"

Surry's eyes were glowering, and it was a frightening sight.

"It means no museum activity till I say so."

"Please, Dad!" The other ear had turned tomato-red in sympathy. "Please. I'll stop smoking."

"It's not the smokes." Surry let go of the ear. "It's the fucking balloons."

"It's Mr. Man's fault," the boy said. "He looked so pathetic, I couldn't resist."

"So it wasn't enough to fuck with Man's head? You had to go down low? And make me look like a cunt?"

"Sorry, Dad."

"And the lap dance is off, you fat faggot."

Somchai did not break. "Please, Dad. I'll be careful. Please let me stay."

"Wait till your mother hears about this."

"That's enough," Pierre said. "Somchai is grounded for two days. Meanwhile, let's get back to work."

Benton was glad to see the young devil suspended, however briefly. The world was evil enough without his mischief.

The rest of the week was busy. Sharky's deliveries started to pour in, the workroom bursting at the seams with Survivors. They huddled together with their gaunt faces and empty eye sockets, their cheeks glinting, their mandibles hanging open in a perpetual trance. Some lacked a skull or pelvis, while others were mere wisps coughed up by blood-drenched fields. The children were hunched low staring in incomprehension, and some of the elderly folk lay broken and spread-eagled in their final moments.

Benton stared at the figures. When the light caught on their teeth, some seemed to be smiling through their bloated skin patches. The scene was as bizarre and gruesome as it could get, but he was glad that the inventory had built up. The specimens were now clamoring for attention, for careful restoration and resurrection, but they were squeezed far too tight, the arm of one raised over another's mangled shoulder, their scraggy forms mingling with implements and electronic components in what had once been Pierre's master bedroom. And Pierre, who valued a neat workplace, was getting increasingly annoyed, with his tools scattered about among the specimens.

Benton was pleased with the crowding because it meant that the collection had to be moved. And as expected, Pierre broached the subject at their Monday morning powwow.

"I mentioned the collection over lunch to Mrs. Aye, the Cambodian Ambassador. She'll be happy to inaugurate the museum, wherever it's hosted. It will do wonders for diplomatic relations."

"Best to have it away from Bangkok," Surry said. "There's not enough flood protection in place."

"You're right," Benton said. "No point soaking in the plains during the monsoon. How about somewhere up at a higher elevation?"

"You mean in the Thai Alps near Loei, in the east?" Surry asked. "Or in the north, in the Golden Triangle?"

"Wherever. Combine a museum visit with mountain treks and home-stays. And maybe Bikram yoga."

Pierre smiled. "Did you have a specific place in mind, Benton?"

"May Tai?" He watched the men carefully after saying that. "Aren't you guys running trials there? You're bound to have local contacts."

"*Mon ami*, the Palin aren't sophisticated enough to set up a museum. It took us years to organize the trials with Michael."

"Michael?"

"The headman," Pierre explained.

"May Tai is a fucking dump," Surry said quickly. "It's so poor even the cops have fled their posts."

"It was just a suggestion," Benton said.

"Actually," Pierre said, staring at his boots, "let's give it more thought."

Benton was pleased to see that the idea had taken hold. He said nothing further, working with the team for the next few days until Pierre brought it up again.

"The lab will stay," Pierre said. "We'll do all the assembly here, then ship to a site in May Tai. Agreed?"

"Sounds good, boss."

"But we'll need an onsite curator," Pierre went on. "Along with staff for tours and maintenance."

"What about you, Benton?" Surry asked, with a grin. "Seeing as you suggested the idea."

"I'm not the right guy," he said, feigning reluctance.

"Why not?" Surry asked. "You seem to get along well with the Survivors."

"I need to think about it."

"Talk to Megumi," Pierre said. "She knows the place well and may be able to find us a site."

"Megumi'll be thrilled," Surry said with a laugh. "She's been missing her Jack."

24. Survivors

The night before Benton left, Pierre invited him to dine at the Peak. Father Dennis had joined them, and the menu included *foie gras* and a splendid Beef Wellington, one of Benton's favorites. It was accompanied by a dark Argentinian wine, a Malbec. After they ate, they finished the wine sitting on the balcony. Pierre's face was glowing in the pale moonlight, which cast a shimmering stain over the sea.

"You live so like a Roman," Father Dennis said. "Up on a hill above the sea, surrounded by art, every meal a feast. While trying to keep the lemures at bay."

"Lemures?" Benton asked.

"Roman for evil spirits," Father Dennis said.

It was a dig at the spirit house Pierre had installed a week earlier at the entrance, peopled with a ghoulish Khmer goddess and her male guardians.

"Had we been Romans," Pierre said, laughing, "we would have to set aside some of our *foie gras* for Vesta."

"Precisely," Father Dennis said, topping his glass up with more Malbec. "That's why St. Augustine had to rail against demon worship."

They heard a shriek just then, followed by a second more high-pitched one. It came from the sea. They stood up to look. It was an upwelling in the gold and black water, layers of dark folding onto each other like convulsing sheets. Then the sheets lifted slowly off, swirling around a vast eye that vanished into the deep. The plughole was as wide as Wat Santisuk, its rolling edge serrated by silvery spray. Birds were circling and screeching above as the flux spun faster, the sea churning around the whirlpool's gaping mouth.

"What the heck's going on?" Benton asked.

"An Ekman monsoon spiral," Pierre said. "Too weak for now, so nothing to be concerned about. The locals of course are superstitious and consider it a bad omen, foretelling destruction."

"It's a reminder," Father Dennis said, "of the Spirit that hovers over the face of the waters."

The spiral was fortunately short-lived, and the birds and sea soon quieted down. After Father Dennis left, Pierre brought out the cognac, and they sat in the moonlight talking.

"Do you really want to head to May Tai, Benton? You came here to retire."

"It's the least I can do," Benton said, heaving a deep breath.

"You've done wonders for the museum. I'm very grateful."

"Thanks. I'm grateful too. For your friendship." Benton took a long sip of his cognac, which was sweet with a whiff of jasmine. "And for helping me get fit—I've never felt so good."

"You're very welcome, my friend. But it's one thing to volunteer, quite another to get down in the trenches. The tribal settlements can be wild and lawless."

"I understand."

"What about your girlfriend?"

"Mimi'll be fine. She needs to grow up, spread her wings."

Pierre shrugged. "Won't you miss the sexual activity?"

Benton stared hard. "I'll be visiting often, I hope."

"Promise me one thing, Benton. Don't ask people about the trials."

"Why not?"

"We don't want them exchanging information about the treatments. They might switch groups or drop out. To add to our worries."

"Trust me. I can be very discrete."

"Very well. Now I have something to show you. Today is September thirtieth, Maman's death anniversary."

And with that, he asked Benton to follow him inside. They went into the museum, to stand with his mother before the grandfather clock. The skeleton with its beret, still formally dressed, stared vacantly at them. A stick of incense was smoldering at her feet.

Benton stood stiffly and watched as Pierre knelt and prostrated thrice, following with a long Buddhist prayer sitting at his mother's feet. He chanted in the rhythmic, singsong fashion of the pros, which suggested that the man had spent time among the monks. Or else he had studied the sutras on YouTube.

When Pierre finally got done and was up on his feet again, the tiger eyes had tears.

"I'm so sorry, Pierre. It's always hard when you lose someone you love."

"Did I ever tell you what happened?"

"No." Benton had a feeling he knew what was coming.

"It started with cancer." He wiped his eyes carefully with a hankie and then blew his nose. "I was away at Cambridge when Father called to say she was seriously ill. When I got to India, Maman had a thin and jaundiced look. I'd never seen her so sick. And right after she kissed me, she vomited."

"What sort of cancer?"

"A pancreatic adenocarcinoma." Pierre paused. "Father had to Whipple her."

"Whipple?"

"An operation where they remove the head of the pancreas and an initial part of the small intestine, along with the bile duct and gallbladder. Father allowed me to watch, seeing as I was by then a final-year medical student."

Pierre stepped up to the remains of his mother and tapped at where her abs would have been.

"You see, he snipped Maman open with a triangular patch right there, above the navel, to expose the peritoneal cavity. It was the one occasion he really took care of her."

Pierre went on, speaking as if he were explaining a medical case history to a student. "It was a pleasure to watch. He neatly cut the bridge between the colon and stomach, moving the colon from the upper part of the abdomen to the lower. After he anchored the lining, Maman's gallbladder came into view. It was severely distended—like a purple pear, due to a tumor having blocked her bile duct."

"I remember your telling me that your father wasn't that nice."

Pierre paused, the tiger eyes glinting with more than a dash of anger. "He was a topnotch surgeon, but a cruel bastard. At home, at work, everywhere. During Maman's procedure, I remember how he suddenly shouted out 'Debakeys!' The nurse was clueless, and Father's eyes started to bulge. Then he abused her, calling her a stupid *motherchoad*! Imagine that behavior in a hospital anywhere in the West! Or even in Thailand! He would have been disbarred immediately."

"Awful. What are Debakeys?"

"A type of forceps. I went and fetched them myself. I was worried that he might attack the nurse. But then he managed to calm down and continued to work methodically. He pushed the stomach out of the way to the upper abdomen. You see, he had to separate the splenic and portal veins from the pancreas before cutting into them. He asked for suction, and I remember how the nurse's hand trembled as she mopped up a rush of yellowish-brown juice."

Benton took a deep breath. "Pierre, if you don't want to go on, it's okay. The details are getting pretty horrendous."

"That's the way the public thinks," Pierre said, shaking his head. "Anything inside the body is horrendous." He made a face, talking in a baby voice. "*Yucky, obscene, disgusting*. Isn't that right, Benton?"

His voice was now raised, and his nostrils were bristling in anger. "Medicine teaches us to admire and love what lies within. Even cancer, our enemy number one, is part of nature, and beautiful in its own way." He tapped his mother's skeleton for effect, making it rattle violently against the clock, which suddenly responded with a triple chime.

Benton waited for the raging timepiece to stop. "I guess it's a mistake," he said slowly, "to look for beauty only in the outward form?"

Pierre didn't answer, and his eyes had a faraway look. "The real highlight was when Father slid out the extracted organs in one nice connected piece, like pipes fitting together. The head of the pancreas and the duodenum looked beautiful, like a purple sausage curled on a testicle. And sitting on top were the gall bladder and common bile duct, as well as a packet of lymph nodes. And do you know what?"

"What?"

He imitated a deep, haughty voice. "'Feel it,' Father said. 'Don't be afraid, son.' I took the organs in my hands and pressed her pancreas, feeling the walnut-sized cancerous mass. It rolled like a marble under my fingers. And may I share something else, my friend?"

"Pierre, my lips are sealed."

"We don't ask for security clearances here, haha! Let me tell you, Benton, that I still have this never-to-be-fulfilled longing. A deep-seated nostalgia to return to the fetal state, to feel the touch of Maman's womb, its smell, its private chamber! Don't you miss that?"

"I was an orphan," Benton reminded him. "But I was close to my aunt."

"It's the same uterine mother-bonding, Benton, only displaced to your caregiver. Anyway, there I was in the smelly operating theater in the Aurobindo Hospital, caressing Maman's insides. I was so excited that I wanted, innocently, to kiss them! And even managed to, after pretending to lift the package up for a sniff."

"Wow. Did your dad notice?"

"Father didn't say a word. He always thought of me as degenerate. And a social failure, unable to make any friends from kindergarten onwards—when it was invariably the other kids who ostracized me! He was never proud of me, would never present me to any of his friends at the club." He stopped, looking at his left boot, before bending down to wipe a speck off it. "He punished me for my animal experiments. Among other things."

"Let's not go there, Pierre." Benton cleared his throat. "Was your mother's cancer surgery a success?"

"It was, but alas, India got back to her, in the form of a UTI. It turned into sepsis, and then her kidneys started shutting down. I had to stay back from college to help out, as Father returned to Bombay to his practice. Poor Maman was throwing up each time she was fed, so I threaded a nasogastric tube through her nose down the esophagus directly into her stomach. She wept as the tube went in, and blood sprinkled from her nostrils. But soon her kidneys got the better of her, and her electrolytes went out of whack. Things headed south from there."

"I'm so sorry, Pierre."

"You know what's striking, Benton? Even after the mind goes, we still have our feelings. On her last morning, I was surprised to hear her speak clearly, reaching out to her friends." He mimicked an elderly lady's voice, beginning high-pitched and ending in a groan. "'Where are they, Pierre, darling? Where are Vann and my lovely Champei?' Then she called out for Montha, her fellow singer and lover who had been executed."

"Isn't Montha your middle name?"

"Yes, he was the only other man who really loved her. Montha was by then little more than a few stray fingers and a skull chip or two somewhere in the Killing Fields. Maman kept groaning and moaning, calling for him in her feeble voice, so to try and cheer her up I dressed up in a two-piece suit with a bow tie and sang Montha's one major hit, the mournful Khmer ballad 'Violon Sneha.' Did a bit of air violin too! It was all for a laugh, but poor Maman fell for it, dazed, clutching onto the IV tube as she listened with her mouth half open."

"When people are on their deathbed there has to be complete honesty, don't you think?"

"Absolutely," Pierre said, saluting his Maman. "I told her that I would find out what happened to her friends. She squeezed my hand with her last ebb of strength and said 'Promise, *kaun proh.*'"

He repeated that last phrase a few times, stroking his mother's metacarpus, obviously overcome in his own peculiar way. He began to whine, and Benton had to stand there beside the man's mother and watch, waiting for the fan belt sound to subside. When it was over, Pierre turned to him, placing his hand on Benton's shoulder.

"Benton, the MIAO-W sou didn't work out."

Benton waited stiffly, hoping the hand would go away. "Aren't you onto another thread now? To deal with that cancer precursor brain stuff you mentioned?"

"Yes. But I don't know how we're going to get those win-win results." His hand now felt limp, even helpless.

"Pierre, what was it you told me about keeping the flame alight?"

"It's just that I've worked for more than a decade on the trials."

"You have to stick with it."

"I came here thinking I would start a new chapter in my life. Joining the fight against cancer. And laying the seeds for the future. All our business plans and visions—I feel like they're going up in smoke!"

"You've done a ton of stuff already, my friend. What was that quote? 'The future belongs to those who believe in the beauty of their dreams.'"

"The person inside doesn't change, Benton."

"It does not," Benton said. "Sadly so."

"And science is hard. The world doesn't understand that. There's so much pressure for results."

"But you'll get there, won't you?" Benton asked. "No matter what."

"We will," Pierre said, nodding slowly. "We have to make sure of that."

"Pierre, if everything falls apart, we still have one consolation."

"What?" Pierre's voice was now eager, like a child's.

"The Survivors. They'll shine on, won't they?"

Pierre nodded. "Lighting up eternity," he said, his eyes glowing. And then they embraced, briefly.

25. The Pastor

The Palin men wore axes on their belts. A warrior lifted one out and held it high, the blade flashing before descending on an infant's tiny fontanel. There was a piercing scream, and a fountain of blood gushed up. The other men in the rice field, led by Pierre and Surry, crowded around for their drinks. The child lay dead on the ground with its damaged head cracked open, while the headman Michael mumbled a prayer.

"You fucking murderer!" Benton shouted. "That poor kid."

"Shush." Megumi slid her palm across his lips. "They're planting blood paddy. Many more will be sacrificed."

"Blood paddy?"

"Rice grown from seedlings soaked in blood. From the heads of our enemies."

He was about to rush at the warriors but found he was unable to move, his body fading into little points of light.

"How are you feeling, Jack?"

Benton gazed up at Megumi from the pillow. He tried to speak, but all that emerged was a gurgle. It would have made more sense to linger on in his dream, where his words remained pristine.

"You passed out in the church," Megumi said.

He stared at her.

"You're in Michael's guest house."

He was in a traditional windowless Palin hut, ventilated by the doorway and the gap between the bamboo walls and the straw thatch. A pile of cushions lay on the floor.

He looked at her smiling face, lit up by the ray of morning sunshine coming through the doorway.

Megumi touched his forehead. She smelled as if she had walked in straight from her garden.

"You have no fever, Jack. Must be the Dutch pancakes in Chiang Mai. Now rest a bit, while I run some errands this morning."

The fog cleared. He remembered that they had arrived in May Tai the previous day. Megumi had greeted Michael with kisses on both cheeks, but the headman, a wizened and shrivel-headed goblin, had stared hard at Benton, as if unused to the sight of a black man. Benton's first impulse was to ask him what he was staring at, but he didn't want to risk a confrontation at this stage of his investigation.

Michael's daughter, a tired looking but gracious lady, served lunch without joining them. The food tasted fresh, obviously made from local produce. Michael chewed slowly, his dentures surprisingly large for his wizened cheeks. Benton tucked into the fiery grilled pork with garden greens, and then enjoyed the delicious burn that followed.

Michael had opened the whisky Megumi had brought as a gift. He wanted to know where Benton's family was, how long he had been with the Foundation and why he had come to Thailand. Most insulting of all was his asking whether he had been born in the US. It made him feel he was back at the Fort, forced to go in for yet another polygraph. But he passed muster.

The last thing he could remember after that was visiting the May Tai dispensary.

He was standing in the dispensary next to a group of wizened old men with weasel faces and bloodshot eyes. They had the sour odor of the elderly, sweetened a little by the flavor of tobacco. One was chewing a leaf between toothless gums, staring blindly at Benton, his tribal grooves like black webbing on his jaw. They did not look much like warriors, reminding him more of the old folk in Baltimore who would gather outside the liquor stores, discussing their affairs while waiting for their outstretched hats to fill with coins.

Someone was screaming from up ahead in the line. He asked one of his neighbors to keep his place and went ahead to investigate.

The source of the screams was a boy of six or seven, his head bent, palm over his ear. He kept hopping on one leg and then another as if something unbearable was trapped in his ear. Benton couldn't help sympathizing, as he had experienced something similar on the hike with Pierre.

The others standing nearby seemed oblivious to his screams, absorbed in their own pains. They included a pregnant teen who was practically doubled up, clutching her stomach. An old lady was seated on the floor with her head in her hands, half-drowsy. Her son or grandson massaged her neck with a steady hand. Then came a pair of two-year-old twins dressed in white frocks, their backs arched, each one's expression frozen in a steely rictus, their only saving grace being that they were holding hands.

Benton returned back to his place and waited, saddened by the sight of all those ailments. The Palin were collectively in a bad state. Yet, thinking logically, none of the people waiting had any of the ophthalmic or porcine side effects he had been hoping to spot.

The pharmacist at the counter looked as weather-beaten as the rest, though he was wearing a tie and a white jacket. He gave some of the supplicants a red capsule dispensed from a tall glass bottle, placing it on their proffered tongues as if it were a sacrament, handing them a paper cone of water to wash it down. Others were taken away for examination. When Benton came to the counter faking stomach pain, the pharmacist led him into an annex with a soiled examining bed, facing a wall with an eye chart and a map of the digestive system. Above it sat a frayed photograph of the man posing in cap and gown.

"I'm Brother Weldon, the pastor." He had pulled out his stethoscope and listened to Benton's chest. "You're wearing a tiger tooth?"

"A gift from a friend."

He palpated Benton's stomach. "Does it hurt here?"

"Higher up. Near the diaphragm."

"Don't worry, it's not appendicitis." He put away his stethoscope. "There have been so many getting sick. The hand of the Lord falls heavy on our people."

Benton noticed a Bible on the desk.

"I used to be a doctor," he lied. "A pathologist. What sort of illnesses are you dealing with?"

"Birth defects. Extra appendages, and also neurofibromatosis, as in the Elephant Man. Insect bites, meningitis, and some other undiagnosed cases among schoolchildren. It's as if the Lord is punishing us because of all the spirit worship."

"Why so many cases?"

"The defects—we don't know why. The meningitis has been traced to parasites."

"I guess the Palin are prone to worms?"

"Yes, but the meningitis outbreak is from rats. Hookworm eggs hatch inside rats, and the larvae pass into their stools. Our people have a taste for snails, which are sometimes contaminated by the rat droppings, and so they pick up the parasites."

"Worms traveling from rats to humans via snails? Interesting… You said you're from here?"

"A Palin born and bred. The church sent me to Virginia for higher studies."

"Wow, I used to live in northern Virginia," Benton said. "We may have run into each other somewhere before."

"We have a center in Chesapeake. To get to business, how many times have you pooped today?"

"I've lost count. Been puking every few hours."

"Are you taking any medication?"

"No."

The pastor took his temperature and BP. Both were normal.

"What about that red capsule?" Benton asked. "I saw you dishing it out to those teens for their stomach pain."

"It's the Tuesday afternoon batch," Brother Weldon said. "For the trial."

"Isn't there anything you can do?" Benton looked at his hands, wishing he was a better liar. "I feel lousy."

The pastor smiled. "The dispensary offers medicine, but only Our Lord Jesus Christ can heal."

Benton nodded. He tapped the Bible. "May I?"

He thumbed through it idly, finding that the script, obviously devised by a missionary, was the same Cyrillic-looking one he had seen on the forehead of the giant wasp. What was its name? HAGANI.

"You will get better soon," Brother Weldon said.

"By the way, do you know someone called Fire? Apparently well-known in the community."

"Fai?"

"Just someone I'd like to meet." He was glad he had suddenly remembered to ask.

Brother Weldon stood up. "If she's the person I'm thinking of— I'm afraid that won't be possible."

"Why?"

"Fai passed away five years ago." He offered a polite smile. "Meanwhile, why don't you drop in to our church? Our evening social is at six this evening. We serve local snacks with beer and homebrewed whisky as well."

He must have turned up at the social, in the hope of meeting more Palin, and paid the price by overindulging in spirits.

He needed to pee and he got up, forcing himself to hobble to the bathroom outside the hut. After using the primitive toilet, he cleared his throat and spat out blood into the hole. It was pink with a bit of froth.

It served him right for going to church. As he returned to his hut, cursing, he heard singing. The words floating into his ears were in Palin, a mewing sound like *su le zmewz nu.* But still familiar, for it was Aunt Zora's favorite gospel tune, which he had the choir sing at her funeral service.

> Hear my cry, hear my call
> Hold my hand lest I fall

Take my hand Precious Lord
Lead me home.

She had found her home all right. While staying in touch, being there for him when it really mattered.

He had been about to tumble over the precipice on the hike with Pierre when his aunt had warned him about the man. "Keep your distance, and don't never cross him."

He clutched onto the hem of her skirt. "I sort of feel sorry for him, Aunt Zora."

"Stay clear, Ben. Don't break no bread with Satan."

26. Blood Paddy

He slept most of the afternoon and was awakened by Megumi with a cup of tea, along with tiny guesthouse biscuits whose edges had been nibbled off. She was wearing her sun hat.

"You look a little rested," she said after their snack. "Let's go visit the museum site. You can ride pillion."

And he did, holding on to Megumi's waist. As she bounced along, everything went by fast, a blur of tribals, pigs and crooked huts against a backdrop of terraced green slopes.

He touched his larynx, trying to concentrate hard on it.

"Where?" He was pleased that he had managed to spit out an ultra-short utterance.

"To a house on top of Elephant Peak."

She braked to avoid a huge water monitor. It hesitated, its forked tongue testing the air, and then shuffled slowly across the road on short, stout legs, until its broad back with a hump-like protuberance disappeared into the undergrowth. It was only after it had gone that he realized that the hump he had seen was a second, probably parasitical, head.

Megumi pointed. "That hill over there is where they grew poppies. Before the government took out the farmers."

After fifteen minutes of driving up a steep road, she came to a stop beside a crumbling wall with a pair of broken black lanterns. The gate had iron spikes, and behind it stood the ruins of a two-story stone mansion.

"To be had for the asking."

"Why?"

"The house has a story. A Chinese jade merchant built it for his daughter. He abandoned it after the poor girl hanged herself when an English captain rejected her. Obviously, if you believe in ghosts..."

She pushed the gate open, and they walked slowly toward the mansion.

The front door was made of teak, the faded red paint still showing through the cracks, with an animal carving on the lintel. There were other carvings on the gables, and crouched on the roof was a headless gargoyle.

Megumi pushed open the door. They entered a grand hall with floor and walls of dark teak. Alongside was a row of lacquer cabinets, their glass now cracked, with a few pieces of porcelain still propped up inside. The long dining table had two broken chairs at each end. The air felt musty.

They could see rooms leading off from the hall, all of them of ample size but in disrepair. At the far end was a staircase.

Megumi went bounding up the stairs, but Benton was too tired to follow her. He sat at the dining table on one of the broken chairs. It wasn't hard to imagine a pale Chinese girl sitting in his spot, falling to pieces along with the house.

He could hear clambering on the floor above, and then a door banged and he heard something crash.

"Megumi?"

She came down slowly, covered in dust and cobwebs. He dusted her off.

"It's a mess up there, Jack—a wardrobe door fell, nearly knocked me down! But the hall will be great for the skeletons."

He pointed to the door at the end of the hall. They passed through a kitchen and scullery, and they came out to a courtyard, still muddy from recent rains, with the remains of a fountain. Benton stepped very slowly and carefully over a headless bronze torso that had toppled on its side. He picked up a stick and prodded a pile of leaves. A barbet rose up and skittered away to a bush, its blur of green feathers making him dizzy.

"We could set up tents here, Jack, and activities. Teach them about the local ecosystem. There's so much space."

He gave her the thumbs up. She was right about the space, but it wasn't going to host any skeletons, not if he had anything to do with it.

The courtyard extended into a garden which ended at the edge of a slope, where a small path descended. Stretching below were the tufts of trees, the beginning of a forest that clothed the eastern slope of Elephant Peak.

"Hang on a sec," Megumi said. "I've spotted an old friend. *Cheirisophus Pontica*, the lamprey plant." She headed down towards the trees, while Benton lingered at the edge, taking a piss behind a clump of bushes with yellow flowers.

The bushes had been squished in places as if an animal had recently crossed through. He had hardly zipped up when he came across some scat, sizable enough to be that of a leopard. A swarm of butterflies with emerald-striped wings gathered over it.

He recognized them, for they were of the same variety that had appeared earlier on the beach with Major Wirachon. Except that the scarlet eyespots which had decorated their hind wings had now morphed into bizarre lip-like shapes, reminiscent of the protruding mouths of certain species of fish. Those mouths, which resembled infant pacifiers, would be perfectly useless for scaring off predators. Then he stopped, spotting something moving in the scat.

It was a brown dung beetle, a lowly creature doing its bit of recycling, but now a butterfly was inspecting it and then unfurling its proboscis to nudge at the beetle, which at first ignored the nuisance and then reared back. Another butterfly prodded the beetle in the rear, and soon a half-dozen of them had pushed it away, hauling it off like a victorious trophy before finally flipping it on its back where it lay wriggling. The entire swarm of newly carnivorous butterflies then advanced, preparing to tuck in.

He hurried away from the insect feast towards the forest path, to catch up with Megumi. The path was muddy among tall trees, with pine cones scattered on the ground like offerings. Soon the path leveled off, and he came to a pond surrounded by flat rocks that looked like seats. The roots of an old banyan stretched like fingers to the banks, and farther on a grey tree trunk extended across the water like a long pillow, its scarlet flowers floating on the glassy surface. In the middle of the pond, a lotus with giant purple petals rested in splendor on the turbid water.

He called out to Megumi but all he heard was a froglike plop, and then a large ripple came towards him from the far end, followed by several others radiating after. The scene was almost Zen-like in its beauty, but the ripples were too large, the plop too slow and slithery to be caused by a frog. It could be a large catfish. Or even a water monitor.

He remembered the double-headed beast he had seen earlier, and then it clicked. *No, it can't fucking be.* The water monitors were not sipping sou cocktails and producing two-headed babies. Nor were those lovely beetle-chasing butterflies fizzing with overloaded sous.

But then there were the worms. The filthy ones like hookworms, long and grey with sharp teeth, that lodged in the intestines of the Palin, feeding off their hosts. Brother Weldon had explained how the snails had accidentally picked up worm larvae from rat feces. The worms had, in turn, lodged deep in the Palin gut as a result of their fondness for a local variant of *escargots à la Bourguignonne*. Could those tubular vermin also be responsible for transmission of Palin sous?

He saw the glint of a Lay's packet in the mud, and then a child's slipper. Kids had been playing there, not too long ago. It was probably a safe place, but one never knew. He called out to Megumi again, but there was no response. He hoped she was okay. An old lady like her should not have been wandering off in a mountain jungle.

He picked up the Lay's packet and slipped it into his pocket. He walked past the end of the pond where he found the path again. He stepped up the pace, hoping to catch up with Megumi, wherever she was.

The worms were on his mind. If they were to blame for sou dispersion across species, DNA from Palin intestines would have to be leaching into the cells of hookworm larvae residing there. Then, when a Palin adult or child took an alfresco dump or skipped hand washing, the larvae would have to infect the creatures who messed around with poop. Butterflies among them. Those frail and short-lived beauties flitting in the breeze would be contaminated with wretched human DNA, which might not sit that well with their own native material, producing all sorts of bizarre results. Like the pacifier fish mouths on the butterflies that had acquired a taste for beetle meat.

But how would intestinal parasites absorb sous from their hosts? As he thought more, it did not seem that farfetched a scenario. If not the entire sou, some of its material for sure. For DNA was not only transmitted from parent to offspring but also jumped around horizontally, rather like viruses, infecting other species. He and Sylvia had watched a PBS documentary which delved into colorful examples of DNA leaping across species, from beetles to pine conifers, from snakes to cows and even to lizards and rhinos. The vehicles in the animal transfers were either bloodsuckers like ticks and mosquitoes or shit-borne parasites like worms.

"Jack, can you hear the birds? Something weird out there."

Megumi was standing holding a plant cutting in a clearing a few dozen yards ahead, where there were numerous small mounds, rather like termite homes, with puffs of vapor emerging from them.

He signaled Megumi to wait, for he had spotted something in a thicket. It was bloodleaf, which he had seen earlier in her video, also called the beefsteak plant because of its glossy, bright-red leaves. In the video it had green veins, but now the veins were dangling in a thin black Daliesque mustache. Every leaf was the same, the veins stripped from their leaf bodies and left to dangle. It was indeed peculiar, as were the distortions on a plant that stood silently nearby in damp soil. It was another local specimen that Dr. Tollendal had identified in her video catalogue, a yellow fungus topped with a giant brown popsicle made up of leaf-like honeycomb folds. Except that in this case the honeycomb had a yellow clown face in each cell, perhaps designed by nature to frighten off birds. Though it was hard to see that silly face making a difference to an ordinary bird unless the bird in question had a longstanding aversion to kitsch.

His ruminations were interrupted by a cry.

"Glue-it, glue-it!"

It was a bunch of birds making a racket. There were dozens of them, looking as if they had emerged from a tub of blue paint. They swarmed above the termite mounds and then swept up in a long curve towards a tall tree growing next to another plant Megumi was hunched over.

"Glue-it!"

He put his hands to his ears so he could think in peace.

So human DNA might be getting into plants. One could only pity the poor bloodleaf and morel, bystanders caught up in the plague of crazy experiments.

Slam dunk, Bento!

He had homed into something much worse than what he had expected. His findings now suggested that there could be a new environmental crisis brewing, on top of all the existing ones. But this one, with the random mixing of genetic material across species, might well be the most fucked-up of all.

He would have to check with Toy if nature had a way out. Perhaps the receiving organism's genome might be smart enough to spot the good, if any, in the transferred DNA and discard the bad. But there would be no guarantees there; it depended on the genome's drive towards fitness. And in any case, for some victims, it was clearly too late… the damage had been done.

The only hope for the others was for the government to stop the trials immediately. Otherwise, everything was going to hell real soon, becoming one of the great disturbances he had heard mentioned by Pierre and Megumi.

He hurried towards her and then froze in his tracks, for he had spotted a child playing near one of the termite mounds. It was a game like hopscotch, and as the girl hopped, she looked up.

"Bev!"

She came running up in her flowery dress, her hand reaching out. He felt a surge of energy as he lifted her up with his forefinger, wafting her into the air. Her dress fell away, along with charred flesh, leaving only a few shards that flew up, backed by wings which, as they folded back like an eagle's, flashed against an iridescent blue.

"Wow!" Megumi pointed. "A fairy bluebird."

"*Whit-whit-wheet*," the bird tweeted. "*Glue-it*."

He understood.

He had sensed a threat but had failed to protect her. But now he knew, from the flag shape formed by her wings, who had taken her. Along with her father.

"*Glue-it*," the bird said softly. She would forgive him.

A muscled wraith flapped its wings beside them, and now the barbet was up on a branch calling *koo-kook* with its thick orange beak.

"Such lovely birds," Megumi was saying. "Great to see them thriving here."

He needed to trust Bev. The voices of loved ones were the few things one could count on. And that meant that someone from May Tai may have wanted to silence Bert, to put a stop to his inquiries. And discovering his abortion work, relayed the information to the Army of God enforcers in Chesapeake, Virginia. Who had come straight to Vienna and done the deed. Taking out poor little Bev as well.

That someone from May Tai would be the munchkin Michael, then. Perhaps the Foundation salary paid for the headman's dental work. And those lavish meals.

Brother Weldon, the benign-looking Chesapeake-trained pharmacist who proclaimed that only Jesus could heal, could have helped make it happen. The man had been evasive about Fai, who was, according to the messages he had seen, Bert's informant and oddly enough, died the same year as Bert.

There were many positive indicators, but ultimately his analysis relied on too many speculative links, and he lacked the hard evidence to pin the Maple Avenue murders on them. And so those thugs and their cohorts would endure, planning new targets for their evil.

His thoughts were interrupted by a figure who came hopping along. It was Daniel Thigpen, with his brilliant smile, though more than a few teeth were missing. He was hobbling on his hands because his legs had been shorn off above the knee, the stumps black and rounded.

"WTF, man?"

"Busking in Dupont Circle, I got high and fell on the fucking tracks. Had to spend a month in a ward at Prince George's."

"So sorry, Daniel," he whispered.

"We were like fucking gods, remember? Doing the hucklebuck."

He hucklebucked away, heading off towards a fallen acorn. As Benton watched him go, amazed at his squirrel-like transformation, a tall man passed by, slim but stooped, wearing outsized Air Jordans.

He put down the books he was carrying.

"We had it good, brother Benton. And then you sold out big time."

"Rr-rat," Benton said.

"That you did, brother. A coward. Refused to confront your identity. Forgot about us."

He knew what the books were. Tetrault's three Fs. Fanon, Freire and Fromm, their names once hot and cited in Benton's prize-winning senior thesis but now remembered by only a few old stalwarts.

"Brother Benton, your heart was always good. That's why she loved you more than anything."

They hugged, and then his former classmate and rival gathered his books and disappeared towards the old mansion.

Encouraged by his presence, others came out from behind the termite mounds. He saw gaunt warriors, tribesmen who had fallen to Palin violence, their heads missing and bellies ripped open. They staggered along in single file chained by the waist to a long bamboo pole, bent double like Russian burlaks, their blood-stained rags burnished with rusty sequins. They stank up such a storm that the birds stopped their twittering to let them pass.

As Benton gazed speechless at the spectacle, he realized that the genetic gifts from the Palin could yield, even in the best case, only fitness. To become a true warrior, one had to go beyond battle readiness and learn two old-fashioned virtues—courage in the face of death and decency towards one's fellow beings.

"What are you looking at, Jack?" Megumi was holding several long green and red plants between her fingers, their stems dangling down like necks.

A sliver of green trickled between the stones, coming to a stop a few yards away.

"Hey, watch it, mister pit viper," Megumi said. "Keep your distance."

The snake's yellow pupil watched them carefully as they stepped back. After a full minute, it slithered quietly away.

"*Merde.*" Megumi brushed off the sweat on her brow. "The residents have given us a warning."

They heard a quick cough, more like a bark, and then two more.

"It means Nigandu is warning us."

"Nigandu?"

"The Palin leopard spirit, who tears out the heart of anyone who tramples on sacred ground."

They exited, with Megumi hurriedly closing the gate behind them.

"Intense," Benton said, scratching his chin.

"I know you're a man of logic, Jack. But be grateful to the Palin, for their sous have put you in touch with the spirits."

If only she knew what damage the sous had wrought. They were a blight on the still fair planet.

Megumi climbed back on the scooter. "You seem shaken. We'll discuss the site later."

Benton held on, his worries mounting, as they returned to the guest house. He collapsed on top of his mattress, glad to be resting and phantom-free. Lying back, he heard the clucking of an anxious hen and then a wail.

"Jack, you're looking green at the gills," Megumi said. "I'm going to call Pierre."

"No." He held his lips tight so the blood wouldn't come oozing out for her to see.

"I need to give him my daily report. I'll say you're thinking hard about the site." She headed out.

He heard the wail again, followed by a series of woofs and howls. It was a jackal. He couldn't understand what it was saying. He wondered if the Palin sous favored understanding birds over other creatures. He shivered, hearing his stomach gurgle. But he wasn't ready to go. The last time he had squatted uneasily as a family of centipedes, each with dozens of little legs, had dragged their reddish-black bodies towards him to feed on his droppings.

He felt worn out, his fingers clenched together like stumps. He was tired of being pummeled by side effects, fed up with all the sorry schemes, subterfuges and self-deceptions of humans. He might have been better off as a centipede, living half-blind in dampness and decay, feeding on the detritus of other creatures.

But he had arrived as a human. A black boy delivered into a nation scarred by race. Orphaned early. Never fully adjusting or fitting in, always playing a part. Until things fell apart and he retired to Thailand. Where he had been down in the dumps until things started to happen.

In recent weeks he had been so full of energy, thinking it would last forever, but now he wasn't feeling good. And meanwhile the stakes had risen, the planet was in free fall and his mission was to do something about it.

He wanted none of it. He was a retiree who needed no responsibilities, least of all fighting a battle a single individual could never win.

All he really desired now was to stroll with Mimi once more on the beach, to see her pale arched feet stepping beside his on the wet brown sand, their footprints crisscrossing the trails of birds and small creatures. To watch her crouch down, her shorts riding high, gathering a shell and scratching the sand off it with a long fingernail. To taste her salty lips, her little tongue hot and hard against his. And then, hand in hand, to retire to his little fan room and begin again his exploration, learning all over again how to best tell her he loved her.

He had called her twice, but she had not picked up. He hoped she still had some of the cash he had handed her for while he was away. After that expense and paying off Oi, he had just enough left until his end-of-month Social Security installment. Following several refusals on his part, Pierre had insisted on paying him a stipend starting in the new year. The extra thousand dollars a month seemed fair compensation for the long hours at the museum and dealing with Surry. But that was still another ten weeks away, and he wasn't likely to see it. And now he was lying in a barn acting like a pig, one who needed to go urgently and squat among worms and shit. While the world was literally going to hell.

Megumi came in. Her cheeks seemed blanched.

"I've got bad news."

"Spill it."

"Toy's had a massive blood clot."

"And?"

"She didn't make it."

He had visited Toy just four days earlier, and though blind and weak, Toy still seemed tough in spirit. She had high-fived him as he left, making him promise to send her his findings.

"I'm sorry, Jack." Megumi touched his hand, and he let it stay there.

"Funeral?"

"Surry's organizing it this weekend. We'll head back for it. But there's one more thing."

"What?"

"Pierre asked about your eyes. I told him they were fine. They are, aren't they?"

27. Bamboo Rat

Benton had liked Toy ever since that first trip to Noi's shack. She was smart enough to get what he was about. What did she say he was? *Like a frog under a coconut shell. Who thought his world was just the coconut.* Very funny. He had hoped all along that she would make it, but the eye medicine had backfired. She had a fantastic future ahead of her if only she hadn't fallen prey to Pierre.

She said she would become a *Krasue*—a yucky ghost. There to remind people of all that was amiss with the world.

The funeral was on Saturday. Megumi, who was snoring next to him, impervious to all existence, had suggested that he prepare the funeral book. He couldn't tell her that he wasn't planning to attend, but he agreed to help with the book. That meant getting in touch with her surviving bandmate, to fish out more details about her and invite her friends. But he had no idea of the drummer's name. He texted Little John, but Nellie didn't know either.

His relapse couldn't have come at a worse time—just when he needed to act, perhaps the most important endeavor of his life.

And meanwhile, the smell of garden herbs from Megumi was stimulating his appetite. He wanted to wake her up, get her to feed him a warm mash. Instead, he heard the first rooster and drifted off to sleep.

He awoke at noon and Megumi had fetched Michael. He was muttering something to her in Palin. Benton gave the wrinkled gnome the once over. He looked like a harmless old man longing for a nice nap on his verandah, with his dentures sparkling in a glass beside him. Not a capo who would be ordering executions.

Megumi and the headman conferred together, and then Michael began spraying the contents of a bottle all over the earthen floor. The liquid was clear with a floral scent.

"It's for your own good, Jack. Kneel down."

He resisted, but Megumi bent down and made him kneel. He felt too weak for further protest, as Michael opened a worn Jansport backpack and placed three human skulls out on the floor. He inserted a joss stick into each and lit them. He mumbled before the makeshift altar, moving his hands in circular motions, intermittently swigging from a bottle and spitting it out voodoo-fashion as vapor. When he was satisfied that the barn was purified, he asked for two hundred baht.

Megumi counted out two crisp bills from her wallet and handed them to him. Michael put them in his rear pocket and then lifted out a thermos from his backpack.

"Soup," Michael said, handing him a cup.

He refused. No more quackery for him. No more fucking poisons.

"It's Himana," Megumi said. "The spirit of the bamboo rat. You've got to get him out."

The soup tasted revolting, like a Thai tom yum made from sewer water and ground stinkbugs, with a distinctly chemical aftertaste. He prayed there were no sous mixed in it, but the concoction looked too primitive for that. The few shreds of meat inside were chewy and disgusting. But he kept it down even as he felt a ringing in his ears and a rush of molten lava into his stomach.

He had not realized there were other onlookers. Men with thick hands, with soil-worn fingernails, and two pale Chinese-looking women who hung their heads low. He scanned their faces, as he had at the dispensary, to see if anyone had odd mutations or other problems. But he spotted nothing.

"Who are you?" Michael began.

The smoke from the incense was hurting Benton's eyes.

"*Tête de noeud*," Megumi said. "Answer him, so you can get well!"

"Benton."

"Your name means nothing," Michael said. "Why are you here?"

"Foundation." His knees were already killing him, and he tried to sit back.

"Kneel like a man," Michael said, in a gravelly voice, as if he were speaking through a cistern.

He kneeled forward.

"Your name is Judas, is it not?"

"No." He managed to keep kneeling. The one thing he did know was that this old and feeble man was not going to be able to take him out.

The onlookers stared at him without sympathy or enthusiasm. The pale women must have been famished, for they were gnawing noisily as they watched the proceedings.

"Tell us where you come from."

"USA."

"No, Africa. What is the name of your tribe?"

The man was right about Africa, but Benton wanted to clarify that he didn't have a tribe. He wanted to explain, as he had long ago to Little John, that he came from a collection of many different migrants, some of whom emerged out of Africa and then moved on to Asia and later to Europe, and others who went from Asia back to Africa and then to America. But he lacked the means to communicate that diversity, and in any case, Michael would not understand a thing.

The headman laughed, his teeth sharp and black in his betel-stained mouth. "So how come Africans are black as night?"

The barn was now wreathed in smoke.

"You are a Muslim, no? And a spy?"

The interrogation continued, absurd and pointless as he had nothing to reveal. He could feel drops of sweat collecting on his neck.

"Sonofabitch!" He put his hand on the back of his burning neck and wiped off the hot drops. They felt like tallow.

"Fat from your soul," Megumi said.

"Who do you spy for?" Michael asked. "You are FDA agent?"

Benton remained silent, waiting to see what was coming next. Megumi, he had to believe, would not let him die.

Michael spat out more vapor, and the drops stopped. The shaman began to sing in a surprisingly high-pitched falsetto, calling out for Himana while his fingers wove a nimble pattern as if he were embroidering a fine Palin waistcoat at lightning speed. Then he reached under his shirt. The old man pulled out a knife and licked the blade, hissing and barking as the sweat formed a puddle around Benton's feet.

The smoke in the barn now had a green glow as insects with hair-like antennae crawled in through the air gap right below the thatch, dangling down with their upturned capuchin faces. A leaf curled down beside them, then an entire plant descended, wrapping its long lip-shaped leaves like hair around his neck, and he could smell rotting flesh. Another green plant with an enormous mouth sucked onto his snout like an octopus, practically pulling his gums out, and then a plant with leathery leaves with red veins tore roughly across his lips, and he could taste blood. He could hear a medley of jungle sounds approaching, turning into a vile cacophony of jackal laughter, terrifying barks and coughs and geckers and gibbers, groans and growls and hisses and hoots, and blood-curdling screeches and whistles and whoops, yaps and yips and yowls. Something was moving on his neck, and he felt his tiger tooth necklace, the one that Pierre had given him, being yanked off. He could hear his own voice trying to scream, to rise above the voice of the jungle.

Michael laughed and cried at the same time, asking Himana to witness the splendid wretchedness of the black *farang*, for he had taken into his body that which had been set aside for other creatures. He asked if the patient was deserving of punishment or forgiveness, and as the onlookers murmured, the knife glittered on high and then he brought it down hard.

Benton fell back as a wave of pain struck his body, ricocheting down to his coccyx. He wanted to cry but would not. His diaphragm was still rising and falling, and then as its pace slowed to short gasps he could feel the sour taste of all his deeds to date, the brackish waters of regret welling up, and he knew that he carried the burden of evil like a snake in its bulging throat. It was getting heavier, unbearable, his breathing now so slow that he was gasping on intake but no, he refused to be extinguished, and then Michael came to him and whispered things in his ear, saying that he had passed the test and now had the true warrior spirit, and he felt bilious on top of the pain which was radiating up into his throat as Megumi handed him a bowl. He opened his mouth wide and then vomited out the morsels from his soup.

28. Wilbur

He woke hours later. His sleep had been dark, deep and dreamless, a tonic of regeneration. He could see moonlight trickling in through the door. The guest hut was clean, devoid of humans, insects, spirits or vapors. Megumi usually slept nearby, but she was not to be seen. It was then that he got the call.

It was her, the voice angelic and unmistakable. Her hello itself meant that he was loved and that the world was worth every atom in it.

"Bento, Pierre tell me you sick."

"Yes."

"You become Wilbur pig man again?"

He didn't know what to say.

"I come help Bento darling."

"Can't."

"Can too," Mimi said. "Granny Devona have same-same problem, *ka*. Get stroke, motor car not work."

"Car?"

"Mimi give Devona *ya*, then she drink so much whisky. Guess what? Motor okay now!"

"*Ya?*"

"Medicine from wild pig brain. Celebo Lyzine. Make you feel better."

"Fuck!"

"Bento, I check already. With your small-small *farang* friend."

"Little John!"

"I ask if Celebo Lyzine good for Bento. He ask girlfriend Nellie. She have Thai boyfriend long time back. He very clever but drug addict. You proud or what, Bento?"

"What?"

"Mimi call him up. Crazy man is biohacker. He say pig brain peptides not strong enough. Need also *Fa Thalai Chon*."

"*Thalai?*"

"Thai name *Heaven Strike Thieves*. Antibacterial antioxidant antiviral anticancer."

"Anticrap."

"Make you whole man, darling. Know what?"

"What?"

"*Khitung muk muk*. I miss you, Bento!" He heard some smooching sounds on the other end.

And so, she had come. He heard the taxi pull up on the dirt road, and it was the happiest moment of his life. She arrived in new stiletto heels and blowing smoke from her cigarette.

They hugged, and she yattered on about inconsequentials, an evening dress, a wonderful new iPhone case, the latest befrienders and unfrienders, the market gossip from Nellie, and it was all good, and he was grateful. He let her fill the syringe she had brought with one of the ampules of Cerebrolysin and stick it smoothly into a vein in his forearm.

"How?"

"My friend Fon teach me. Naughty girl."

Mimi then expertly emptied the contents of another capsule on his tongue. It was horribly bitter. She insisted that he take the medicine for a whole week. She would stay for three days, during which he was to rest in the hut, and she would go into the village and fetch him food.

At first, she begged him not to use a condom. "I make baby with you, Bento."

He insisted, rolling the sheath on himself. "School first," he reminded her.

"Okay, pig man. Mimi study, become brilliant. Then have smart baby!"

Seeing him erect, she shook him and laughed. "Old man with power!"

But soon he lay spent in her arms.

"You tired, honey?" She stroked his chest hair. "Old sperm good, Bento. So many Thai use to make nice baby."

Her face was resting on his cheek. "I love you, Mimi."

"Liar!" She tickled his ear with her nail. "You buy me new necklace?"

"You bet I will. You deserve it." He fingered her tattoo.

Megumi came in then. They were still relaxing in bed.

"Jack, those *roubignoles* again!" She laughed. "You must be feeling way better—but call when done. Pierre has been asking about the site."

He didn't care about the site, because he was on the honeymoon he had always wanted. With a teenaged caregiver. At the end of which he felt complete again. His language deficit had almost vanished, though he wasn't entirely sure whether it was the medicine or her presence. Or the exercise he was getting. His biceps and pecs were already thinner, which Mimi said was lost water weight. And his curiosity had returned. The first thing he wanted to know was what he was on. He looked up *Heaven Strike Thieves*. It turned out to be creat, a green plant known to science as *Andrographis Paniculata*. It was widely used as a traditional medicine, and its benefits were being studied by a group of doctors at the medical school in Chiang Mai University.

The morning of her departure, he reminded her about the children who had been zombified. "You have to tell Pierre. About your *ya*. So he can inform the government."

"Daddy say Pierre is bad man. Not go near him."

So Sharky was cutting his losses.

"Have Nellie and her ex explain about these two meds to Major Wirachon," Benton said. "They should also chat with these Thai doctors in Chiang Mai." He wrote down Wirachon's contact and the address of the Chiang Mai website and placed the note in her hand.

She closed her fist, high-fived him, and then proceeded to give him a fake *muay thai* kick on the jaw.

He held on to her foot and kissed it.

"You kinky old man, Wilbur!" She withdrew it gently and left.

29. Dispensary

He sat up in bed, feeling pressure in his stomach. The moon was full and yellow, the night silent except for a rustle in the leaves. He felt a strange mental fatigue as if part of his brain had been carefully excised, while still allowing the remainder to concentrate on what was needed.

He looked at his watch. It was four a.m., and he was trying to remember what had happened to him the previous week. Had his angel really come? Had Mimi really been there?

He knew she had because he had phoned her a few hours earlier, just before he hit the sack. She was nervous, but also excited, waiting in Bangkok with their tickets in hand. Sharky had agreed to give her a big chunk. It was a wedding present of sorts. He said that as soon as he tied up the Klub and his other businesses he too was heading out to Cambodia.

Benton had asked Megumi the day before about the *Andrographis*, and she was all praise for the plant and its properties. She was happy her Jack was back, she said, giving him a hug. And he knew, though she reported to Pierre, that she was rooting for him.

He slung on his backpack and headed in the moonlight towards his bike. He released the footbrake and then pushed the Yamaha out over the soft soil towards the road. Once there, he pointed it downhill, away from the abandoned school, and let it roll.

He turned left near a brook and then saw the dispensary building on his right. He parked against a tree and walked into the back garden.

It was dense with tall trees, a leaf of which fell on his hand. It smelled of mango. He could hear an owl with its hunting *toowit* cry, and then the jackal, howling for its mate. He turned his phone light on and walked towards the back door. It was secured with a bolt and a heavy brass padlock. A branch was scratching against the window in the slight breeze. He pushed against the glass, feeling something scurry away under his shoulder, but the window didn't yield.

He shone the light into the glass, which was dulled with grime. There was no choice but to bash it in, which he did by flinging a fallen mango at it. It shivered into shards that skittered and chinked across the floor. He reached in quickly and pulled at the handle, opening the door. He walked in, his feet crunching on broken glass.

He saw the usual picture of the Thai King Bhumibol, in a jacket with gold airline-style epaulets, wearing a panoply of medals, including one with a glorious Garuda bird with outstretched wings sitting on a vertically rotated Thai flag. Next to that sat a picture of an old, long-whiskered Chinese man in a red, silk mandarin jacket with rolled sleeves and frog buttons in gold brocade. His face resembled that of Brother Weldon.

On the table were mushrooms and fungi in neat packets next to a pair of rusty scales. There was also a printed book in Chinese, probably a *materia medica*. It was open with a cracked tortoiseshell used as a paperweight.

There were shelves opposite with jars of what looked like pickled fruit or organs. And bottles of shredded roots of different colors—white, black, yellow, even red. He noticed a stepladder under the desk and dragged it out. He climbed slowly up. The top shelf was full of packets of tea. Behind them was a set of plastic jars. Shining the phone, he managed to discern the handwritten Thai characters วัน on some of the labels. He couldn't remember what the วั was, though he knew the น was an *n*. If only he had paid more attention when Mimi played the Thai alphabet song to him on her phone, but he was focused then on her lips.

He unscrewed one of the jars. Inside were blue capsules. He collected some in his handkerchief and then split open one in his palm.

Out came a white powder, which he took in his fingertips and spread on his tongue. He recognized it immediately. It had the stinkbug-sewer flavor of the soup the shaman Michael had fed him in that bizarre ritual. He spat it right out, unwilling to subject himself to more hallucinations and purging.

He was about to open the second jar when he saw a piece of paper stuck to the back of the shelf. Thankfully, the writing was in English. He opened the other jars. He saw the red capsules he was expecting, as well as white pills—and also pink pills, yellow capsules, violet ones, and some with a sickly green color. He stuffed them into his backpack, squishing them.

He picked up the piece of paper and climbed down slowly. He sat at the table, resting his head for a minute on the open pages of the Chinese *materia medica*. He closed his eyes, needing to get his head together while there was so little time left. After a few deep breaths, he raised his head again and spread the piece of paper flat on the book. He picked up the tortoise-shell paperweight and placed it on top. Then he fished out his phone, and holding it in his left palm began to type.

30. Codes

October 16, 2014
May Tai, Thailand

Hey Mimi-bird,

I'm writing this while remembering that farewell *muay thai* kick and your delicious toes, my love! I already miss you awfully, even though it's been only two days. I don't know what I've done to deserve you and all that you've done for me—including saving this old pigman's precious life!

But this time Wilbur's in serious doo-doo, darling. He's sending this email because he doesn't know what will happen. He's going to write his thoughts down so that as soon as he hits "send," you'll receive a complete brain dump. He wants you to know what he has found out, and he wants the world to hear it through you. Because Wilbur doesn't have a good feeling about the future and whether he'll be able to make it out okay.

There's something else I've been meaning to get off my chest. Mimi, I know it has all been a game on your part. You act dumb just because you think other folks, Wilbur included, aren't as smart as you. And you also think acting like you don't give a fuck is cute—which it is, in a way. But you need to grow up. You're not a kid anymore. There's nothing wrong in showing off your mental chops.

I know you're smarter than many of the folks I worked with. And your school Principal already told me that you're the brightest he's seen in years. You tried to keep your smarts secret from everyone. The Principal told me how you acted up in class. Like the first time your teacher asked you to come up to the board and write the formula for the volume of a cylinder. You pretended like you were dumbfounded, scratching your nose before writing *pizza* in huge letters, which had the kids laughing so loud they were ready to wet their pants.

You're always saying "School sucks!" because you want to stay popular with Fon and her crowd. But I can tell you that Fon and the rest aren't your kind. They're going nowhere and are more like parasites, spreading their legs and living off the generosity of others. I know you think I'm being mean and crude, but at this stage I'm no longer bothered with being polite. It's high time you dumped Fon's ass.

You, my dear, are destined for something much greater than your pals in school. Mimi is going to be very successful! Trust me, honey. Your life is going to be rich. I'm not talking about having lots of money for accessories. That you may have too. But those riches are of a different kind.

Enough said—you're probably pissed off already by the lecture. Well, you love solving puzzles, don't you? And I'm not talking about Sudoku. I have a puzzle here that will get you all riled up. I want you to share the solution when we find it—which we will, hopefully, before I get to the end of this letter. Share the solution with Nellie and ask her to help get the word out about what's happening to the Palin as well as Thais. Tell her to sing it in the marketplace, at the Pub, wherever—the more people are empowered, the better. Nellie and Little John will protect you from any fallout because I trust them.

I'm going to type as fast as I can and I hope I get done in time because I'm sitting somewhere that I'm not fucking supposed to be. It's going to be daylight soon, and your Wilbur has got to be out before that, or the sleazeballs who work here will find Wilbur and then he's going to be diced up and sent to the sausage factory. Meanwhile my tongue is running loose like I'm drunk so forgive the f-words if they show up.

The puzzle? This is what I found on a piece of paper.

POLAND, NOREÑA, ASSISI, THAILAND, RAINBOY, ASSISI

Can you tell me what that means? Three distinct place names (yes, Assisi is a place!), with one repeated, indicating a pattern. It's a code, kiddo, for something important.

The Ñ? You spotted that right away, didn't you? Here's a hint: it's a symbol of Spain and suggests a Spanish name, and probably stands for yet another place. The odd man out, as you already guessed, is Rainboy.

The place names have very little in common except for the thread of Catholicism. Poland is Catholic, and Assisi is the home of St. Francis, a famous saint who grew up in wealth but gave it all up and was known for his love of all living creatures. Sort of like Lord Buddha, you think?

I know you're drumming your fingers or smoking impatiently. The codes? I'm getting there, baby. I first thought they had something to do with religion. But I'm sitting in front of the flag of your hospitable yet thoroughly fucked-up country. And your flag pattern:

red white blue white red. That makes me think flag colors are relevant, not religion. Thank God!

Easy, eh? Assisi's flag is rather simple compared to the Thai one: blue and red. You'll have googled Poland by the time you read this. The Poles are tough people, let me tell you. When I worked in Washington we used to track Polish government officials who had been smuggling arms to the leader of Iraq, Saddam Hussein. I don't have to google their flag. I can recall two horizontal stripes, white followed by red.

I gave you a hint about Noreña. You've looked it up by now, as I have had to with this dang slow-mo phone, and have found that it's in Asturias, Spain. It's a place that you may never visit, as it's mainly known for its hefty bean stew. Its flag is the reverse of Assisi: red and blue.

Like any clever girl, you're keeping a scratchpad. I'm willing to bet that a whole minute before you actually read this sentence, you had already written this out:

POLAND: [WHITE RED], NOREÑA: [RED BLUE], ASSISI: [BLUE RED],

THAILAND: [RED WHITE BLUE WHITE RED], RAINBOY: ??, ASSISI: [BLUE RED]

The puzzle is pretty neat, isn't it? What's Rainboy, you're asking? Is it a nickname like Wilbur? Clearly not a place-name with a flag. I'm typing slowly now because I have been searching again in parallel. I tried *rainboy flag* but found only music videos and other junk, including an article on eyewitnesses to the paranormal. I even did an image search for flags red blue white. I clicked for more than five minutes through the flags. Nothing fucking relevant.

The key is not to give up, something my aunt Zora taught me years ago. I was about to, when

I came to a white, red and blue flag that linked to a Wikimedia commons image file for unused formats. The documentation was in Croatian, but I didn't even have to look. The author of that file? You guessed it: Rainboy.

You've already put that in your scratchpad. And you're pissed off, because I made you wait so long for the interesting part.

POLAND: [WHITE RED], NOREÑA: [RED BLUE], ASSISI: [BLUE RED],

THAILAND: [RED WHITE BLUE WHITE RED], RAINBOY: [WHITE RED BLUE],

ASSISI: [BLUE RED]

You don't like quintuplets in the midst of pairs, do you Mimi? And the list can't be reparsed so as to have all triplets. Try partitioning into pairs, and you get what? Eight pairs?

What's so cool about eight, Mimi-bird? I know it's a lucky number in Thailand, with all those vanity license plates with **888**. But seven would be nicer, because it's really a magic number. You may already know that. So let's try seven. When in doubt, eliminate.

[WHITE RED], [RED BLUE], [BLUE RED], [RED ~~WHITE~~ BLUE], [~~WHITE~~ RED WHITE],

[RED BLUE], [BLUE RED]

There are seven rows. What are seven things that are famous? There's the seven deadly sins. And seven colors of the rainbow, and maybe seven lipstick shades. Of course not. And the days of the week. You bet! All that trouble for a fucking weekly calendar!

Sunday	WHITE	RED
Monday	RED	BLUE
Tuesday	BLUE	RED
Wednesday	RED	BLUE
Thursday	RED	WHITE
Friday	RED	BLUE
Saturday	BLUE	RED

There are two entries for each day of the week. You're guessing day and night? Or morning and afternoon? I should have told you earlier, I'm sitting in a dispensary. Where they hand out medicines. Get the hell out, Wilbur, you're screaming!

The code. You saw of course that there are only three elements: white, red, and blue, and three pairs, ignoring the internal order of the pair. Why didn't I guess earlier that it's a code for three treatments being compared? That's the problem with analysis, my sweet. Like life, it only makes sense, if at all, in hindsight.

When you run trials, comparing different treatments, you probably have the same number of people in each group. Over a couple of years, that would amount to a sizable chunk of data. Actually, five days out of seven, it's only the red and blue being compared. What is the third pair doing here, red and white, compared only twice?

The pills that slimebucket Pierre slipped into my dish—at the banquet where we first met—were white. So those had to be the pills with sous. About half an hour ago, I found some blue capsules here that tasted exactly like the disgusting Himana soup from the shaman Michael!

Blue for homebrew. There's really only one choice left for red. For drug trials, you need a placebo, a drug that's inert. So that you can compare drugs that have real effects versus those that have nothing useful in them, to see which works better. Sometimes the inert ones work fine because people believe that they will get better! Hell, when my aunt Zora was bedridden with her final illness, they gave her an injection of distilled water that got her up and about for two days, shouting the praises of the Lord!

Meanwhile, you have gotten ahead of me and have already filled out this table:

Sunday	SOU	PLACEBO
Monday	PLACEBO	HOMEBREW
Tuesday	HOMEBREW	PLACEBO
Wednesday	PLACEBO	HOMEBREW
Thursday	PLACEBO	SOU
Friday	PLACEBO	HOMEBREW
Saturday	HOMEBREW	PLACEBO

And you also figured out what stands out from the data. Namely: the sous are being compared rarely, with the homebrew taking most of its place.

Why? Because the sous have nasty and uncontrollable side effects, sometimes fatal, like in the case of poor Toy, not to mention near misses, like me. The homebrew, I'm guessing, is probably significantly better than a placebo. When reporting the results, the data can easily be fudged by collapsing the sou and homebrew together and palming the results off as coming from the sous. Any side effects of the sou in these trials will remain few as a proportion of sou and homebrew together.

Which basically means that Pierre will be broadcasting to the world at large how amazing these newfangled high-tech Palin-harvested sous really are. While ignoring all the damage they have caused. You know about the side effects on humans, but I don't have time to explain the shit that's happening in the rest of creation.

I can hear a peacock, Mimi. It's like the cry of a child in danger. It's now half-past five. Dawn will be breaking any time soon.

You're scratching your nose. If you're going to fake the results, you're thinking, why even bother to test the sous? May as well just test the homebrew and compare it against the placebos, claiming the homebrew results for the sous. But maybe you forgot one thing. Pierre, despite his criminal mind, is actually a brilliant scientist. And scientists are driven by curiosity. Pierre would want to know how good the sous really are.

You have one more question? Get to it fast, honey, or I'm history. Why didn't he bakeoff sou versus homebrew? I'm guessing he didn't. If he did, the result from the comparison of the latest science against ancient tribal magic would have been too much for him to bear.

These trials were just for cancer prevention. If the cancer treatment trials were done along the same lines, with mysticism in place of modern medicine, and word got out about it, it would be equally scandalous. Because making a sick person die is just as bad as making a healthy person sick.

Of course, getting any word out would also mean the end of Pierre's multinational pie-in-the-sky business dream. That's why it's so fucking dangerous if Pierre hears that any of this has gotten out. Like I said, trust the ones I've asked you to trust. And, of course, your dad Sharky. But nobody else. Promise me that.

I hear the rooster again, and it's time to go.

A thousand hugs & xxxx xxxxxx! Wilbur is your lover forever.

Benton Sims, Ph.D.

31. Finale

Benton fished Major Wirachon's card out of his wallet. He dialed the number, it rang eleven times, and there was no answer. Nor was there any voicemail.

The moon had vanished, and dawn had broken. The rooster crowed thrice, the last cry ending in a gurgle, like blood curdling from a slit throat. He felt his heartbeat quickening. It was time to get going. But he had to try once more. He called again. No answer. He texted an all-uppercase message to him, hoping it would reach and get his attention.

> SAWADEE KHRAB, URGENT, PLS CALL BACK.
>
> MAIN FINDING: BULSANI FOUNDATION SCAMMING US FIRMS PAYING FOR CANCER DRUG TRIALS.
>
> CHARGES:
>
> 1. FAKING PERMISSION FORMS & RESULTS.
>
> 2. REPLACING GMO DRUGS WITH TRIBAL MEDICINES.
>
> 3. GMOS CAUSING EXTREME/FATAL SIDE-EFFECTS.
>
> 4. MAY BE INFECTING HILL COUNTRY FLORA & FAUNA.
>
> KEY EVIDENCE, INCL. SAMPLES & DATA, IN MY POSSESSION.
>
> P. S. DID NELLIE CONTACT YOU? FOR WILD BOARS: TRY CEREBROLYSIN + ANDROGRAPHIS. AND LOVE.

Wirachon wasn't the brightest of men, but he hated the Palin as well as Pierre, and the fact that the doctor had Cambodian blood would make his victory especially sweet. Maybe busting the outfit would get the major another promotion. Benton didn't really understand what made Thais like him tick. But he hoped to hell the samples he had were good enough for the government.

He would have liked to finger Michael as well, and maybe Brother Weldon, the Army of God and everyone else, but he had no hard evidence against them. The testimony of the bluebird-spirit of a murdered child, obtained by an aging *farang* prone to drug-induced hallucinations, would never be admissible, not even in a Thai court.

He slipped out through the back door and left the dispensary. He headed back to the bike, exhausted now.

He wondered about his friend Pierre. He could visualize Wirachon and his team arriving at the Peak. They would seize all his rare statues and paintings. The Survivors would be in a panic as they were packed off to Cambodia. Or perhaps they were destined for a *Lang Pa Cha* space-saving funeral. They would survive all right, but in some other form, dispersed into natural materials.

It was unlikely that Pierre would let himself be paraded and photographed in leg irons like other criminals. The rat-infested Bangkok Hilton, aka Bang Kwang Prison, was not for him. He would probably bid a teary adieu to his Maman and throw himself off the balcony, to be gobbled up by his monsoon spiral. Or else the doctor could swallow a handful of his own designer concoctions.

He climbed on the Yamaha, his backpack slung behind him.

There would be no pleasure in seeing Pierre go. After the deaths of Siri and Toy, he wanted no more. Pierre had trusted him, extending a slimy paw of friendship. If they had stayed friends long enough, Pierre might even have redeemed himself. Realizing at last that however much nature might be poked and prodded, he was not a smart enough scientist to outwit it. Or Benton Sims, for that matter.

He almost wished he hadn't sent the message to Wirachon, but he had done it because it was right, and now what he had to do was get going and join Mimi. He couldn't wait to pick her up and take off.

Benton started the Yamaha and heard a branch crack. A spotted wood owl flew up, hooting low. He was about to flick on the accelerator when a tall figure came out of a thicket, and the look on the man's face, even in the gloom of morning, froze Benton in place. The man was dressed in black, striding purposefully like a monk in walking meditation, but with his fingers hovering on his belt.

"My oh my," Surry said, purring softly. "It's our friend Jack."

Glossary

Agacea Xanthicles: morel or fungus from which Megumi extracted a green curd-like mucilage.

Agyneia Coccinea: plant also known as glochidion coccineum, with pink, garlic-like fruits, used for wound healing in traditional Thai medicine.

Andrographis Paniculata: plant also known as creat or green chireta, widely used in traditional medicine in South and Southeast Asia.

Angkor Wat: 12th Century temple complex in Cambodia, one of the world's largest religious monuments.

appam: South Indian pancake made with rice and coconut milk, known as 'hoppers' in Sri Lanka.

asparaginase: chemotherapy drug derived from E. coli or other bacteria.

Axenfeld syndrome: a condition marked by eye abnormalities such as off-center pupils, extra holes in the iris, and corneal oddities.

babysan: 'native child' in Japanese-derived slang used by US soldiers in Korea and Vietnam.

bar fine: customary fee for taking a bar girl out for sex in Thailand.

Bayon Buddha: giant Bodhisattva face carved on rock, among several at Bayon Temple in Angkor Wat, Cambodia.

beta-blocker: medicine to lower blood pressure by blocking the effects of the hormone adrenaline.

billets-doux: 'love letters,' from French.

biltong: South African air-dried meat jerky.

black-hat hacker: a computer programmer who finds vulnerabilities in other people's computer systems, stealing information or damaging them for fun, financial gain, or other malicious purposes. Black hats are those who remain unreformed, compared to white hats, who use an awareness of hacking methods for the benefit of society.

blast: short for myeloblast, a stem cell found in bone marrow. A clear symptom of leukemia is the overproduction of abnormal blasts that are unable to develop into mature white blood cells.

BMI: Body Mass Index, a formula for measuring how fat a person is.

bodhisattva: in Mahayana Buddhism, a being or deity who postpones his own nirvana in order to help others.

boetie: 'brother' in Afrikaans.

bong proh: 'older brother' in Khmer.

bor bor: Cambodian rice porridge, flavored with lemongrass and whatever is at hand.

brae: 'barbecue' in Afrikaans.

Bundolo: 'I kill' in Mangani, the ape language spoken by Tarzan.

bun khun: Thai phrase for a favor, obligation, or good turn that has to be paid back, as in the case of a grown child helping out an aged parent.

burlak: barge hauler in the time of the Russian Empire.

bushido: honor code of the samurai.

calpain: a protein involved in numerous cell activities, including necrosis and decomposition.

Calpastatin: a protein that inhibits the activity of calpains.

caoutchouc: a variety of rubber, also known as 'India rubber.'

charcutier: 'pork butcher', from French.

Cheirisophus Pontica: a plant with an enormous lamprey-like funnel-mouth that caressed Megumi's neck.

chickenshit foreigner: alternative English translation of Thai phrase 'farang ki nok' or 'birdshit foreigner.'

conjee: Asian rice porridge.

Coptis Teeta: a variety of buttercup, also called 'Yunnan goldthread', used in traditional Chinese medicine.

Dioscorea Hispida: Asiatic bitter yam, called 'kloi' in Thai, a food source with tubers containing the toxin dioscorine.

Eleuthero Senticosus: eleuthero or Siberian ginseng, used in traditional Chinese medicine.

Entertainer rag: classic piano rag written by Scott Joplin in 1902.

fan: generic term for 'girlfriend,' 'boyfriend,' 'lover,' or even 'spouse' in Thai.

farang: 'foreigner' (usually white person) in Thai. Derived from Persian 'farang' meaning Germanic tribe of Franks.

File Salvage: a program for recovering deleted files on a computer system.

Form 86: A standard form used in applications for security clearances, also known as the Questionnaire for Investigation Processing.

FOXC1 gene: a gene involved in regulating the growth of the embryo and eyes. Defects in the gene can cause glaucoma and Axenfeld syndrome.

gene therapy: using genes to prevent or treat disease, by knocking out a defective gene, replacing it with a healthy copy, or introducing a new gene.

girlfriend experience: vacation rental of a prostitute, popular among well-heeled sex tourists in Thailand.

Git: an open-source software system that keeps track of different versions of a system's files and code changes.

gkin kao rue yang: 'have you eaten or not?' in Thai.

gluai jun: 'sandalwood banana' in Thai.

GMO: genetically modified organism, with its genetic makeup modified in a laboratory.

GPG: Open source encryption tools to ensure privacy of electronic communication.

Ha: Palin soul.

Hagani: Palin wasp spirit that enters through the ear and swells up on the wax, driving the faithless mad.

hi-so: Thai pidgin English slang for 'high society.'

Hieronymus Elegans: a plant with cnidarian-like flowers straddled in Megumi's video by a sun-spangling spider web.

hijra: an Indian eunuch or transgender person earning a living as a street performer.

Himana: Palin bamboo rat spirit, inflicting stomach ailments on people consuming forbidden fruits and plants. Himana is appeased only when victim consumes gallbladder of a black dog.

hotnot: racist term for so-called 'colored' (or 'brown') Khoisan people in South Africa's Western Cape. Derived from equivalent racial and racist term 'Hottentot.'

in utero: inside the womb.

in vitro fertilization: egg and sperm being united outside the body.

indels: insertions and deletions of one or more nucleotides in DNA sequence. While indels have their uses in forensics, they are also implicated in certain cancers.

Irisene Herbstii: Herbst's bloodleaf, also known as chicken gizzard or beefsteak plant.

Ixora Coccinea: jungle geranium or jungle flame, used in traditional Indian medicine.

jai dee: 'good-hearted' in Thai.

jai yen yen: literally 'cool-hearted' or 'calm and composed' in Thai.

jep: 'it hurts' in Thai.

Jorani: Palin crocodile spirit delivering deathbed punishment.

jou poes: widely-used profanity in Afrikaans (literally: 'your pussy').

ka: polite particle used to end sentence by female speaker.

kabadiwala: 'junk dealer' or 'ragpicker' in Hindustani.

kaffir: racist slur for black person in Afrikaans. Derived from Arabic word for 'non-believer.'

Karen long-neck: a subgroup of the Burmese Red Karen tribe, whose women wear brass neck coils that elongate their necks.

kaun proh: 'son' in Khmer.

khao niao: Thai dish of sticky rice.

khitung: 'miss' or 'long for' in Thai.

khotord: 'sorry' or 'excuse me' in Thai.

khrab: polite particle used to end sentence by male speaker.

khun: honorific prefix used before a Thai given name.

kloi: Asian bitter yam in Thai.

Krasue: Thai ghost appearing as beautiful young woman with internal organs dangling from neck and will-o'-the-wisp-like glow. A staple of Thai horror movies.

kratom: mitragyna speciosa plant whose leaves when chewed have opioid-like effects.

kroeg: 'bar' or 'pub' in Afrikaans.

kroeung: Cambodian curry paste.

Krungthep: 'City of Angels' in Thai, short name for Bangkok.

lamut: 'sapodilla', also known as Mexican zapota, in Thai.

lamyai: 'longan' (fruit) in Thai.

Land Of Smiles: A marketing slogan for Thailand. The Thais, who do smile a lot, have terms for thirteen different types of smiles, some far from innocent.

Lang Pa Cha: Thai ritual called Cleaning and Tidying of the Cemetery, where bodies unclaimed by relatives are dug up and cremated according to Buddhist rites.

Loi Krathong: Thai festival involving krathong or 'floating baskets' set free at night on a river, symbolizing letting go of the past and propitiation of river goddess. In some parts, floating lanterns are launched into the night sky.

ma leeaow: 'has arrived' in Thai.

maengpong: 'scorpion' in Thai.

mafuang: 'star fruit' or 'carambola' in Thai.

mai bpen rai: 'no worries' or 'never mind' in Thai.

mai pet: 'not spicy' in Thai.

mak mak: 'a lot' in Thai.

mamasan: 'native mother' in Japanese-derived slang used by US soldiers in Korea and Vietnam.

Mamisu: Palin soul representing consciousness, leaving the body each night during sleep.

mangkhud: 'mangosteen' in Thai.

manpla: 'lifesaver' in Thai, the glochidion sphaerogynum plant that is toxic to Westerners but useful in Palin chemotherapy.

Mara: A tempter demon who assaulted the Buddha as he sat meditating during the night of his final enlightenment, trying to seduce the Buddha with a vision of beautiful women.

materia medica: traditional pharmacological cookbook.

méchant: 'naughty boy' in French.

MENTIS: an early warning system used by Benton at NSA to help analysts by creating visualizations of possible terrorist threats. MENTIS significantly failed to predict the 9/11 attacks.

methotrexate: drug variously used in chemotherapy, autoimmune disorders like rheumatoid arthritis, abortions, and food manufacturing.

Millettia Brandisiana: a plant with leathery leaves and tomentose fruits used in traditional Chinese medicine.

moo pa: 'wild boar' in Thai.

muay thai: Thai boxing sport requiring vigorous punching, kicking, elbowing, and blocking.

muk muk: 'a lot' in Thai.

Musini: Palim forest guardian spirit, causing birth defects in offspring of anyone who cuts down the sacred yang na tree.

Ni: Palin spirit.

Nifah: Palin shaman or sorcerer.

Nigandu: Palin leopard spirit who tears the heart out of those who trample on hallowed ground.

noi-na: 'custard apple' in Thai.

oi: 'sugar-cane' in Thai.

paw: 'father' in Thai.

petit filou: 'young rascal' in French.

phasa arai: 'what language?' in Thai.

piñata: treat-filled container (usually papier-mâché) that is smashed with sticks as part of a celebration.

placebo: an inert or 'sham' substance that is not intended to have any therapeutic value, used as a control in clinical experiments.

Play-Doh: modeling putty used by children to create toys.

polygraph: a highly unreliable lie-detection device based on physiological indicators, popular in US intelligence and law enforcement agencies.

prik kee nu: 'mouse shit pepper' in Thai, very spicy.

PSA: prostate-specific antigen, measured in blood to screen for prostate cancer.

pseudogene: (referred to as sou) a DNA segment that is a leftover from a gene that is no longer in use, with some of the underlying gene's functionality being disabled. Sous make up almost half the human genome. Some sous produce proteins that attack cancer tumors.

qi gong: Chinese exercise to regulate qi, or life energy.

rak: 'love' in Thai.

riak wa arai: 'what is it called?' in Thai.

rock-water rating: a scale used at the San Paulo hospital to measure Benton's stool consistency, from one, meaning rock, to ten, for water.

roubignoles: 'testicles' in French.

sabay sabay: 'feeling fine and relaxed' in Thai.

sai ua: a grilled pork sausage stuffed with meat, herbs and spices (literally: 'intestine stuffed') popular in northern Thailand and Burma.

sanae dum: 'black magic' in Thai.

Sang Som: brand of rum brewed in Thailand.

satay: Indonesian skewered meat, popular throughout Southeast Asia.

saukaulat: 'chocolate' in Pierre's pidgin Khmer.

sawadee: 'hello,' 'goodbye,' or 'be well' in Thai.

seppuku: Japanese ritual suicide or 'harakiri,' carried out by disembowelment.

SIGINT: signals intelligence, a general term for electronic interception by intelligence agencies.

Singha: a popular lager beer brand brewed in Thailand.

soi: 'side-street' in Thai.

somtom: Thai papaya salad.

sou: a convenient synonym for 'pseudogene,' defined above.

sukonta: 'fragrance' in Thai.

TAENIA: AI-based who's who system used in Benton's work at NSA, automatically collecting personal data from public, government and corporate records as well as chat, email and other online presence.

tap: 'liver' in Thai.

thanaka: sunscreen face paste made from wood bark, used by Burmese women.

the Fort: slang for National Security Agency (NSA), headquartered in Fort Meade, Maryland, where Benton worked.

u ti nai: 'where are you?' in Thai.

UNIPROT: a freely-accessible database containing detailed information about proteins and their biological functions.

va t'en: 'get out' or 'scram' in French.

wai: Thai greeting with slight bow and palms pressed together in front of chest as in prayer. One does not wai those of lesser status.

wat: 'Buddhist temple' in Thai.

ya: 'medicine' in Thai.

yang na tree: Dipterocarpus alatus, whose resin and bark are used in traditional medicine throughout Southeast Asia.

Yidosi: Palin whirlpool spirit.

An excerpt from

Ultimate Loot

A new novel by

Mani

To be released soon

Mani

1. Mimi

The last call for boarding had come on, and there was still no sign of Benton's bearded face.

Mimi had taken the bus to the airport in Bangkok, just like Benton had instructed and queued at the Thai Airways check-in counter behind a turbaned giant who reeked of beer and garlic. A pair of clueless Chinese girls created a scene by repacking their carry-ons.

She was supposed to head together with Benton to Phnom Penh, where she would take care of business with her dad's friend Father Darcy, and then, once Benton had made the arrangements, they were going to fly off to America where they would start a new life together. She was looking forward to it—living and working among the smartest people in the world.

But Benton had not shown up. That was the problem with the elderly. They forgot important things, like Devona forgetting her only grandchild's birthday, making Mimi cry, as she was now doing standing at the boarding gate with the sun on her face.

She wiped her eyes with a tissue and noticed that her mascara had come off.

"Your passport?"

She dug it out yet again from her threadbare Vuitton bag, which was the first thing she would change when she got to New York. Because that was where she was heading, Benton or no Benton. It was his loss, missing out on a nice time with her. She could see herself standing tall in a pair of Michael Antonios on the terrace of a

Manhattan skyscraper, snapping selfies of the jagged skyline, wowing Fon and her other friends back home.

"Australian?"

She nodded, still sniffing. She had never been to her father's homeland. But she was fully aware from everything he had told her that Australia sucked.

Once on board she slipped into her window seat. The seats were narrow and hemmed together on either side of a narrow aisle, and it felt hot, with a smell of engine oil. Stretching her legs out, she tucked her bag behind her ankles. Inside was her laptop with the stuff Father Darcy needed, as well as an envelope with five hundred US dollars from her father, to tide her over until things calmed down.

The fat man next to her was eyeing her legs. She let him gape, while peering out of the window at the runway and the wet fields. Out of the shimmering haze a heron appeared, spreading its silvery wings before settling on the mud.

She felt a knot in her stomach and crossed her legs together. She couldn't be airsick when the plane hadn't even moved, so why did she feel like throwing up? She breathed deeply, like the monk at Wat Santisuk had taught her, trying to make the light of peace shine inside, making believe the world was a friendly and loving place.

"First time?" The fatty's voice was smooth, with an accent that was either Italian or Lebanese. Why Lebanese, she didn't know, but she had seen a movie where a Lebanese smuggler sounded like that.

His fingers, she noticed from the window reflection, were resting on a book. His pinky had a green onyx ring carved with a scarab.

"American?"

She exhaled, and then turned towards him, straightening out her leg and flattening the skirt above her knee.

"I go New York," she said.

"You're headed the wrong way, miss. This flight's to Phnom Penh."

"Yes, after that New York."

"Studying in Thailand?"

"You ask too many question, mister."

The man laughed as she turned away. An announcement came on, informing them of a delay due to a missing passenger's baggage having to be removed. She took out the emergency instructions card and fanned herself.

Her suspension for skipping class was going to end right after the October break. She was glad she was never heading back. Because school sucked. She hadn't learned a thing there, and she had to deal with boys like Surasak who said mean, hurtful things about girls who slept with old snake-heads. But she was willing to forgive them, for they were just boys who didn't understand a thing about love. And despite the malicious gossip, she had managed to stay popular. In computer class, they had given her a standing ovation when she presented her animation project. *Panda Bunny* was about a martial arts fighter whose fantastic airborne kicks she had stayed up all night perfecting. She knew the moves well, as she had been learning *muay thai* boxing. But the teacher's eyes had turned away from the fast-moving images on the screen. He was focused instead on her spooky black lipstick and the fact that she happened to have her shirt buttons open.

"You are headed for the gutter," the teacher said, wagging a finger. "Like your friend Fon."

The teacher had no business picking on her best friend, who had dropped out of their class to work in a Pattaya bar. Especially when Fon was making more money than he ever would.

Now it was Mimi who had a long-term cash problem. Her father had promised an allowance, but only if she continued with her education. But she had other plans, with Benton.

He had sent her a long email, but it was his voice that she missed most. They had spoken two days earlier when he had called from May Tai, in the mountains near Chiang Mai.

"When you come, Bento? You forget me?"

"I'll be there... at the airport." He was trying to sound upbeat, but his voice was tense and full of throat clearings. "Like... I told you, Mimi-bird. Hang in there."

The line got cut off, and then his phone wouldn't answer, but she knew what it was all about. Benton was going to bust the Foundation, with its deadly drug trials carried out among the hill tribes. After which, he had predicted, the shit was going to hit the fan.

Exposing anything in Thailand was risking one's neck, and she had to admire Benton for that. And the Foundation deserved to be brought down, for it was run by Dr. Pierre, who her father said was corrupt to the core. But why should Benton be the man to do it? Instead of trying in his old age to fix the wrongs of the world, he would have been better off focusing on their life together. They could have been snuggling in bed eating ice cream, licking each other's cones like those snow bunnies on the lovely card he had given her for her birthday.

In her rush to catch the airport bus, she had left it behind, tucked between the panda and the pair of lion cubs on her pillow.

Her collection of stuffed animals brought to mind a Bugs Bunny cartoon Benton had shared with her hoping she would learn American English. She really loved the animations, which were based on the classic Twelve Principles for creating the illusion of life. But she couldn't get the slang.

"Bento, 'land that big lug' mean what?"

"What's the sentence, love?"

"HEY SISTER IF YOU WANNA LAND THAT BIG LUG YER GOIN ABOUT IT THE WRONG WAY."

"Land means get hitched," Benton said. "And lug is a heavy, stupid guy, like me."

"But then it say you gotta play hard to get," she said, laughing.

He laughed with her, stroking her cheek with his thumb, which made her tingle all over.

As for the actual feelings of love, the cartoons and even the more serious movies like the Thai afternoon soaps always distorted them. For no amount of eye-catching scenes with lovey-dovey words could express those inner emotions, the delirious, champagne-pop exhilaration she had felt when she and Benton had celebrated their first month anniversary by dining on baby back ribs by candlelight.

And now even the most terrific soundtrack could not capture her loneliness, the sense that her heart was about to be broken.

An announcement came on, and then they were moving. The aircraft gathered speed, the wheels bouncing on the potholes on the runway, the engines roaring as the plane lifted off. She watched Bangkok shrink before her eyes, its cars and pedestrians dissolving into specks and then being obliterated, and the skyscrapers flattening into squat little boxes. The plane howled and shuddered as the city yielded to the countryside with its ancient temple spires and the orderly rectangles of green rice-fields and silvery canals, and then she could see a brown river snaking through a valley, which disappeared as they headed up into the clouds, where the plane floated and bumped about for a few minutes before soaring and bearing her like an arrow towards the sun that had now appeared in all its fury. She snapped the window screen down as the plane turned its nose and leveled off, heading east.

The flight reached ten thousand feet, and the clamor of the engines subsided. People settled back in their seats, and the captain came on the PA, apologizing for the delay. It was a short flight, but they would serve drinks to make up.

Mimi asked for a glass of red wine. The stewardess needed to see an ID. She showed her passport.

"Sorry Madam. It says you are seventeen."

"Passport wrong," she said, as the lady turned away.

The fat man smiled and slipped his glass over. She nodded her thanks and drained it.

He laughed. "So you're Australian."

"Dad from Australia. Mama Thai."

"Your dad is Crocodile Dundee?"

"Hey what you call Dad?"

"Relax. Have another drink?"

She avoided his eyes as they waited for more wine.

"You are a brave girl," he said softly, glancing at the oversize gold watch glistening on her wrist. "Come visit me in Phnom Penh and you may have all the drinks you like." He slipped a business card over.

She stared at him. "You try pick me up, mister?"

The man sighed and returned to his book.

Mani

She wondered if she could bring herself to fuck the fatty for pocket money, because a couple of sessions might earn her enough for three nights in a fancy Manhattan hotel. She figured she could manage it, though it would not be enjoyable at all. The man's green eyes were creepy and as for the pink rolls of flesh on his neck and his pale lobster-claw hands—it would be like chowing down on cold fish curry! Though she knew how to get the fatty all excited at first so he couldn't hold it in for more than a few seconds.

And now there was the bad-girl guilt she was already feeling at the thought of deceiving Benton, though it would serve him right for having stood her up.

Benton would have to bring along some serious cash, for once they got to New York they would be going out on the town, to shop and to sample her favorite cuts of steak and some of those fantastic Italian desserts he had told her about. But she wasn't a spendthrift. To save money, she would cook for him, but where would she get ingredients like galangal? Without which there would be no soups like *tom yum* or *tom kha gai* to warm their bellies and remind them of back home.

She figured that ten grand would be the bare minimum to set her up in New York. After that, if she was smart, she could make a killing as a fashion designer or even an animator. Her class had loved *Panda Bunny*, and there was no reason Americans wouldn't go for it.

Her father had taught her that having money did not make you free, but it could buy you time, which was the most precious resource on earth.

As she thought harder about her financial future, her eye fell on the fatty's book. It had a bull's head on the cover, and the page he was reading was made up of characters topped with swirls and hats. It was probably Lebanese, if there was such a language. The decorative swirls and hats would be like those Thai vowels which had markings on top. She could not make out more, except for the fact that one of the characters was repeated thrice, under different shaped hats. It was probably a letter standing for a common consonant, like *T* in English or น in Thai. Then she noticed that one of the lines ended with a shape that looked like a horn or sword, which seemed odd.

She slipped the fatty's business card into her handbag. The script was like a puzzle, which she knew would linger at the back of her mind until it was solved.

About the Author

Mani is a writer, scientist, and professor who retired early from Silicon Valley to Thailand, where he volunteered in the Golden Triangle with the hill-tribe fictionalized in *Toxic Spirits*. Born in India and educated across four continents, he studied creative writing at Penn (with Carlos Fuentes), at Bread Loaf (with Patricia Hampl), and at Harvard (with Paul Harding). Prior to working in Silicon Valley, he was based in Washington, DC and Boston as a professor as well as a scientist at a not-for-profit think-tank advising the US government on advanced AI technology. His work affiliations have included Georgetown University (Associate Professor), Yahoo (Senior Director), Cambridge University (Visiting Fellow), MITRE (Senior Principal Scientist), Brandeis University (Visiting Scholar), and MIT (Research Affiliate).

Mani's six previous books (two of which have been translated into Japanese) include *The Imagined Moment*, on the computing of time in narrative. His stories and essays have been published in *3:AM Magazine, Aeon, Apple Valley Review, Drunken Boat* (Finalist for the Pan Literary Award, also one of Story South's Million Writers Award Notable Stories of 2007), *Eclectica, New World Writing, Nimrod* (Finalist for Katherine Anne Porter Prize), *PANK, Short Fiction Journal, Slow Trains, Storgy, Unsung Stories, Word Riot*, and many other venues.

Toxic Spirits is the first volume of a trilogy dealing with the effects of unfettered venality on marginalized Southeast Asian communities. The sequel is devoted to the looting of Asian antiquities, and the final volume is set amid the devastation of reckless dam building along the Mekong River.